Also by Peter Green

The Hit and Run

A SHOT IN THE DARK

PETER GREEN

iUniverse, Inc.
New York   Bloomington

A SHOT IN THE DARK

iUniverse books may be ordered through booksellers or by contacting:

iUniverse
1663 Liberty Drive
Bloomington, IN 47403
www.iuniverse.com
1-800-Authors (1-800-288-4677)

Because of the dynamic nature of the Internet, any Web addresses or links contained in this book may have changed since publication and may no longer be valid. The views expressed in this work are solely those of the author and do not necessarily reflect the views of the publisher, and the publisher hereby disclaims any responsibility for them.

ISBN: 978-1-4401-7412-4 (sc)
ISBN: 978-1-4401-7413-1 (ebk)

Printed in the United States of America

iUniverse rev. date: 10/8/2009

This book is dedicated to Susan my very best friend and the love of my life.

Acknowledgements

Thanks to Susan once more for her guidance, patience and insight. She is my editor, proofreader, inspiration and driving force. It would have been impossible to accomplish this work without her. Also many thanks to my dear friend Judy Richter, who has encouraged my writing from the start when we first met at Sarah Lawrence. Finally my everlasting gratitude goes out to Vidal Sassoon, who brought me to America and in turn made all things possible.

Wednesday

Chapter 1

Jason Friendly is fourteen minutes into his run when he hears a loud noise. It sounds like a car back firing, but he can't be sure. He looks around and doesn't see anything or hear anything except for some birds clattering in the trees close by. He checks his watch. He thinks he should be further along by now. Someplace in town instead of down by the railroad tracks, which is where he is. This was not the only distraction Jason's had on this evening's run. The first was back at the library.

The library used to be a train station and stands close by the railroad tracks. It was abandoned in the late seventies when they closed down the line. That's when the library took the space. It's been that long since the station's been used for its original purpose, but here now, as Jason jogs up to the parking lot, stands a train. Stopped at the old platform. People spilling from its cars. Looking, Jason thinks, like it did in the old days. Someone's opened the gate in the safety-fence. Passengers wander through it into the parking lot and dribble into Jason's path, slowing him down. He catches snippets of their conversations as he navigates his way through them. "Trouble on the line," wafts over them like a gentle refrain. Then the chatter dies down, and the people thin out and Jason's jogging away from the library and along the cinder track that parallels the train line.

It's when Jason turns towards town that he hears it. The noise that sounds like a car backfiring. The birds squawk for a bit then there's nothing. Not an engine firing up or even a yell. Just the night noises, his panting, and the noise of his shoes slapping the ground as he jogs in place. He checks his watch to see how far behind he is and bares down to try and make up some lost time. Soon he's through the town, up the other side of the golf course, across the greens, and home. He calls it an "orbit" and it usually takes him twenty minutes. This time it takes twenty-four. Once in a while he likes to do it twice. Tonight is one of those times.

When he reaches the library the second time around, the parking lot is deserted and the train and its passengers are all gone. There's not a sign that they were there. Not a cigarette butt or candy wrapper or a discarded tissue. Even the safety-fence gate is closed. He wonders if he imagined it, that perhaps an endorphin kicked in and he's on some sort of a runner's high. Or maybe it's a "Twilight Zone" thing and someone out there is playing tricks on him. Then something catches his eye up ahead. Pencil beams of light stabbing at the dark. Someone lights a flare and eerie shadows move urgently across the horizon. Jason hears sirens and sees cars with flashing lights converge on the baseball field up ahead. He runs towards them with renewed vigor. As he gets closer a policeman looms out of the darkness. Someone he knows. Guarding the perimeter of whatever's happening up there.

"Frankie," says Jason, panting. "What's going on?"

Frankie the Cop is turned out perfectly. That's what the kids call him. Frankie the Cop. They hate him. The kids. He's always rousting them and driving them crazy. Frankie the Cop is thirty-five and looks younger. Twelve years in with a razor sharp crease in his trousers and a belt full of equipment that gleams and creaks with his every movement. He shakes Jason's outstretched hand and says grimly, "We've got a dead lady up there." It's possessive, the way he says it. Like it's the department's body, not the family's. Or the husband's. Or whoever it's supposed to belong to. It now belongs to the Columbia Police Department is how Frankie makes it sound. "She's been shot in the chest," he says, stepping back a pace. Not wanting to get a whiff of the steam rising up from Jason's body. "It wasn't a robbery or sexual stuff, leastways it doesn't look that way. She's got all her clothes on." He looks towards the lights, wishing he was there instead here on the edge of things in the cold and dark. "No sign of a struggle," he adds as an after thought.

Jason stops his jitterbugging and catches his breath.

Frankie's radio crackles to life. A soft monotone pours out information that's got nothing to do with him. He turns the volume down. "You always run here?" he asks.

"Most nights," says Jason and tells Frankie about the noise he heard. "It could've been a shot," he speculates. "There were no cars around. I looked. I was farther up the track," he points up ahead, "there, as you turn towards town."

"They'll want to talk to you about that," Frankie says and they head towards the lights.

Jason asks him, "Did you see the train?" He's half expecting to hear it never happened, but Frankie saw it too.

"A train hasn't stopped in years," he says and scratches his head. "Remember how we used to play here all the time when we were kids? Shagging fly balls when the people got off the train and then watching them scatter for cover. One time someone hit an old geezer. After that," he laughs, "they checked the schedules before they let us play."

Jason smiles. He even remembers who hit the old man. "Any idea who she is?" he says, going back to the dead woman.

They watch as another car makes its way cautiously across the baseball field and comes to a halt where the other prowlers are parked.

"Never seen her before," says Frankie lifting his chin towards the new arrival. "That's Jimmy Dugan making his entrance over there. C'mon, he'll want to talk to you."

Chapter 2

Detective Jimmy Dugan parks his unmarked Chevy next to the prowlers in the middle of the baseball field. He leaves his lights on to illuminate the crime scene the way the other cars have done and hopes his battery doesn't give out on him. Lucy was playing in the car earlier and she left the radio on. Lucy is Mary Harwood's ten year old daughter. Mary Harwood is Jimmy's girl friend. She's close to forty so "girl" is a bit of an exaggeration. Jimmy gets out of the car and walks towards the uniforms standing near the body.

Jimmy Dugan is a paunchy fifty-three. He's five feet nine with stringy gray hair that needs cutting and combing. There's a twinkle in his green eyes and his chubby shopworn face has a look of intelligence and sensitivity to it. He got the call at 9.00 pm. They'd just finished eating, him and Mary Harwood, and were sitting on the deck for the first time this year, staring up at a moonless sky hoping to see a shooting star. They've been together a while, these two. Since Jimmy figured out who killed Thomas Harwood, Mary's husband, and found the $2 million he was stealing from her. That was a couple of years ago. She thinks it's because of Jimmy that she got anything at all, but it's not the money that keeps them together. They like each other is the thing.

The crime scene has tape all around it. A large rectangle has been cordoned off. The body lies in the middle. Jimmy hears noises coming from all directions. Leaves crunching. Twigs snapping. Men calling out to one another in the dark, and muttered curses that carry on the still night air. A crisp-looking sergeant detaches himself from the uniforms and walks towards him. This sergeant never smiles. Jimmy wonders what it's like to live with a guy like that. He's always so serious, this man. Always on the case. He wears an immaculate uniform, the whitest shirt Jimmy's ever seen, and his peaked hat and silver buttons glitter and twinkle in the floodlights. "Shot in the chest," the sergeant says without preamble. "One wound as far as I can see. There's a handbag lying next to her. A couple of things have fallen out. Keys. A wallet." He rattles it off barely moving his lips.

As long as Jimmy's known him the sergeant's been like this. Straight-faced and serious, and very good at his job. "Not theft then?" he asks.

"Doesn't look that way. There's money stuffed in the wallet and the credit cards are still there.

"Suicide?"

The sergeant shakes his head, "There's no weapon we can see, and anyway the angle's all wrong."

Jason Friendly and Frankie the Cop emerge from the dark just then.

"Who's that guy?" says Jimmy. Trying to see in the dim light.

"Jason Friendly," says the sergeant. He gives Jason a nod and his version of a smile. A slight creasing of the cheeks and a glimpse of teeth.

"What's he doing here?" asks Jimmy. He can barely make Jason out. This is a new thing with him, this not seeing so good in the dark. It goes along with the crick in his back and the leg cramps that arrive with increasing regularity. Driving at night's becoming a problem too. Now this. Not being able to recognize Jason Friendly at fifty yards. He wonders if this is how it's going to be from now on. More of his parts not working so good.

The sergeant says Jason looks like he's been jogging.

"He could do with some meat on him," says Jimmy. It's all he can make out in the dim light, Jason's nobbly bones hanging on a dirty white torso. He's got that emaciated look runners often have. He's six feet two of concave chest, sinewy muscle and pale flesh. His sweaty tee shirt and muddy shorts hang on him like they're too big. His handsome face is unshaven and streaked with perspiration, and his black wavy hair is matted down and plastered to his head.

"Who found her?" Jimmy wants to know.

"Some kid sneaking a cigarette."

"How old?"

"Twelve," says the sergeant.

Jimmy thinks he started earlier. Eleven. Maybe even ten. He can't remember now. "Where is he?"

"He was all shook up, so I sent him home in a black and white." The Sergeant hands Jimmy the address. "It seemed to cheer him up."

"You make all the calls?" asks Jimmy.

The sergeant says he did. The calls Jimmy wants to know about are the ones to the state troopers, the county CID, a crime scene crew, the medical examiner and the police chief. It's not that Jimmy thinks the sergeant wouldn't have made them, it's just that it's Jimmy's job to ask.

He's wondering now what the front runner in the mayoral race is doing at a murder scene in jogging gear. He hopes he's not looking for a little free publicity. Politicians like to do that during a campaign. Show up at a crime scene with a smile on their face looking for the cameras, hoping for a sound bite, or a quote, or an opportunity to pump themselves up and make themselves look important. "Mr. Friendly," he says, smiling. "What brings you here?" They meet in the middle of the baseball field where the lights from the cars and spotlights have faded and the banter around the crime scene is barely audible.

Frankie the Cop announces that Jason has some information he thinks they should hear, then he takes a step backwards and leaves Jason standing alone in front of them.

Jimmy gives Frankie a smile and thanks him.

The sergeant tells him to go back to his assignment.

Frankie disappears into the dark.

Jason turns to face the two cops. His long arms dangle by his side and steam rises from his body.

"Whatcha got?" Jimmy asks, still smiling, but making sure he's up wind.

It's a good thing they're not trying to impress each other, these two. Jimmy's wearing faded jeans and an old sweatshirt and there's a days worth of stubble on his moon-like face. Jason is mud-spattered and sweat-streaked and looks like a drowned rat. Jimmy's got the cleaner sneakers, but the only thing shiny about him is the badge that hangs around his neck.

"I think I heard a shot," says Jason

"Why a shot?" says Jimmy.

"Well, I didn't think it was a shot at first. It's only after Frankie told me what happened I thought it might be."

"What did you think it was at first?" asks Jimmy.

"A car back firing, only there weren't any cars around."

"How'd you know?"

"I looked." Jason wipes a sweaty forehead with the back of his hand. "I was right about here when I heard it."

They all look around. Where they're standing is a fair way from the road, but you'd see a car if there was one to be seen.

"Any idea what time it was?" says Jimmy.

"8:43," says Jason.

They're surprised. Witnesses aren't usually so precise. "Why so sure?" asks Jimmy

"I checked to see how I was doing."

"Doing?"

"On my time," says Jason. "This is my jogging route."

"Always this way?"

Jason nods. "I was telling Frankie what a strange night it's been."

Jimmy's making some notes. He looks up now. "Something else happen?"

"The train," says Jason. "Didn't you see it?"

Jimmy said he didn't.

"When I came by the first time there was a train stopped at the library."

"The first time?"

"This is my second time around."

Jimmy thinks runners are amazing. He sees them on the side of the road all the time gasping for breath, sweating like pigs and looking like they're going to drop dead from a heart attack. "A train?" he asks. "Here?"

"There." Jason points to the illuminated parking lot by the library. "It was the strangest thing. People were getting off and milling around, but when I came by the second time the train was gone and so were they. Not a trace of them. For a moment I thought I imagined it, but Frankie saw it too."

"He's right," says the sergeant. "A train pulled out fifteen minutes ago."

"Why'd it stop?" asks Jimmy.

"Trouble at Grand Central is what they said. Everything got backed up. I don't think it's ever happened before. Not since they closed the station down."

"I wonder if she was on it?" says Jimmy, talking about the victim. Jimmy's been a Columbia detective for fifteen years. Before that he lived in Brooklyn and was a detective in the NYPD, a good one too until he found his wife in bed with his best friend. It was down hill all the way after that. First came the divorce, then the drinking. Or was it the other way around? Either way he began to make mistakes. Small ones at first, but then a couple of big ones where people almost got hurt. So after some not so friendly advice from his boss he managed to pull himself together and dry himself out. He went to all the meetings and followed the program to the letter and by the time he was finished he was clean and sober and anxious to move on. He wanted a place where no one knew him and he could make a fresh start. Columbia fit the bill. The year he arrived was the year they opened the library.

Jason's going on about today's commuter. How it was a mistake to close the station in the first place since there's not enough trains running now. "I'd have made a better fight of it," he says in his 'vote for me' voice.

Jimmy likes him. Jason's defended a lot of kids he caught, some grown ups too, and he's always treated him with respect. Not like most defense attorneys who only want to make him look foolish on the stand and rip him a new asshole. But now, in spite of this mutual respect they've got going for each other, Jimmy finds himself looking Jason over for flaws. It's a cop thing. Something you do when someone gets killed. You look at everyone with jaundiced eyes under those circumstances. "So let me get this straight," he says, looking at his notes. "You're out jogging. When you get to about here you hear a noise you think is a shot. Then you find Frankie and tell him what you heard. Is that about it?"

Jason says no. "I heard the noise my first time around."

"Not a shot?"

"I didn't think so. Not then. I thought it was a car back firing."

"When did you think it was a shot?"

"When Frankie told me what happened."

"And you bumped into Frankie your second time around?"

"Right," says Jason

Jimmy makes some alterations in his notes then goes through a list of questions. Did Jason see anyone? Did he see a flash? Could he be sure which direction the noise came from? Was there anything unusual he remembers besides the train? Can he recall anything suspicious? Anything? Anything at all? And to all of Jimmy's questions Jason answers no. All he heard was a noise he thought was a car back firing, but could've been a shot. He can give them nothing else except for when it happened. 8:43 precisely.

Jimmy can't think of anything else to ask him. He puts the pen and notepad in his back pocket and asks Jason if he'd like to look at the crime scene. He figures the future mayor of Columbia is entitled to a little courtesy after all of this cooperation.

The idea takes Jason by surprise. He's only seen a corpse once in his life and he's not so anxious to repeat the experience. It was at his friend's father's wake. An open casket affair he wasn't expecting. The old man wore a blue suit and a beret. His skin was waxen and shiny. Relatives wandered over to kneel and pray at his side. Some even talked to him. One-sided conversations from people who had things to get off their chest. Kids went up to him like he was still alive. When no one was near they clustered around him and chattered and giggled. One kid even adjusted the beret that slipped to the side of the old man's head.

By the time Jason makes up his mind to look at the dead woman, Jimmy and the sergeant are almost at the body. Jason follows after them, but not quickly.

Chapter 3

They're all there now. Everyone you'd expect to see at the scene of a crime. The medical examiner. The crime scene crew. State troopers in Smokey the Bear hats and creaking leather. Columbia's finest, some in civvies, most in uniform. The county guys are on their way. Floodlights illuminate the scene like it's the middle of the day and there are cops everywhere you look. The press is kept at a distance, but more of them are showing up. Cars are parked haphazardly at the edge of the baseball field. A few TV trucks are lined up on the side of the road. Technicians raise their dishes readying for transmission. Reporters joined umbilically to cameramen crisscross the area looking for prey. A small crowd gathers held back by saw-horse barricades being unloaded from a truck. The perimeter where the body lies is marked off at waist level by a six inch yellow tape that snaps and rattles in the in the cool night breeze. CRIME SCENE is written across it in large black letters. A narrow path of wooden planking stretches from a gap in the perimeter to where the body is. When they get there the medical examiner is just wrapping up his preliminary examination. The crime scene crew, two men and a woman in white overalls with large equipment cases, wait anxiously for him to finish up so they can get their own show on the road. They smile at the new arrivals, then go back to their conversation and cigarettes.

Jimmy stands at the end of the path waiting to speak to the ME, but as the medical examiner wobbles towards them on the narrow planking he speaks to Jason first. "Jason," he says in a high pitched croak. "What are you doing here?" His bushy eyebrows rise. Questioning. One bony hand carries a black bag, the other is outstretched to maintain his balance and, when that's established, to shake Jason's hand.

The sergeant gets a thin smile.

Jimmy gets nothing.

The medical examiner, one Eustace Rawlings, is a prissy little man with a narrow point of view and no sense of humor. He wears a dated, blue double-breasted pinstripe suit and a thin bow tie. His oily gray hair has a razor sharp side part and is cut in a short back and sides. He wears steel rimmed glasses and looks remarkably like Harry Truman. He was born and raised in Columbia and distrusts anyone who wasn't.

Jason tells him he thinks he might have heard a shot.

9

The ME's a friend of Jason's father. He attended Jason's christening and his confirmation and dozens of other pleasant functions that took place under the Friendly's hospitable roof. Even now they belong to the same club, Rolling Hills, Columbia's center of power. He looks Jason up and down wondering why Jason's dressed in his underwear looking like something the cat dragged in.

Jason explains that he was jogging.

The ME gives him an understanding smile. "A glass of scotch is more my speed."

They both grin at that. It's an understatement. The ME's got a reputation as a serious drinker at the club. It's an inside joke. The ME turns disdainfully towards Jimmy. He's reluctant to talk to him or look in his direction. They don't like each other is the thing, going back to when Jimmy first got to Columbia all battered and bruised hoping for some peace and quiet. Instead he got the ME who made him jump through hoops till Jimmy got all Brooklyn on him and told him to go and fuck himself. The ME backed off after that, but neither of them forgot what happened back then.

"She's been shot in the chest," the ME snaps out. Anxious to get their business over and done with. "I'd say from a high-powered rifle. She was killed instantly from maybe as much as five hundred yards. Over there," he points to the edge of the woods where it's blackest, "judging by the way she fell. The bullet went right through her. You'll need to find it or a casing to be sure what rifle we're looking for."

Jimmy lets the insult pass and tells the sergeant to put some guys on it. "How long's she been dead?" he asks.

"About an hour judging by the body temperature."

Jimmy looks at his watch. 9:50. Jason heard the noise at 8:43. An hour would be about right. "Did you see the train, Doc?" he asks.

The ME flinches. He hates being called Doc, especially in front of people. He thinks the term is synonymous with "Gunsmoke" and that people will associate him with that scratchy old geezer on the TV show instead of the dapper looking leading citizen he sees himself as. "A train hasn't stopped here in fifteen years," he sniffs. "Before your time I think."

The sergeant fills the ME in on the train story and gets a grunt for his trouble. Then the ME makes his goodbyes. He tells Jason he'll see him at the club over the weekend, and gives the sergeant a friendly salute. He brushes by Jimmy neither talking to him or looking in his direction and disappears into the darkness.

"I see you two are still close," says Jason.

"Like two peas," says Jimmy with a touch of pride and asks Jason what it looked like.

"The train?"

Jimmy nods.

"Like I stepped into another dimension," says Jason, which, as it turns out, was not so far from the truth.

Chapter 4

The crime scene crew is about to get to work when Jimmy calls them off. He must see the body first, he tells them. He needs to get a feel for the setting and see if anything strikes him before they rip the place apart. He walks across the plank onto the plastic sheet laid next to the dead woman, leans down and pulls back the blanket that covers her. There's nothing to see except for a large crimson patch on her white blouse over her right breast. Lying next to her is a black patent leather handbag with a long shoulder strap. It's on its side and like the sergeant said her wallet, keys and some loose change have fallen on the ground. She's a pretty little thing about five feet five. Early thirties. Smartly dressed in a grey tailored suit and black stilettos a tad on the raunchy side. Her shoulder length curly black hair surrounds her face like a wavy frame. It's got something in it that makes it look shiny and lank. Her cherubic lips are delicately painted with bright red lipstick. Her closed eyes are highlighted with eyeshadow and mascara and her perfectly oval face is made whiter by a liberal application of face powder. She looks so peaceful, this elegant young lady, lying with her eyes closed at the edge of the baseball field. It's like she got tired when she came to this spot and decided to lie down and rest for a while. She looks almost perfect if it weren't for the angry red blotch on the front of her shirt.

Jimmy checks out the site but there's nothing to see. No footprints. Or litter. Nothing to give him a heads up on how to proceed. There's hustle and bustle going on all around him. Cell phones go off. He hears snatches of conversations. A distant siren gets louder. The meat wagon this time. Coming for the body. This body. Asleep at his feet. He thinks there should be quiet out here on this hallowed ground. A tent or something. Out of respect for her, this innocent young thing. But the cacophony continues and gets louder still.

Jason is standing alone, back from the perimeter observing the activity. The stone faced sergeant is off taking care of other things. Jason watches him as he gives people orders and points in different directions.

Jimmy catches his eye. "Wanna take a look?" he asks.

Jason's not enthusiastic and shakes his head.

Jimmy smiles. "C'mon man. You're gonna have to do it all the time if you get to be mayor. Murder scenes. Open casket affairs. It's good practice for you."

Jason says he can do without this type of practice. He's not joking either. His face is a mask of terror. He doesn't want to see this body in the worst possible way. He hates dead things but now all eyes are suddenly upon him. Photographers with telescopic lenses have got him in their sights and point their cameras his way. A phalanx of them. On tripods. Like artillery. Watching his every move and capturing every second of his uncertainty. The crowd sees him too. He takes the look of horror off of his face and replaces it with something more dignified. Then he tells himself it's just another photo-op and how great he'll look in the papers tomorrow, him being the Johnny On The Spot and all. When he gets to the body he gives Jimmy a sheepish grin.

Jimmy nods encouragement.

Jason looks down at dead woman. There's a second where nothing happens - then he gives out with a terrible gasp, runs past Jimmy across the wooden path and into the bushes where he throws up.

Jimmy is shocked.

Jason emerges from the bushes on unsteady feet. He takes a second to compose himself then blurts out, "I know her." Then he says it to himself again, softly, "I know her," and wipes his face with his tee shirt. There are tears in his eyes and his face is a mask of sorrow and pain.

"Who is she?" Jimmy wants to know.

"Her name is Sandra Ellison."

"From here?"

Jason shakes his head, "New York," he says sadly. "She lives in the City."

Jimmy's alert now. His antennas are flashing. It's the first thing he learned at the Academy, to watch for coincidences. Ninety-nine times out of a hundred a coincidence has something to do with the business at hand. Like now for instance. A woman is found dead at the edge of the baseball field. It looks like she came off a train that stopped at the old station, something that hasn't happened in fifteen years. A jogger passing through not long after she's discovered knows who she is. Now that's a coincidence.

Jason is very upset. His head hangs down and his bony shoulders are slumped. He's taken on a rubbery appearance, all gangly and elbow joints. The story tumbles out of him in fits and starts. An explanation. The reason he knows who she is and why he's so upset. "She's an attorney from New York," he says between sniffs. "We're working on something together. How is this possible?" he asks the heavens. He holds his head between his hands like it might fall off his shoulders.

"What sort of thing?" Jimmy asks.

There's more sniffling then Jason says, "She's got a client in the City who's buying some land here. I'm her associate on the deal."

"When did you see her last?"

Jason's eyes tear up some more. "Today," he says and covers his face with his hands.

"Today?" says Jimmy. Alarm bells go off again.

Jason nods.

"Where?"

"Albany."

Jimmy gives a sniff. His nose is running. He takes out a tissue and blows it with a loud honk. He can hear the cameras clicking and wonders if they got him blowing his nose. It's not how he'd like to be seen, with his finger up his nostril, but he's sure if he's in the papers tomorrow, that'll be the shot they'll use. "How come Albany?" he asks.

"I met her for lunch."

"In Albany?"

"It's not so far," says Jason. "There were papers to go over and things to sign. She was in Albany for some other stuff. It's a timing thing. We needed to get everything done for the closing. I said I'd meet her up there to get it finished. To impress her. To get more work out of her, if there was any more to be had."

Jimmy's gets out his notebook. When he's finished scribbling he nudges Jason away from the perimeter and the cameras, and the prying eyes. When they get to a spot that seems secluded he asks, "No fight?"

Jason's face stiffens. "Excuse me?"

"Did you have a fight with her? Harsh words? A disagreement? Anything like that?"

"About what?" Jason wants to know.

"Anything. The deal. Personal stuff."

"No," he says sadly. "There was no fight."

"No problems that couldn't be ironed out?"

Jason shakes his head.

Jimmy writes it all down. "Anything going on between the two of you?"

Color seeps into Jason's face. "Like what?" he asks.

"You know," says Jimmy.

"No, I don't know," Jason snaps and wipes his mouth with the back of his hand.

"Intimacy," says Jimmy.

"No," says Jason. "There was nothing going on between us."

Jimmy takes a different tack. "You own a rifle, Jason?" he asks. He figures he might as well get it out of the way while the guy's already pissed at him.

Jason purses his lips. "No, Jimmy," he says tersely. "I don't own a rifle." He hopes there aren't any reporters around to hear their exchange. He looks around nervously.

Jimmy doesn't care what Jason thinks about him. He sees a different person in front of him now. Not the next mayor of Columbia, or a person out to get a little free publicity, but someone who's part of an unexpected coincidence.

Sandra Ellison

Chapter 5

Sandra Ellison's lunch with Jason went pretty much the way she thought it would. She's kissing him off is what she's doing, and there's no easy way to do a thing like that. He took it well, if you think that storming out of the restaurant and sticking her with the check meant things went okay, but she didn't mind. She was glad to see the back of him. They'd had a good time and he was nice enough in a country club sort of way, but it's action she likes. Bright lights, parties and everything else in between. She's a City girl. She lives there, works there and plays there as hard as she can. The one time she stayed at Jason's house she thought she'd put on twenty years. His world revolves around that country club they've got going there. Rolling Hills. The center of Columbia's gravity. They lunched there, went home for a quickie, then back for dinner, dancing and knowing looks from all his buddies. She hated it. Hated them. They had these gooey smiles on their faces like they had something special going on she wasn't part of. Join us, their smiles said, and become one of us. Then you'll see what we're so smug about. No thanks, said hers, never in a million years.

Closing the deal was all she cared about. Her deal. The biggest deal she's ever been involved in. For a piece of land just outside of Columbia that looked, when she first took the job, like it couldn't be done. But she'd been persistent. And tenacious. And finally got the two parties to agree to something so creative she'd already gotten three clients from it. "We'll use a local boy to work with the town and county people," she told the client, "And I'll do the closing and everything else in between." Someone recommended Jason Friendly. He was happy to get the work. She used him fearlessly and shamelessly, but now it was time to move on. The deal was done and so was she. It was time to end the relationship such as it was. He was bringing the last things up to Albany for her to sign. That's where she was now. Albany. Working on another deal. Jason had no idea what she had in store for him.

They met for a late lunch at a place she knew just off the Albany mall, a cute little bistro with checkered tablecloths and a French menu. She made sure they sat in the back away from prying eyes and gave him the bad news between the coffee and dessert. He must have figured that their brief affair gave him some leverage for more work judging by the surprised look on his face. He lost on both counts and looked like he wanted to throttle her after she'd told him it was time for them to move on. Instead he stood up, muttered something unintelligible and, red faced and fuming, stormed out of the restaurant. She finished her coffee and stayed for dessert. Then she paid the check, got a cab to the station and caught the 5:30 express back to New York.

The train took off at a breakneck speed that quickly degenerated into a ten mile an hour crawl. Sandra went through her brief case and sorted through her papers, then made some notes. The train made little progress. She went to the bathroom, then back to the notes and papers. The train went even slower. She checked her cell phone for messages. There's one from Marc. Her lover and main squeeze. She's been with him for a couple of months now. He lives on 57th St. A brand new building. Two bedrooms. Big bucks. She left his bed this morning for the meeting in Albany. He drives her wild, him and his endless supply of coke. She can't wait to see him and she hits the redial button to tell him so, but there's no signal. It's why she never got the call in the first place. It's a dead zone. She'll have to wait for the train to move to a different location before she can call him.

She met Marc Hilliard on a Wednesday night at Babbette's on 52nd St. At the bar while she was waiting for someone else. A hot-shot bond trader she thought had possibilities. Marc came in alone, looked around and walked straight towards her. He was dark and handsome and wore a black suit with thin lapels and a black open necked-shirt. His hair was spiky and short. His smile was full of gleaming teeth and his deep blue eyes sparkled with anticipation. He sat next to her, looked around, gave her a crooked smile and took a hit so quickly no one near them had any idea what he'd just done. He flashed the vial at her and raised a questioning eyebrow.

She smiled demurely and shook her head.

"Someplace else?" he inquired.

She smiled at him again. "Why not?" she thought and slowly nodded. The bond trader was late and she'd had enough of squeaky clean any way. Jason Friendly had taken care of that for her and even though she was still seeing him she figured it would be nice to get down and dirty for a while.

She thought Marc was a coke dealer that first time. His place gave her that impression. Everything was black. The walls, the furniture, even the drawn shades. His black phone rang constantly and there were quick bursts of conversation that used the word gram a lot. It's a coke pad, she was sure of it, she'd been in enough of them to know. She's two months into the relationship now and she's absolutely sure.

The train ground to a halt. She looked out the window. It's dark, that's how long they've been traveling. They were standing at an unused station. The conductor came through the car. A dumpy looking guy in a worn out uniform of blue serge and a shiny cap that had seen better days. "Trouble at Grand Central," he said sauntering down the aisle. "Gonna be here for a while folks. We're stopped at a platform. You can get out and stretch your legs if you want." Then he was on to the next car.

People got up and moved around and stretched and yawned. Conversations started up. Some of the passengers got out onto the platform, others soon followed. Sandra watched them from her seat. She's cautious that way. Never the first to do something. Always holding back to see how things play out. She'd like a hit is what she was thinking. Something to perk her up from this miserable journey that's taking forever. That and a cigarette. So after a while she got off the train to look for some seclusion.

It's not a real station, she can see that now, just the platform's left. What was once the station is now a library. Somebody opened the gate separating the platform from the building and people spilled through it into the parking lot. Sandra thought it was wrong, legally. Even getting off the train seemed odd. What about liability? Who's responsible if someone gets hurt? But it's got nothing to do with her, and now having gotten a feel for her surroundings she wandered to the end of the platform and down the stairs to the edge of the woods.

If she looked back she could see the lights of the train and the parking lot, but where she stood was pitch black. She took out her silver vial, unscrewed the top and scooped out a pile of cocaine with the little spoon and snorted it up one nostril, then the other. It was an exquisite moment as the drug charged through her brain like a stampede of white lightning. "Hot damn," she whispered and gave her head a little shake as she exhaled. She felt so good. So perfect. Because of the deal she'd pulled off. And the money she was going to make. And handsome Marc waiting for her with all of that coke. A spasm of euphoria coursed through body her in a delicious wave of pleasure. Neurons and endorphins danced in her brain like fireworks on the Fourth of July. She'd never been so happy.

She's about to light a cigarette when the lights start to dim. It happens so quickly there's no time to react. There's just a hint of pain, but it's too brief to register. Then there's nothing. Only blackness. And just like that

Sandra Ellison's life is over. Like someone reached in and turned off the set. Her set. That's how quickly it happened. She was dead before she hit the ground.

Chapter 6

Jimmy has the sergeant pull the crew together and tells them to start moving out from the perimeter to see what they can find. They have eight guys with them, almost the entire shift, spreading out slowly, their flashlights sweeping the ground in front of them. Jimmy watches as the beams bob off in different directions then goes over to see how Jason's doing. He's white. Even in the dark Jimmy can see it. "C'mon," he says kindly, "I'll have someone drive you home."

"I'll walk, thanks," says Jason, still smarting from Jimmy's questions. He wants no favors from him. He thinks the walk will do him good and give him a chance to think things through.

Jimmy shrugs. He says he's going to need a statement from him and probably the county CID boys will want to talk to him. He's talking to Jason's back now as Jason marches resolutely away into the dark.

As if on cue the county CID cops show up, late as usual. Detectives Arlis Smith and Burt Monahan are from the Criminal Investigation Division of Westchester County. The CID is the county's support system for police departments who don't have the resources to mount an effective investigation of a major crime. Murder is considered a major crime. Jimmy is Columbia's only detective, so the town qualifies for their help. Smith and Monahan have made late entrances an art form. They do it on purpose so that everyone can see them coming. They're prima donnas. Divas. The best the county has, or so they think. The only thing missing for their entrance is a brass band.

Jimmy's glad to see them. He's not so crazy about digging into a local up-and-comer like Jason Friendly. He's noticed those guys at the Rolling Hills Country Club don't forget things so quickly. Let Smith and Monahan do the dirty work is what he's thinking as he watches them walk towards him.

The CID boys have a history with Jimmy. They worked with him on the murder of Mary's husband, Thomas Harwood. It's the last murder they had in Columbia. They tried to ace Jimmy out of the action, the collar and all the publicity, but Jimmy solved the crime. So it was Jimmy who got all the action, the collar and all the publicity. Not such a good thing for divas and prima donnas. This time they'd like to keep the proceedings friendly. A "let bygones be bygones" sort of thing.

Jimmy's always thought Smith and Monahan was a great name for a hat company. It's hard to know why since the boys don't wear hats. It's just something that pops into his head every time he sees them. *Smith and Monahan. Hats For All Seasons.* He once told them he thought they'd be much better off in the hat business. It was over something on the Harwood case. They looked at him like he was crazy. So did everyone else.

"How you doing?" says Smith.

Monahan gives Jimmy a mock salute.

Monahan's a big guy in a rumpled gray single breasted suit, a white shirt and blue striped tie. His face is square and features a flat nose like a prize fighter, mottled skin, a tight mouth and beady eyes. Smith is just the opposite. He's thin and short, and wears a blue blazer, gray pants and a pale blue open necked shirt. His face is long and pinched with a beaky nose, thin lips, and big eyes with almost no eyebrows. Both of them are in their mid to late forties. Laurel and Hardy is everyone's nickname for them because they're a big guy and a little guy that look kind of silly if you're walking behind them.

"Whatcha got?" asks Smith

Jimmy gives them the run down.

The boys nod effusively after every point Jimmy makes, then it's their turn. They ask a few unnecessary questions to keep the pot boiling, then make a big deal out of promising to keep Jimmy in the loop, saying the same thing over and over so no one gets the wrong idea. He can poke around wherever he wants they say like he's getting a special dispensation. Or he can do what he likes they say with smiles and winks and a cloyingly forced friendliness. Yes Jimmy. No Jimmy. Three bags full Jimmy signaling obsequiously they want no trouble with him this time around, but making it clear, nevertheless, that this is their case now and they're taking it over.

Jimmy loves the whole performance. He figures he's entitled to a little ass kissing. He's cool about it and doesn't rub it in, but he loves the sucking up all the same. The truth is he's got a soft spot for these two even though they tried to screw him. They're part of his history with Mary.

The first time he met Mary was when he had to tell her her husband had been found dead on the side of the road. All Jimmy wanted to do was to put his arms around her and hold her. There was something about her that made him melt inside. Jimmy asked her out after the case was closed and everything calmed down. Well, for a cup of coffee anyway. He bumped into her on the street and got all tongue-tied when he realized who it was. His head was down and he wasn't looking where he was going, then bam. There she was. Staggering back from him. And he, unable to speak.

Not winded, but tongue-tied. And blushing. Fumbling like an awkward teenager. An overweight not so spiffy looking teenager. Blurting out words that barely made any sense.

He missed her after the case was closed. It surprised him he felt that way. He thought of calling her a couple of times, but his shyness got the better of him. Now here she was, standing in front of him after he slammed into her. She could see he was not equipped for this sort of thing. When it looked like he'd pulled himself together she told him how parched she was, it being such a hot day and all, and how what she'd really like is something to drink. Then he, since they were standing in front of a coffee shop , asked if she thought a cup of coffee might do the trick. It was their first date. A coffee shop on Main Street three years ago. It got easier after that.

"Who's that guy?" Monahan wants to know, looking at Jason marching off into the night.

"He *was* going to be our next mayor," says Jimmy.

"What's that mean?" asks Smith.

"He's leading in the race. Now I think he's had it."

"Why's that?" says Smith.

"He's probably going to get some bad publicity."

"Because of how he's dressed?" says Smith.

Jimmy shakes his head. "Because he knows the victim."

"No kidding," says Monahan.

"What are the odds?" says Smith.

"Especially," says Jimmy, "when you figure a train hasn't stopped here in fifteen years."

"What train?" asks Monahan.

Jimmy tells them about the train and his assumption that Sandra Ellison was on it.

"You think this or you know it for sure?" asks Smith.

"The tech guys are going over her stuff now, but it looks that way. She lives in New York. She was going home. She was in Albany all day. That's where the train came from."

"How'd you know she was in Albany?" asks Monahan.

"And lives in the City?" says Smith.

"Jason had lunch with her there."

"In Albany?" says Monahan.

"That's what he said."

Smith wants to know why.

"They had some business to take care of. They're attorneys."

A groan rises up from the boys. They don't like attorneys.

"Why couldn't they do their business here?" asks Monahan.

Jimmy shrugs. "Jason said she was working on something else up there and he was doing her a favor. Whatever it was they needed to get it done quickly. Something about a closing."

"Some favor," says Smith.

The boys want to know if Jimmy has any theories. They're solicitous about it like they really care, but nothing could be further from the truth. They don't give a shit what he thinks and whatever he says they'd like to shove up his ass, but they want this thing to go smoothly so they paint their faces with genuine interest and hang on his every word.

Jimmy says he doesn't have any theories, and tells them they should talk to Jason themselves and make up their own minds.

The boys like this, the way Jimmy's treating them, and do some pontificating of their own. They say they'll speak to Jason like he suggests, paying tribute to the idea and giving Jimmy the credit for it, only they'll do it in the morning after they've got their ducks in a row. Then they tell him, in the only awkward moment of their exchange, that they're officially taking over. They've got a speech ready in case things get difficult, but they can see by the look on Jimmy's face they won't be needing it. It's not what usually happens in these small towns. When they show up the case is theirs. Those are the rules. The local cops don't like it and usually aren't very friendly, but not this time. Jimmy looks like he's really pleased to see them. And he is. Really pleased to see them. Only too happy to have this one taken off his shoulders.

The big guy and the little guy continue to cluck away, pecking at the dirt and shoveling the shit. If he wants to go home, they say, it's okay by them. Or not, they say. Whatever he feels like doing, they say. "That all right with you, Jimmy?" they want to know. All smiles and cheerfulness.

Jimmy says it's fine by him and, after saying good night to them, trundles off in the direction of his car. Only too happy to surrender things into the fumbling hands of Smith and Monahan that well-known hat company who can't find their way out of a paper bag unless someone shows them the way.

Chapter 7

As Jimmy heads towards his car, Frankie the Cop emerges from the gloom and sidles up to him. He says he has something he thinks might be helpful and makes it clear he doesn't want to speak to him in front of Smith and Monahan. The boys are standing near the body about a hundred yards away, comparing notes and deciding what to do. The unsmiling sergeant hovers by their side now not Jimmy's, waiting for them to give him instructions. Jimmy walks Frankie in the opposite direction, over to a clump of bushes out of earshot.

Frankie says in a low whisper, "I think Jason was banging the victim." He looks at Jimmy waiting for some reaction. Some sign this fabulous piece of information has saved the day.

"How'd you know?" Jimmy asks. Not impressed.

"I saw them."

"Doing it?"

"I saw them together," Frankie says. Wary now. Not sure how things are going here.

Jimmy waits for something else. When it's clear there is nothing he says, "How do you know they were doing it?"

"They always had that look about them. You know, all dreamy like."

"When you saw them."

"Yes."

"How many times was that?"

"What?"

"That you saw them."

Frankie gives it some thought. "A couple. Maybe."

Jimmy digests this. "You see them fighting?"

Frankie says no.

"See him make any threats towards her?"

Frankie did not. He shifts his weight and keeps his eyes on the ground. "But they definitely went out is what I'm saying here. I don't know if they were doing it, you'll have to ask him that, but WE all thought they were."

"We?"

"The guys."

"What guys?"

"The football team," says Frankie. "From high school. We still play ball together once in a while. Jason told us he was going out with someone. We figured it must be her. She's the only one we've seen him with. We all made a big deal about it because it's been a while since that's happened."

Jimmy remembered what Jason told him, that there was nothing going on between him and Sandra Ellison. He wonders why he'd lie about it. "When you bumped into him tonight, which direction was he coming from?"

"The Library. He lives up that way." The cop points towards the hill.

Jimmy looks, then he watches a photographer taking shots of the crime scene. The guy looks like a wind up toy. Stop, shoot. Crouch, shoot. Shoot again. All in herky jerky movements. Jimmy runs his fingers through his hair and says, "So what do you think, Frankie? You think your buddy could've done this thing?"

Frankie blinks. He's surprised by the question. He shifts his feet, takes off his hat, slicks his hair back with his free hand and places the hat back on his head in one motion. It's something he's done a thousand times only this time it looks like a tick. Like he's nervous which he is, and doesn't know what to say, which he doesn't. "Jason?" he asks. Making sure we're on the same page here.

Jimmy nods. "You think he could've done it?"

There's another long pause then Frankie says hesitatingly, "Anything's possible, I suppose. But I got to tell you Jimmy, when I bumped into him he didn't look like anyone who'd just knocked someone off."

"What did he look like?"

"Someone who's been jogging. "

"And how's that?"

"Hot, sweaty and out of breath."

"He could've taken the shot and got back on the path and you'd be none the wiser. He'd still be hot, sweaty and out of breath, and there's no reason you wouldn't believe every word he told you."

The cop agrees it's true, "But he didn't have that look about him, you know what I mean?"

Jimmy did. He felt the same way.

"Jason's got all sorts of tics when things aren't going right for him and I've seen every one of them," says Frankie. "I'd have picked it up if something was going on."

Jimmy agrees. He didn't think Jason had that look either. "And if he shot her where did he get the rifle from?" he asks. "And how could he plan for a train to stop when it's the first time it's happened in fifteen years?"

Frankie the Cop has no idea.

Neither has Jimmy.

Thursday

Chapter 8

Jimmy wakes up with a start and checks the clock. It's 6:30. The alarm is set for 7:00. He reaches over, turns it off and stares out of the glass doors that lead to the deck. Three bird feeders of varying sizes are suspended from a nearby tree limb. Jimmy watches the birds zoom in and out to it. It's the usual suspects. Juncos, cardinals, chickadees, titmice, and some different sized woodpeckers. Once in a while a new guy shows up. He'll hang around for a day or two then he's gone. It's a good day when that happens, but not today. It's just the usual crowd. Some flying in from the tree line, some coming from the shrubs and bushes by the side of the deck. Those from the tree line have the furthest to fly. Suddenly a hawk swoops down and catches a titmouse in mid-flight. Jimmy sits up and blinks. He shuffles to the glass doors and peers out. The hawk stares up at him from the grass. The titmouse is clutched in its claws. Jimmy opens the door hoping to scare the hawk into letting the bird go, but as he steps onto the deck the hawk flies off taking the titmouse with it.

When he gets to the station the parking lot is crammed full of press cars and news trucks with extended antennas and big logos painted on their sides. Jimmy swears under his breath. A large white van is parked in his spot. It looks like some sort of command post with people buzzing in and out of it clutching papers and files. He's forced to park across the road in front of the pizza parlor. He figures it'll cost him an earful the next time he wants a slice. Gino's always complaining to him about people taking his parking spots. He says it costs him money, but it won't cost him any money today. He'll be making a fortune off of all of those reporters camped outside the station house.

Jimmy parks the car and crosses the road to the station. Inside he gives the desk sergeant a friendly nod and heads to his office. He's got a lot of paperwork to catch up on and a ton of calls to make. Finally he's summoned for a pow-wow by the Chief. On the way he's buttonholed by a couple of uniforms. Fans. Guys that like to hear his war stories. They give him the, 'hi's' and, 'how's it goings,' hoping he'll tell them something good, but he can't stop he says. He'll be late for the meeting. Everyone knows about the meeting with Smith and Monahan. The boys have made their presence felt throughout the station. The uniforms wish Jimmy luck as he squeezes past them. One of them gives his back a pat and a rub. He's not so keen on the rubbing part, he thinks it's creepy. It's always the same guy too. A kid a couple of years in. A toucher. Always putting his hands on people, Jimmy's noticed. No one seems to mind, only him. He wishes the kid would keep his hands to himself.

They're all there when he walks into the chief's office. Smith and Monahan are slouched in their chairs sipping coffee from Styrofoam cups. The Skipper, that's what Jimmy likes to call the chief of police, is behind his desk holding a container of coffee of his own. He's perfectly attired in a spotless uniform with gleaming buttons, shiny insignia and a chest full of ribbons.

There's no coffee for Jimmy. There's an empty chair next to Smith and after getting the nod from the Skipper, Jimmy sits down on it.

The chief is a beefy looking man with piercing blue eyes, a flat pockmarked nose, a scowl that looks permanent and a meaty face made larger Jimmy can't help noticing, by a fresh crew cut. Another fresh crew cut. Jimmy figures the man must be getting his hair cut twice a week now. It certainly looks like it's just been done and he's always got that, 'fresh from the barber,' smell about him. The chief's gray metal desk is covered with piles of papers, mounds of files, three phones, a computer and a copy of today's local paper. On the walls are pictures going back a hundred years of previous chiefs of police in sepia tones and out-of-date uniforms.

The chief starts the meeting by declaring that all hell has broken loose. "It's because Jason's running for mayor," he explains to the slouching boys. "It makes for good headlines." He glances at the paper to make the point. A picture of Jason in running gear sweat stained and bedraggled is plastered on the front page with a headline that reads, "Leading mayoral candidate at murder scene.'"

The Skipper wants to make sure everyone's on the same page here. He insists on no freelance interviews by anyone, everything must go through him. That way only his picture will show up in the papers and on the television screens. "The press are driving me crazy," he tells them. "And the switchboard's lit up like a Christmas tree." There's the slightest hint of panic in his voice when he says this. Almost like the media frenzy has taken him by surprise.

Monahan is the next to talk. He says, speaking on behalf of his partner Smith, that they've got no problem not talking to the press and hope that everyone in the department is told the same thing.

The chief breaks in here and performs a quick tap dance about the tight ship he runs at the station and how no one would dare to disobey him.

After that, Monahan makes a small speech about the wonderful cooperation they've had so far. He skillfully lays on the soft soap, puffing up Jimmy like a hot air balloon and schmoozing the chief like he's his long lost aunt. Then he turns to his notebook and, in a voice more formal than the one he's been using, brings them up to date.

"The victim's name is Sandra Ellison. 28. Single. An attorney with Kibbins and Frader on 56th and Park in New York. They specialize in real estate. She lives alone and owns a two bedroom apartment at 536 East 79th St.. We've established that she was on the train that stopped at the library last night. Witnesses confirm this. She was on her way back to New York. She was in Albany all day with a client. She had a late lunch there with Jason Friendly. Albany police confirm her movements. Witnesses at the restaurant say Jason and Sandra had a fight towards the end of the meal. That he left mad and stuck her with the check. The staff at the restaurant say she didn't seem too upset about it and remained there for dessert and coffee. A canvass of the murder scene has been started," Monahan looks up to make sure they're all listening. "We're waiting for progress reports. No luck on shell casings yet. We've been looking where the ME told us to, now we've widened the search. The NYPD is contacting Sandra Ellison's friends, family and co-workers to see if there's anything there. Then there's this cocaine wrinkle."

"What cocaine wrinkle?" asks the chief. He glares at Jimmy, thinking he should've been told about this wrinkle beforehand.

Jimmy has no idea what they're talking about.

The boys like that. A little friction on the home team is always good for a laugh. Monahan continues like nothing's happened, but he can't wait to yuk it up with Smith when they get back in the car. "They found a vial of cocaine in Sandra Ellison's handbag," he says. "And the call on her cell phone was from a known cocaine dealer named Marc Hilliard."

Smith takes up the tale. "We went to see Jason Friendly this morning."

Jimmy asks, "What time?"

"About 7:15," says Monahan.

"We gave him the third degree," says Smith. "We asked him about the fight with Sandra in Albany. What were they fighting about, that sort of thing. Then things got hairy."

"When we brought up the coke," throws in Monahan.

"That's when it got hairy," says Smith. "He threatened to lawyer up and threw us out."

Jimmy looks sympathetic.

So does the chief.

Jimmy says a lawyer threatening to lawyer up sounds like a lyric from a rap song.

Everyone chortles.

Smith's got nothing else to say.

Now it's Jimmy's turn. He tells them what officer Frankie told him.

"That's the guy you were talking to in the dark?" asks Monahan.

Jimmy says it was.

The Chief is alert now. He's looking at Jimmy all beady eyed, waiting for an explanation. Thinking to himself, "that's two things he should've told me."

The boys are loving it.

Jimmy says, "He thought Jason was having an affair with Ellison."

"The cop says that?" says Smith.

Jimmy nods.

Monahan says, "How come he didn't tell us?"

"Shy, I guess," says Jimmy and quickly moves on. "I'm going over to Jason's later. I need him to sign a statement." He says he'll try and mend the fences for them while he's there. The boys technique is well known. He can only imagine what they said to Jason for him to throw them out of his house.

The boys are grateful for Jimmy's efforts and outdo themselves in singing his praises and kissing his ass.

Jimmy laps it up.

So does the Skipper.

Brooklyn

Chapter 9

Jimmy was hot back then. In Brooklyn. When he was a detective. N.Y.P.D. Williamsburg Division. Jimmy Dugan. Thirty-five. Five feet nine all muscle and moxie. Hotter than a pistol. Walking through the building with that swagger of his. Wetting a finger and touching his ass going, SSSSS, that's how hot he was. With the slicked back hair and sharp looking suits and those ties. He had a thing for ties. They put him in an elite squad, courtesy of the captain. "Part of your education, kid," he told him. "One day you'll be running the place." That's how hot he was.

It was a steamy afternoon in late August. There'd been no rain for days. Everything was dry and dusty and hot. Jimmy is out with his partner, a guy called Curtis. "Don't be calling me no Curt," he told Jimmy that first day they're teamed up, "it's Curtis." Curtis is a big black man elegantly turned out with a knife edge crease in the trousers of his dark blue mohair suit and highly polished Bally shoes. Jimmy looked good too. He always looked good. Wearing all black today. Black slacks, black open necked shirt, black summer sport coat and black slip-ons. They all looked like that, the other members of the unit. Sharp, hot, gelled and hungry. The lieutenant looked even sharper.

The squad was an anti-crime unit targeting areas that might lead them to larger fish. This time it's the fences they're looking at. Jimmy and Curtis were sent to interview one working out of a pawn shop on Broadway underneath the El. It's what they call a go-see. A roust. To let the guy know they're there and push him just a little. The whole unit in their fancy-looking clothes and heavily styled hair, is out doing the same thing. Shaking up the fences to see what falls out.

The place they went to was a grimy storefront next to a laundromat on a block crammed full of people of every persuasion. Chassids and Puerto Ricans. Mexicans and Russians. Chinese and Slavs. Black and white. Straight and gay. Salt and pepper and everything in between. The melting pot in all its glory. All of them rushing this way and that like rats in a lab experiment. A three-ball sign of the pawnbroker hung outside the filthy premises. The window was crammed full of musical instruments, some hanging from the ceiling, some piled on cases. All of them were dusty and cobwebbed. Tarnished trumpets and dull trombones lay higgledy piggledy on the window floor. Guitars were tumbled one on top of the other in a rudimentary display. A banjo had a special place close to the glass. It was the only thing that was clean. Probably a new addition. Inside was just as bad. Boxes piled in every direction and instruments wherever you looked. At the back of the store was a counter with a grill. Behind that, sitting on a stool wearing a dealer's visor and a jeweler's glass in one eye, was the man they'd come to see. Murray Fisher. Caucasian. 45, looks older. Five foot seven, looks shorter. 160 pounds, looks fatter. Gray hair. Balding. Brown eyes. Pasty face. Murray Fisher. Owner. Fence.

Murray the Fence, seeing the very obvious cops come storming into his place of business, decides to do the only thing his addled brain can come up with on such short notice. He draws the gun he has ready for the robber he's sure will one day come and hold him up. It's registered and legal and has never been fired. Till now, that is. Murray takes aim at the cop in the front. The thin one. The white one. The one not in a suit, who's just now beginning to make a move of his own.

Jimmy's the man in front. The one Murray's aiming his gun at. Jimmy Dugan. Our Jimmy. Out there in front. Just ahead of Curtis, not Curt. Screaming at the top of his voice "Gun. Gun" and drawing his own weapon as he leaps horizontally. Falling. Falling. Onto a pile of boxes. Squeezing off a shot as he falls. At the same instant, the pawnbroker pulls his own trigger, but Jimmy's not there any more. He's lying in the pile of boxes. The shot he got off slammed into the pawnbroker's shoulder and put him out of action. The pawnbroker's bullet went between Jimmy and Curtis, bouncing off a tuba and settling in a squeezebox that made a plinking plonking sound.

It's a close call. The closest Jimmy's ever had. Back at the station house he's debriefed, questioned, shrunk and offered counseling. After all of that they sent him home, telling him to take tomorrow off and to take more time off if he thinks he needs it.

He drove home listening to Dave Mathews. At full blast. Adrenalin pumping in his brain. Wild thoughts charging through his head. Quick images flash in his mind, then he's back to the pawnbroker. And that filthy store. And the guy. Murray the Fence. Whoever heard of a guy called Murray pulling a gun? Drawing down on him like a western shoot-out. Like Gary fucking Cooper. And now on top of the rush he's still feeling and the trembling in his belly, he's getting horny. Jimmy can't believe it. He could've been shot. Or maimed. And here he is with a hard-on. He laughs. Then his mind goes to Vicki. His Vicki. Beautiful Vicki. Home from work early these days. Maybe there now. Waiting for him. To comfort him. And hold him in her arms. And tell him everything's gonna be all right. His brain is speeding like a meteor. His dick is as hard as a rock.

They rent a walkup in Park Slope. The good part where the streets are quiet and the neighbors are decent. Jimmy and Vicki. In their two bedroom apartment with the drop down living room and big bay window. They make out pretty good, the two of them. She's a teacher and he does okay as a cop. They're high school sweethearts married ten years. No kids. She wants them, he doesn't. He doesn't tell her this. He says he wants them too, just not yet. But he doesn't want them at all. Ever.

He found a spot at the top of the street, parked and hot-footed it to their building. He bounded up the stairs, opened the door and burst into the apartment with an expectant look on his face and a huge erection in his trousers.

And there she was. Vicki. His high school sweetheart. The love of his life. Married ten years now. In their bedroom. On their bed. Naked as a babe. In the arms of his friend. His best friend. Who'd not heard his entrance. And continued to pump himself wildly into Jimmy's horror stricken wife.

Chapter 10

Jason Friendly's road looks more like a war zone than a quiet residential street on the edge of a golf course. The press have removed themselves from the station house and are now camped by the hedgerow at the edge of Jason's property. A sea of cameras face the house. Reporters gather in tight knots smoking cigarettes and swapping stories. Vans and trucks line the road. There's even a lunch wagon tucked near the center of the action. One of those quilted silver paneled affairs you see selling coffee and sandwiches to construction crews. This time he's making a killing off of the press who've got nothing else to do but drink his liquids and eat his food.

A lone uniform guards Jason's walkway.

Jimmy has to park his car a quarter of a mile from the house. By the time he gets there he's winded and irritable. He pushes past a group of guys with cameras and fends off a reporter trying to shove a microphone in his face with his briefcase. He gives the uniform a grin as he breaks free and says, "How's it going Brian?"

Brian's an old timer like Jimmy. Rumpled crumpled and been around the block a few times. "Better get me some help, Jimmy. What if they rush me?"

"You can handle it," says Jimmy full of confidence. He likes Brian. "You'll finally get to shoot off that weapon of yours. You've been wanting to do that as long as I've known you, but you better be quick." He whips out his cell phone and calls the station house. When he gets off he tells Brian the troopers are on their way. "I see a Wyatt Earp thing here, Brian. The reporters rush you. You draw your weapon and fire a warning shot in the air. They stop. You make your speech. They can overpower you but not before you take some of them with you, sort of thing. Then you point your gun at some guy and tell him he's the first to go. That's when they all back off and you look like a hero."

Brian opens the gate and says he thinks he'll wait for the troopers to show up.

"Suit yourself," says Jimmy, and trundles up the pathway to Jason's front door.

The photographers shoot off a barrage while he waits for the door to open.

A haggard looking Jason appears wearing sweat pants, a baggy tee shirt and nothing on his feet. His face needs shaving, sleep is still in his eyes and his hair looks like he stuck his finger in a light socket. "Oh it's you," he says without enthusiasm.

Shutters click like a cicada party.

"What do you want?" he asks rudely, running a hand through his scruffy hair. He gives Jimmy's beat-up briefcase an impolite squint.

"We have to talk," says Jimmy. Without waiting to be invited he pushes past Jason into the small foyer. Once inside he can't help noticing how fresh the house smells, unlike his own place that has that funky odor of cat pee compliments of Felix, his pet with an attitude.

"Those CID guys were here this morning," Jason grumbles.

Jimmy says he heard about it.

Jason closes the door. The noise from the street disappears. "7:15 seems early for an interview don't you think?"

Jimmy agrees that it is.

"Not even a call to say they're on their way."

Jimmy shakes his head sympathetically.

"They got me out of bed, the bastards. Not very dignified for a mayoral candidate, not that it matters any more. The way those guys were talking it's the end of my political career anyway."

"How's that?" asks Jimmy.

"This cocaine thing."

Jimmy screwed up his face.

"They're saying if she did cocaine, I did it too. That's what you do when you hang with someone, was their point."

Jimmy raises an eyebrow.

"Who cares about that? What's it got to do with Sandra's death? In any event, I did NOT use that stuff," says Jason emphatically. "She did, but I didn't." He sighs despondently. "Who's going to believe me anyway. I can see the headlines now."

Jimmy tells him how the boys have a reputation for heavy handedness. That their bark is worse than their bite and he shouldn't worry about it.

"Don't worry about it. Easy for you to say." Jason looks out the window which drives the photographers into a frenzy of picture taking. "My political career's up in smoke. My practice is ruined." Jason catches Jimmy's frown and explains. "Three clients left me today, good ones too. They said they're uncomfortable with this type of exposure. Murder's nothing they want anything to do with. As if I actually did the thing. They said they liked it when I was running for mayor. It gave them something to brag about.

Once this cocaine thing hits the papers, it'll be a miracle I have any practice left at all."

He leads the way to a sunroom at the back of the house. It's got floor to ceiling windows on three sides that make you feel like you're sitting in the middle of the garden. The fourth side opens up into the foyer. Wooden beams grace the ceiling and a thick maroon carpet covers the floor. Jason gestures to a chair. "Sit down," he says and sits down himself in one of two armchairs that face each other across a coffee table. "All I did was try to do the right thing and look what I got for my trouble." He shakes his head disgustedly. "Is this what happens when you step up? No wonder no one wants to get involved. It's not like Smith and Monahan don't know who I am. We've worked on a dozen cases together. You should've seen how they went at me this morning, Jimmy. You'd have thought I killed ten babies."

Jimmy makes the excuses again, trying to smooth things over. He knows what went on here. That Smith and Monahan aren't called Laurel and Hardy for nothing. It's not just a tall guy and a short guy walking down the street that got them the name. They're clowns is the truth of it. Heavy-handed gumshoes from another era who leave a trail of destruction wherever they go. They've got a good arrest record and that's what the bosses care about. How they get it doesn't concern them. The boys don't believe in tact, or etiquette and use a routine that went out with the ark. Going at their prey with crude questions, menacing looks and just a hint of violence. It's something you'd see in a fifties movie minus the light that shines in the suspect's eyes.

Jason begins to calm down. He leans back in his chair and cracks his knuckles.

Jimmy says, "And Sandra Ellison?"

"What about her?"

"You were going out with her?"

Jason looks uncomfortable.

"You told me nothing was going on."

"We had an affair," says Jason sheepishly.

"Had?"

"She broke it off yesterday."

"Why'd you lie to me?"

There's a long silence.

Jimmy waits.

Jason says, "It's a guy thing."

"A guy thing?"

"I don't like getting dumped, you can understand that can't you. I guess pride got the better of me. It was easier to say nothing than to explain she broke it off in front of everyone. Especially because I had no idea it was coming."

"She took you by surprise?"

"You could say that."

"Did she give you a reason?"

"Time to move on. That sort of thing."

"She hurt your feelings?"

"A little."

"And after that?"

"I drove back to Columbia."

"Angry?"

"Not enough to kill her if that's where you're going with this."

Jimmy thinks it would be smart to leave him alone for a while. He spends a little time rummaging around in his briefcase for Jason's statement. "I need you to sign this," he says finally and hands it to him. "Or write me a new one if you like. Whatever you want is fine by me so long as it's signed and I get it soon."

Jason snatches it away from him and gives it a glance. "You want me to do this now?" He shakes his head. "I don't think so, Jimmy. I'm in no condition to sign anything. I can't even think straight."

"When then?"

Jason gives the sheet another look. "Later this afternoon, but probably tomorrow."

Jimmy gets up to go. Almost as an afterthought he says, "Nothing else you can tell me to put you in the clear is there?" It was a poor choice of words. He knew it the minute it popped out of his mouth.

"In the clear?" Jason explodes. "Like I'm a suspect, is that what's going on here? You think I'm a suspect? You did the same thing to me last night. Slipped something in on the sly. The rifle, that was it. 'Did I own a rifle?' Who do you think you are? Just because I knew her you think I killed her, that's it? That's the logic? And now you know I slept with her," he's up now, looming over Jimmy, "that must seal the deal altogether. You've got your jealousy motive, the drugs. It sounds like a detective's wet dream."

Jimmy stares at him in silence.

Jason's not done. "You're no better than those mutts I saw this morning. I could've kept on running last night. You know that, don't you? I didn't have to stop. I wish I had now. I'd have saved myself a lot whole of trouble and you and your buddies wouldn't have anyone to sink your teeth into."

"C'mon Jason, it's not like that and you know it. You're getting yourself worked up for nothing. No one thinks you did anything, we're just following procedure. All of us. Gathering information. Putting the bits together. You know how it works. You've seen it done for your own clients. It's just unfortunate you're part of the process this time." He wheels out the apologies again and makes a few more excuses for Smith and Monahan.

Jason flops back in the armchair. "It's not so nice when the shoe's on the other foot, Jimmy. One minute I'm going to be the mayor the next I'm a drug addicted murderer."

Jimmy gives him a rueful smile. "What about this guy Marc Hilliard?"

"Your friends asked me the same thing."

"What did you tell them?"

"That I have no idea who he is."

"Never heard Sandra mention him?"

"No."

"Or see her take a call from him?"

"No."

"How much coke did she do?"

"The weekend we spent together she went through a gram."

Jimmy thinks a gram's a lot. If you do a gram through the weekend you generally don't stop on Monday. You get yourself some more. "You think this drug thing was the reason she was killed?"

"How should I know."

"Maybe Hilliard got jealous of you?" says Jimmy. "Or frightened she'd say something about him to you. She ever say anything along those lines?"

Jason shakes his head. "I told you, I never heard his name before."

"Or the fact that he was a dealer?"

"I just told you, I've never heard his name before."

"But you know she did coke?"

"Yes."

"Ever ask her where she got it from?"

"No."

"Never say 'a friend needs a gram, can you get me some?'"

"Certainly not."

Jimmy looks around the room. It's so sunny and bright. He thinks he could do the same thing in his own house. Put floor to ceiling windows on his screened-in porch and turn it into a sun room. Something else for Felix to piss on. Then he looks back at Jason. He doesn't look like he could kill a fly. He's about to end the interview when Jason leans forward and looks like he's going to say something. It takes him a while to get his thoughts together, then he tells Jimmy about the death threats he's been getting.

Jason Friendly

Chapter 11

It was nice to be back in Columbia. He'd been away for too long. Four years of college, then law school, and then seven years in New York with a top law firm. His father knew one of the senior partners from the club and got him the spot. Now, finally, he's opening his own law shop on Main Street. In one of those turn-of-the-century houses with a cupola and shutters and a wrap-around porch with rocking chairs and hummingbird feeders. He bought it for a song. There was a recession on and real estate prices were in the toilet. There's an elegant reception area, a well-stocked library, two smaller offices and Jason's big one. The place has an ambience of professionalism and charm. Attorney Friendly at your service. Estates. Civil suits. A defense, if that's what you're looking for. Closings. Some pro bono work, but not too much if you don't mind we're just getting started here. And specializing, when all was said and done, in real estate. Jason Friendly. Local hero, one time high school football star, volunteer fireman and home town boy made good.

He's going to live upstairs above the offices on the ground floor, but he lived with his parents while the place was being fixed up. What was supposed to take three months took six and the builder, a swarthy Irishman who led a band of South American immigrants, wanted a lot more money at the end of the process. They finished the upstairs first, and Jason moved in two weeks before the downstairs opened for business. That's when the funny business started. His second day in the apartment, furniture arrived he didn't order. A couch and a chair, both paid for with his credit card. He stopped the card, but it was too late to stop the deliveries. Lamps, dressers and a bed all showed up over the next few days. Jason called the cops. They sent Jimmy over, but there was nothing he could do. He figured someone must have gotten hold of one of Jason's credit card receipts and the call to the furniture store couldn't be traced.

On the first day of business five florists each delivered three dozen roses. The place looked like a funeral home. All of it paid for with another of Jason's cards. On day two, applicants showed up for jobs he hadn't posted. It was a cruel trick to play on people trying to make an impression for a job that didn't exist. Day three of business, the five pizza parlors in the area each delivered five pizzas all paid for by another of his cards. He cancelled every one of them and ordered new ones.

Jimmy got nowhere with his investigation. The pizzas were ordered from pay phones. So were the flowers. The credit card people put their own guys on it and they didn't make any more progress than Jimmy. The second week of business the mail was full of porn. Jason's new secretary was appalled. They got to guessing what the next thing would be, but after that nothing happened. In the end Jimmy thought they were pranks by Jason's friends, the club crowd, or his old high school friends - something like that.

Jason's practice was a hit. Everyone gave him work. Rolling Hills Country Club. The town. All his old connections. He had to hire another attorney to help with the load. A year later the hang-ups began. First in the office, then in his apartment. After a couple of nightmare days and nights, he called Jimmy who had the phones tapped. The calls stopped and there was no luck tracing them. Then strange messages kept showing up on the answering machine. Lines from Clint Eastwood movies like, "Do you feel lucky, punk?" and "Make my day." Then the mail was suddenly full of travel brochures and mail order catalogues. Waves of the stuff arrived for weeks on end, then it trickled to a stop. Jimmy put it down to an angry client or someone Jason had beaten in court.

Nothing happened after that until Jason won the marathon. It was a couple of years later and by then he was living in his parents' house, since they moved to Florida. The day he won the race, Jason put the trophy on the mantle over the fireplace in the living room. The next day the trophy was in the sunroom. A week later, he found it somewhere else. He thought the place was haunted because other things kept moving around too and papers weren't where they were supposed to be. Eventually it stopped. But every now and then something strange would happen - an occasional flat tire from nails scattered in the driveway, or the mailbox stuffed with dog shit. Silly things like that. It really didn't matter, so Jason didn't call the police. The economy was booming, real estate values were soaring, everyone was refinancing their mortgages and his practice was a gold mine.

It was Richard Charkham's idea for Jason to run for mayor. Richard was a fellow club member and a marketing guru with a lot of notches on his belt. He'd done amazing things for this product and that, and now he wanted to try his hand at politics. Charkham stood for nothing, believed in nothing, and didn't have a single idea for Jason's campaign. He couldn't care less about the sick, the poor and the disenfranchised, or anything else for that matter. All he saw was Jason Friendly, this shining local star with the perfect features, sparkling white teeth and a very engaging smile. He thought that Jason Friendly was a wonderfully marketable product who, if handled correctly, should be able to beat the crap out of anything the opposition put up, no matter what they stood for. It's an argument Charham's been making for years. That if you put a good looking, articulate guy up for office and, providing his positions aren't radical and you have plenty of money behind you, you can get him elected. The power of marketing, Charkham believed, ruled over all other aspects of the business of politics.

It's a cloudy Friday morning. Jason's throwing his hat in the ring. They've got more than enough signatures for the application and all the money they need to run an effective campaign. They're expecting more funding to roll in as the campaign swings into gear. A crowd of Columbia's finest gathers on the lawn in front of the Jason's office for his, "I Have a Dream" speech. It's been finely crafted by an expensive speech writer who sets forth in stirring rhetoric how Jason will make things better for all the citizens of Columbia.

Jason's parents are up from Florida for the occasion. Everyone's pleased to see them especially the Rolling Hills crowd who clap them on their backs and tell them what a nice boy Jason turned out to be. They all remember a time when no one thought they'd ever get to say that. They stand all bunched together smiling benignly at the rest of the citizens of Columbia, those that is that don't belong to the club.

Jason's speech is well received. He gets high marks from the media and he's way up in the polls. It's no contest, really. People approach him like he's won. The press offers him advice like he's already in office. Who he should use. What he should do. There's even a rumor going around that his opposition wants to throw in the towel.

The next Monday a truck draws up to the house, backs into the driveway and unloads a dozen enormous wreaths that need stands to hold them upright. They look like the things gangsters send to a funeral. Big and garish and over-the-top. "Sorry for your loss," says the driver. "Where'd ya want them?"

"What loss?" says Jason. "There must be some mistake."

The driver shakes his head, reaches into the cab and hands Jason an invoice. It's no mistake. The invoice says twelve assorted wreaths to be delivered to Jason's house and there's his address. Charged to Jason's credit card. Ordered over the phone three days ago.

"Take them back," Jason insists.

The driver says he can't.

"Why not?"

"We're not allowed to. Sign here," and he hands Jason a clipboard.

Jason won't take it. "I'm not signing anything."

"Don't matter," says the driver. "I'm unloading them anyway. You can have them inside or out, but if you're gonna cop an attitude I'll leave them on the front lawn.

Jason doesn't know what to do. Wreaths on the front lawn won't help the campaign any. Wreaths in the house will suffocate him they're so huge. He's about tell the guy to put them in the back when the driver says, "I almost forgot. There's a card for you," and he reaches into the cab and gets it for him.

Inside a plain, sealed white envelope is a white card with cut out letters pasted together to form a message. At first Jason can't read it. Then he thinks it's some kind of joke. Then he goes cold when he puts it all together. The card reads,

> KEEP RUNNING AND YOU'LL DIE.
> THIS IS WHAT YOUR FUNERAL
> WILL LOOK LIKE.

Chapter 12

The sun streams through the big windows of Jason's sunroom. The sky is a clear blue. Huge robins scoot across the lawn looking for worms. The flower beds are ablaze with crocuses and daffodils. Azaleas and rhododendrons fit snugly into one another making colorful tiers of reds and purples and white. Spring is at its best in Jason Friendly's back yard, but not so inside the house. Jason looks drained. It's the first time he's told anyone about the death threats. He thinks this must be what confession is like for the Catholics. The release that comes from telling someone something that's been bottled up for a while. He feels better already.

Jimmy's recalling the pranks that happened when Jason first opened the office. "Must be three years ago now."

Jason says, "Close to four."

Jimmy remembers those days pretty well. Jason was a prick of the first order back then. Cocky, arrogant and generally a pain in the ass. Jimmy didn't care for him. He had a way of talking to you, not down to you exactly, more like through you. That's how lawyers did things in New York was what Jimmy remembered and Jason embraced the manner with a passion. He was quick to assert himself and distant, and aloof. He affected a general air of superiority because he was an educated man and he assumed you were not. It was only later that they developed this mutual respect they've got going for each other. Jimmy did his job though, he remembers that quite clearly. He tapped the phones and checked the records, and tracked down all the public phones used to order things, but in the end he figured it was a welcome home sort of thing for his new practice. A hazing. A frat boy thing. Maybe. "Any more silly stuff going on?" he asks .

"Like I said – things moving around. Nails in the driveway. Someone messing with the car."

"Anything taken from the house?"

Jason shakes his head.

"What about the car?"

"Some rummaging in the glove compartment."

"How come you never reported it?"

"I guess I'm conditioned to crazy things happening by now. It wasn't such a big deal. I figured I'd let sleeping dogs lie. If I made a thing about it every time something happened I'd have a tough time making a living in this town let alone run for mayor. This bunch like a low profile unless you're going for the glory. Other than that they want you to keep your head down or they'll keep it down for you."

"What bunch?" asks Jimmy. He already knows the answer. He just wants to hear Jason's take on it now that he's on the other side.

"The people at the club. You know what they're like there. Stuffed shirts with all their rules and regulations. I saw them cut a guy off once about something they thought he did, even though he didn't. When they realized they were wrong, they did nothing to rectify it. Not even an apology. The poor man had to move away things got so bad for him. I can't afford that sort of thing happening to me. Nothing was taken, there was no real damage done so why bother? But I'll tell you this, I knew when someone was here. I could always tell when they'd been around."

Jason goes over to an oak sideboard that takes up most of foyer. He rummages in one of the drawers until he finds what he's looking for and hands Jimmy six envelopes bundled together by a rubber band. All of them are addressed to Jason with press kit letters. Each one has a different postmark. Inside are sheets of white paper with words cut out from newspapers each with a different message. 'YOU'RE GONNA DIE,' says one. 'YOU'LL NEVER WALK AGAIN,' says another. The others have the same sort of sentiment.

"These came after the wreaths and the wreaths came after you threw your hat into the ring?"

Jason says, "That's right."

"Why bring it up now?"

"I thought you'd be interested."

"I am," says Jimmy. "And I'll be happy to look into it for you." But he doesn't see what it has to do with Sandra Ellison's death.

Neither did anyone else.

Chapter 13

Jimmy's back in the chief's office. Everyone's in their usual places. The chief sits at his desk holding a mug of coffee. A beauty shop fragrance wafts off of him. Jimmy thinks he might have been to the barber yet again and wonders how often the chief is getting his hair cut these days. Smith and Monahan have coffees too. So does Jimmy this time, one of the gang now. They're served by the Skipper's perky young secretary who flits among them like an exuberant butterfly. Lighting here and there dispensing sugar and cream there and then, when they've all got what they want, she flutters out the door.

The boys heap mounds of praise on Jimmy for mending the fences with Jason for them. They want no trouble from that direction. Jason could still be the next mayor, for chrissakes, and they'll have made themselves an important enemy. Jimmy's done them a real favor here, "And don't think we don't appreciate it," they say in unison. For now, that is.

Jimmy accepts their thanks with great aplomb. He's not taken in by their over-the-top verbiage, but enjoys it just the same. The chief glows as the love-fest reaches a crescendo. Jimmy's his star. The man that made the boys think favorably on the his humble department. The chief's already calculating the parameters of the equation. That the worst that can happen here is that they won't spell his name right in their report. The best that can happen is that he gets his picture in the papers and lots of free publicity. Anyplace in between is fine with him. He beams at everyone, anticipating all the good things that are coming his way. Then he gives his full attention to Jimmy, who's telling them about the death threats Jason's been getting and all the weird stuff that happened when Jason opened up his practice. No one seems impressed with this information. No one seems to care. When Jimmy's finished the Skipper says, "That was years ago."

"But not the death threats," says Jimmy. "That started when he decided to run for mayor."

"What's any of it got to do with Sandra Ellison's death?" asks Smith.

Jimmy shakes his head. "You got me. He said he thought I'd be interested. He also said he wished he never stopped that night to tell us he heard the shot. "

"Meaning he's got nothing to do with it," says Monahan.

"Right," says Jimmy.

"We all know that," says the chief.

The boys nod in agreement.

"But *he* doesn't," says Jimmy. "He thinks you think he did it."

"He said that?" asks Smith.

Jimmy says he did.

"What an asshole," says Monahan.

The phone rings. The chief picks it up, listens, then hands it to Jimmy. A furious Jason Friendly is on the other end. He says he's watching TV and they're saying everything he just told Jimmy. About his relationship with Sandra Ellison and the cocaine they found in her bag. "Where'd they get their information from, Jimmy? Answer me that."

"Not from me," says Jimmy.

"It's word for word with what I told you."

"So?"

"What do mean, 'So?' Why'd you do that?"

"Do what?"

"Run to the press."

"Who says I did?"

"It's word for word."

"So you said."

"Well?"

"Well what? Plenty of people could've told them that stuff. You've got waiters up in Albany who saw you fighting. All those folks who saw you at the crime scene. A good reporter could piece the story together with their eyes closed. Anyway it's the truth, isn't it?"

"It's no one's business."

"C'mon counselor, you're running for office. It's everyone's business. It goes with the territory, but it still didn't come from me."

"I'm ruined," Jason moans. "The club's notified me they no longer require my services. My work for the town's been cancelled. Clients are pulling out in droves."

Jimmy doesn't know what to say. Jason doesn't either and that's the end of their conversation. They're all watching Jimmy.

"What did he say?" asks the chief.

"He's upset about what they're saying on TV."

"About what?" asks the chief.

"Him," says Jimmy.

Smith is indignant. "Like it's our fault he was doing her."

"Or he likes his coke," says Monahan.

"What an asshole," says Smith.

"Amen to that," grunts Monahan.

There's a knock on the door. A head appears in the opening. It belonging to a gangly young uniform with shiny black hair and pimply white skin. His eyes are wide with excitement as he enters the room and hands the chief a note. He's barely able to contain his enthusiasm as he waits for a reply. There's a feeling of a suppressed energy that's subtly released in the slightest of his movements.

The chief looks stern, but there's amusement in his eyes. He reads the note then tells the kid he can go.

The uniform takes it all in for the briefest of seconds then scurries out the door, desperate to find someone he can share his experience with.

The chief clears his throat and appraises his audience with a squinty stare. Then, in formal tones, he announces that they've found a cartridge-case behind the shops fifteen hundred yards from Sandra Ellison's body in the same direction the ME suggested, only farther away.

Brooklyn

Chapter 14

Freeze frame. No one moves. Jimmy stands in the doorway. Motionless. His mouth hangs open. Disbelief is on his face. Then pain, and hurt. She's lying naked on her back. On the bed. Their bed. Vicki. His wife. Lying perfectly still. Her knees pulled back and far apart. Looking at him. Jimmy. Her childhood sweetheart. Her eyes are wide. Her face is drained of color. Her lips form an agonized O. Her arms are around her lover. Jimmy's best friend. Who hovers naked above her. His ass raised high for another thrust. He's still inside her. Just a little. Just the tip. Inside Vicki. His wife. His childhood sweetheart. His face is turned towards Jimmy, a masque of despair flashes across it as pleasure turns to pain. They stay that way for an eternity. Each locked in position while their brains perform gymnastics they never thought possible. Every detail burns itself into Jimmy's mind. His eyes are like cameras. Not seeing. Recording. White flesh. Snap. Soft light. Snap. Mole on hip. Click. Swollen lips. Flash. Messed up bed. Snap. Bedside table. Snap. Book. Snap. It's the book that gets to him. By the bed. By them. While they do this. Click. But last night when he put the book down and turned out the light, they whispered in the dark and made gentle love and fell asleep in each other's arms. In this bed. Snap. The one they've been rolling around on. Flash. The details sear themselves into his brain. His pants. Snap. His brown pants. Flash. His brown pants with the silver buckled belt.

Jimmy's first instinct is the gun. To blast them. To shoot them. To blow them away. But his brain's already done it. And their bodies twitch. And blood splatters the wall. It's real, this image. He feels every part of it. Every emotion, but there's no satisfaction in it. Or joy. Or sense of release. And his hand drops to his side not wanting to shoot them any more. The moment has passed. He needs to get away from them now. From this nightmare. He turns on his heels, grabs the Jack Daniels from the sideboard and staggers down the stairs and up the street to his car. Then he drives. And drives. Without knowing where he's going. For what seems like an eternity.

Betray. Betrayed. Betrayer. Betrayal. The words pounds away in his brain like a bizarre mantra. Throbbing like a trombone. Waa. Waa. Waaaaa. He can't get it out of his head. Her face. His face. The sweat. And funk. And messed up sheets. How could it happen? How long had it been going on? The two of them. In his bed. Where they made love last night. Him and Vicki. So soft and tender. To be blindsided. So completely ambushed. He barely knows what he's doing. Scenes play in his head each focusing on something different. Things he saw, but didn't register. With those eyes. Those camera eyes. Missing nothing. Click. His dick. Flash. Sticking in her. Snap. Just a little. Click. Her hair matted and damp. Snap. Her underwear. A piece here. Another there.

Alcohol helps for the rest of the day. Then every day after that. He's drunk when he gets to his mother's house. Her of the pinched face and sharp tongue. He's never going back, he tells her. His mother. Mrs. Sympathetic. Who gets that "I told you so" look on her face when he tells her his story. Offering platitudes for solace as it pours out of him. She knew it all along, "But it's not for me to say," she says in the voice of a martyr who's endured the truth and is finally proven correct. There's nothing she doesn't know this hawk-like being. She'd have set him straight, she tells him, if he'd have only come to her. At the beginning. Before they got married. "But not you. Not Mr. Big Shot. And now look what's happened."

Jimmy goes to his room for some clothes. The dent is still in the wall where his old man flung him. Dad and his buddy Jim Beam. Before he lost his job and walked out on them. Jimmy and Mom, the worlds greatest authority. He fills a duffel bag with clothes. Sweat pants. A wind breaker. Sweatshirts from high school. Tee-shirts from his youth. Underwear he hasn't seen in years. Sweat socks with the smell of the locker room. Old friends from before. When they were high school sweethearts. Him and Vicki. And none of this happened.

He's back in the car now nipping at the Jack. Swigging at the Jack. Driving. And driving. Heading for the shore. Music loud. Country. Twangy and sad. He parks at the beach and stumbles for a dune. The bottle of Jack is wrapped in a sweatshirt. He finds a spot, sinks down in the sand and sobs as he assesses his world that's come crashing down around him. He goes AWOL for a week and sobers up enough to tell the department he needs more time. Fuck them. Fuck you. Then he's back in the car. To Travis Tritt. And Willie Nelson. And all those old cowboys singing their sad songs. To him, it turns out. And Jack. Always Jack. Straight from the bottle.

If you stop going to the gym and drink yourself into a stupor every day, muscle quicky turns to fat. So long six pack hello flab. He's dirty and unshaven. His hair is long and lank. His jeans and tee shirt have been on him for a week. Six weeks into his new regimen he's a bloated mass of blotchy flesh. That sharp looking detective in custom made suits no longer exists. The change is startling. He's holed up with a buddy who gives him a bed and all the booze he can drink. Which he does. To get numb. And erase that image. That freeze frame. When they all stared at each other. His wife and best friend. The details haunt him. His shirt. Flash. And his shorts. Click. And the hits keep coming.

The department sends someone over to see what shape he's in. He'll be carrying a gun when he comes back. If he's not right things can go wrong. If things go wrong it'll come down on them. So they sent someone to check him out. It's ten in the morning. Jimmy's miserable and drunk. He's red eyed, foul breathed, unshaven, unwashed and in his underwear. Tears roll down his cheeks as he opens the door. This is how he's doing. He's drunk by ten. Throwing up at eleven. And teary eyed and depressed for the rest of the day. Won't you come in, he says in an attempt at civility and trips over a pillow and ends up on the couch sprawled out like a sack of oatmeal. The man from the department is appalled and dismayed to find Jimmy this way. Someone on his way up not six weeks ago. A comer. Someone they had their eye on, the bosses, but no more. Cross his name off the list. What a mess there could have been. All because his friend was screwing his wife is what they heard through the grapevine, and not because of a bad reaction to the shooting. They send him for counseling and give him more time to pull himself together, but still he drinks. It's how he likes things these days. Soft and fuzzy. But still it's not enough to deaden that image. That silent montage he can't get out of his head.

He's way out there now. Farther than he's ever been before. Where it's bleakest. And coldest. And he wraps himself up in it. His misery. His overcoat of lead. Unable to shuck it. Not even wanting to. It's so welcoming. And familiar. As he sinks lower. And lower. Into his depression.

He drives all the time now, him and Jack, in that blurry haze he's gotten used to. With the music loud. Always loud. Bob Marley today with it's jaunty beat. Only it's not jaunty, it's sad. And melancholy. And takes Jimmy back to the Islands with Vicki. His high school sweetheart. Who stared at him naked. And sweaty. Mid fuck. He revels in it. His misery. His depression. Slopping in deep troughs of comforting sadness. Aching with despair. Tears rolling down his face as Bob pounds out that reggae beat.

His mother reaches him at his friend's. She's got a softer tone this time. More cajoling. Less wanting to be right. "Come off the edge," she begs him.

"Please, Jimmy. Do it for me. Stop this nonsense," in a voice he's never heard before. Almost motherly. Only "nonsense" echoes through his brain. It's what he's heard all his life. Nonsense. So dismissive. So disrespectful. Like it's silly, what he's going through. What he's doing. Nonsense, is how she lumps things together she doesn't understand. Only Jack is not nonsense. It's all he likes now. Chugging it down like soda-pop now. Numb from the booze. From Jack. He's two months in and spiraling down. Bleak upon bleak. Black upon blackest. Someone packed his things and left them at his mother's. Vicki? His buddy? What the fuck. On the stoop. Cartons of clothes from another life. His mother gets hold of him again. Mrs. Sympathetic. "You better get this outta my place, Jimmy. I've got no room for it," she tells him. Always there for him. Standing right behind him.

It's another bad day. He's driving in Westchester trying to exorcize his demons. Trying to blot the images out. Trying to blot everything out. He's spilled his coffee and banged up his knee and his hands are trembling like he's got Parkinson's. He drops things all the time now. His brain is fuzzy and full of cotton. Every bone in his body aches. His wife and best friend live inside his head no matter how loud he turns up the music. Every aspect of them. Every detail. All signs point to more of the same. Conversations confirm this in a recent monologue of self-pity and misery. How nothing, not even walking down the street, goes right for him. Segueing quickly into his failed marriage. His failed friendship. And the upcoming divorce he wants nothing to do with. It's a symphony of pain. An aria of sadness. A tragic opera that plays in his head along with the hollow feeling he's always got in the pit of his stomach. That constant sense of loss. Like someone died, but not just anyone. That person you loved most of all. The one you worshipped. And adored. And whispered secrets to in the dark. Gone. Out of your life. Just like that. Like some evil magicians trick.

He wonders how much more he can take of this. Driving. And drinking. And crying. All the time now. Every waking moment now. He's starting to think he'd like to end it, but it's not that easy. He's got requirements. An agenda. It must be quick. And painless. And no one must know. It must look like an accident, so he'll be buried right. And no one's ashamed of him. A bridge looks good for this purpose. You drive into it as fast as you can and it's over in a second. But bridges have guard rails to protect them from the traffic. He's been driving for weeks and hasn't seen one yet. Till now, that is. On this most awful of days. On a quiet Westchester road. He sees a bridge with no guard rails. That beckons to him as he drives. Then comes his epiphany. Nurtured by Jack Daniels and fear, and his ultimate good sense. That no matter how bad things are they can't be as bad this. As what he's thinking of doing now. Nothing can be as bad as that. As ending it all. And as he's thinking these thoughts the bridge races by him and disappears in the rear view mirror. He shakes himself off. Exhaling like he's been under water for too long. Breaking the surface to sanity. No longer wanting to slam his car into the bridge he's found. Or any other bridge for that matter. All he wants to do now is dry himself out, clean himself up and start someplace new.

Chapter 15

The town of Columbia is nestled in the northern hills of Westchester not far from the Hudson River. There's a main drag where the shops are and a number of side streets full old houses converted long ago into apartments and offices. The shops are small. None of your Gaps and Banana Republics here if you don't mind. There's a deli. A drugstore. A pizza parlor, beauty salon and a hardware store. Small businesses like that. The real estate boom is taking its time getting this far up-county and property values have increased slowly. Trains don't stop here any more. The bowling alley and the A&P closed last year. So did one of three local colleges. On the plus side the Higginbottoms sold their farm to a developer who plans to chop it up into five-acre lots and put up Mc Mansions for the newly rich.

The uniforms found the shell casing behind the first strip mall you come to after you get off the Parkway and take Route #35 into town. At the back of the shops is a small parking lot for two rows of cars, one faces the stores the other faces the woods. To the right, where the parking lot and tree line ends is the baseball field and running track. It's at the edge of the parking lot where the woods begin that they found it. Underneath a tree the gunman used to sight his rifle.

Jimmy arrives before everyone else and parks his car next to a couple of cruisers. As he walks to where they found the casing a gangly policeman comes towards him who doesn't look old enough to be wearing the uniform. His face is very serious. "We never touched a thing," he says defensively.

Jimmy smiles. "Good job."

"We taped off the area and made sure no one disturbed the site."

"Well done," says Jimmy, still smiling.

"We used the cartridge case as a central point and spread out another five hundred yards, but we didn't come up with anything else."

Jimmy's still smiling. "Anything else?"

The policeman is all wound up. He's with two other cops. They let him make the report because he's never done it before, him being so young and all. "There's a piece of paper we found near the shell casing," he says excitedly. "Like I said, we never touched anything, but it looks like a credit card receipt."

"Just lying there?" Jimmy asks.

"See for yourself. It's a bit muddied, but we think," he looks over at his buddies who are watching and grinning at him, "it was dropped by whoever took the shot."

"And why do *we* think that?" asks Jimmy. He's getting a kick out of the kid's enthusiasm.

"It looks like it fell out of his pocket and he stepped on it."

Jimmy can see what he means. The receipt is firmly embedded in the mud. At first glance he didn't see it. The area around the base of the tree is trodden down. Someone was standing there for sure but there's no clear foot print. No cigarette butts. Nothing else but the casing and not far from it the credit card receipt. From the Texaco station off Main Street. The number, in spite of the mud, is clearly visible. Jimmy's telling the kid to have the number traced when Smith and Monahan arrive. Jimmy tells the cop to hurry then turns to the boys and shows them what they found.

Jimmy thinks it's a wonder the uniforms found anything at all what with all the underbrush around. The spot where the shooter stood is a little way in from the parking lot hidden by bushes and brush. You could stand there for days and no one would see you. It's also dark. The tree canopy is thick here and no sunlight penetrates. He can also see that if you lined up the tree where the shooter stood to the spot where Jason was when he heard the shot and Sandra Ellison's body, it's a straight line. He points this out to Smith and Monahan. The boys take a look and agree with him, but they can't make up their minds what it means. "Probably just a coincidence," says Smith, then they turn their backs on him and continue their deliberations. It's not exactly rude the way they do it, but it's not very friendly either.

The chief arrives. Jimmy shows him the site and tells him what he just told the boys, that it's a straight line from the shell casings to Jason to Sandra Ellison. "What did they say?" The chief points his chin in the direction of Smith and Monahan.

"They think it's a coincidence.

"And you?"

"I think it's an odd coincidence."

The chief frowns.

The crime scene crew turns up. They take photographs of the shell casing from every conceivable angle, and the receipt. They measure things. And take earth samples. And take more pictures. Then the public make their appearance. First a few. Then more. Then some press arrives, scurrying about with microphones and recording machines. One has a cameramen in tow. Another has a notepad in his hand. All of them asking questions of anyone who will stop and talk to them. The site is suddenly alive with people. The place looks like a kicked over ant hill.

The kid comes back and whispers something in Jimmy's ear.

"Well?" says Smith.

Jimmy says the credit card receipt is from a card in the name of Jason Friendly.

Chapter 16

Smith and Monahan order up a search warrant for Jason's house quicker than you can order breakfast at a diner and get it just as fast. It would've taken Jimmy days to get one. The chief says he'll see them all back at the station. Jimmy and the boys get in their cars and make their way to Jason's house. As they get to the front gate a state trooper arrives with his lights flashing and his siren blasting. He screeches to a halt and is standing in front of the boys in a single bound, ram rod straight, search warrant in hand and Ray Bans glinting in the afternoon sun. It's a fabulous entrance and it drives the press wild. They surge forward in a wave of flashes, shutter clicking, and microphones waving in the air like snakes at a revival meeting. Smith and Monahan take possession of the document just inside the gate. The cop assigned to guard the house stretches out his arms to hold back the gathering crowd and watches the proceedings with fascinated amusement. Jimmy stands next to him, arms folded, enjoying the show. The hand over ceremony is brief. The boys are somber. Monahan praises the trooper for the speed of the delivery, solemnly shakes his hand and sends him on his way.

The trooper gives the boys a crisp salute, turns smartly on his heels, fights his way through the reporters to get to his car and drives off in a cloud of dust. There's more shutter clicking and flashing as the press struggles to record his exit. They push in front of each other and stand in the middle of the road trying for one last shot for their anxious public and hungry editors. When the car's gone they disperse in a pack of chattering and laughter, the sins of elbowing and pushing and even trampling over a fallen comrade who is just now dusting himself down and cleaning himself off, forgiven till the next time.

Armed with the newly acquired warrant and ignoring the pelting of reporter's questions, Smith and Monahan march resolutely up Jason's pathway and knock on his front door. Jimmy trails a couple of steps behind them.

Jason appears at the door looking haggard and distraught. His eyes have the dull look of a person in shock. He's cleaned himself up since Jimmy last saw him. He still hasn't shaved, but his hair is neater and he's wearing jeans, sneakers and a flannel shirt. Standing next to him is a pudgy looking man with sparkling blue eyes wearing a blue suit that somehow makes him appear larger than he really is. His head is completely shaved. He identifies himself as Jason's lawyer and gravely accepts the warrant on Jason's behalf. He reads it in silence, his lips mouthing every word, and when he's finished he advises Jason to stand aside and let everyone in. It is fortuitous that he's there to supervise the proceedings. He'd stopped by to confer with Jason believing that all was well. That even though Jason had been roughed up by the detectives that morning, no harm had been done and Jason had nothing to be concerned about. The knock on the door was a surprise. The search warrant more so. The lawyer looks concerned for his number one amigo and his shoulders slump ever so slightly.

Jason's frothing at the mouth and bars the door till his attorney puts a hand on his arm and gently shakes his head. "What do you want?" says Jason sounding slightly hysterical. "I thought everything was okay. What's happened? Will someone please tell me what's happened?"

Jimmy looks at the boys. It's their case. Let them take care of the niceties.

"Something's come up," says Smith.

Monahan nods in agreement.

"What?" says Jason.

There's a shaking of heads from the boys. "Sorry," says Smith. "Can't tell you that."

Jason looks like he's going to explode. "I have a right to know what you're looking for in my house."

The lawyer tries to calm Jason down then whispers something in his ear that deflates Jason before their eyes. His hands flop to his side. He gives out with an exasperated snort and walks away.

Jimmy's arranged for three uniforms to help them with the search. They're big burly men and enter the house now and fill up the hallway. They shake hands with Smith and Monahan then they all get to work. Three two-man teams, a detective and a blue, scurrying about the house like noisy children. Opening doors and cabinets. Picking things up and moving them around. It goes on like that for quite a while until Monahan in the basement comes up with something. Monahan's partner Sergeant Lewis goes upstairs to make the announcement. Jason's standing in the hallway when the call is made. He's incredulous. "What?" he shouts. "What did you find? There's nothing down there to find. It's a basement for chrissakes." He shakes his head like he can't believe what's going on.

The lawyer, whose shiny bald head comes to Jason's shoulder, looks dumpy and sad. He's out of his depth here as things keep getting worse for his dearest friend. Pangs of doubt are begining to nibble at the edges of his loyalty.

Everyone troops down to the basement, jostling each other to get a better view. On the far wall where it's darkest, boxes are piled to the ceiling in a higgledy piggledy manner. Half way up a rifle case peaks out. Sergeant Lewis begins to take pictures of it.

Jason shakes his head and says, "That's not mine," over and over like a needle stuck on a record player. He's a picture of misery and fear, and his face is a pasty grey. The boys lick their lips and circle him like hungry wolves. The lawyer, pale and shocked from this new revelation, stands next to him trying to protect him with his pudgy body. Things are not going how he'd expected them to. This is not the situation Jason described when he consented to represent him this morning.

A uniform puts on rubber gloves and gives them a theatrical snap. He checks to make sure Sergeant Lewis has finished his photography then pulls the case from its hiding place. A cascade of cartons tumble to the floor raising a small cloud of dust. Someone sneezes. Then someone else. The uniform up-ends a couple of boxes and lays the case on top of them. He looks to the boys who nod for him to continue. He snaps the fasteners and opens the lid. Everyone leans forward to see. Inside is a Remington .303 freshly oiled and polished. There's also a snipers scope that fits snugly into a green felt depression. Smith puts his nose to the barrel and announces mournfully, "It's been fired recently."

"It's not mine," says Jason, starting up again.

"Then whose is it?" says Monahan, irritably.

"I don't know," says Jason. Shaking his head in despair.

Smith is doubtful. "What's it doing here if it's not yours?"

"I don't know," says Jason.

"Don't know. Not mine," mimics Smith.

"You're saying you've never seen the case or the rifle before?' says Monahan.

"Never."

"Same as you don't know how that receipt got near the shell casing we found this morning," Monahan sneers.

Jason and the attorney say in unison, "What receipt?"

"We found a credit card receipt where the shooter stood," says Monahan.

Jason looks from one to the other, "And?"

"It's in your name."

Jason doesn't know what to say to that. Every revelation pulls him in deeper. He looks at his attorney hoping he'll come up with something. The attorney looks at him balefully and shrugs. He's sorry he showed up now. He mops his sweaty brow with a large white handkerchief and runs it over his bald head before returning it to his pocket. He's beginning to be concerned about how things are going to look in this tightly knit community of theirs, his best friend being a murderer and all.

The uniform closes the rifle case and snaps off his rubber gloves. Monahan tells Sergeant Lewis to get it to the lab as quickly as he can. Smith says he'll call ahead to expedite the situation. They'll remain here, he says, at Jason's house and wait for the results. The two remaining cops go back to searching the house. Everyone else, Jimmy, the boys and Jason and his attorney, end up in the back room where Jimmy and Jason sat that morning. The threatening letters are still strewn across the coffee table. No one looks at them or pays them any mind. Instead the boys lace into Jason some more.

"You think the victim knew the shooter," asks Monahan.

Jason snaps angrily, "How should I know?"

"What do you think?" asks Smith.

"I don't see how it's possible," huffs Jason.

"Why's that?" says Monahan.

"It was an unscheduled stop. How could he know she'd get off that train?"

"You did," says Smith.

Jason is suddenly full of righteous indignation. "I did not," he says.

"Yes you did," says Smith, raising his voice. "You saw her on your first go round. Your first orbit. Isn't that what you call it, counselor? An orbit? You recognized her. You were still pissed at her because she dumped you. Seeing her again was like waving a red flag in your face. You ran home, got the gun and shot her. It's as simple as that."

"What about the noise I heard?"

"You made it up."

"Why?"

"Because you bumped into Officer Frankie."

The boys give him the cold stare.

"That's my motive? Because she dumped me?"

"Maybe it was business stuff," Smith speculates. "Could be anything really."

"Anything," repeats Monahan.

Jason can't believe what he's hearing. He looks like he's having a heart attack. "You're both crazy," he splutters. "I killed her because she dumped me, that's what you're thinking?"

"C'mon Jason. You're the one who told Jimmy you were screwing her."

"You're making this up, aren't you?"

The boys stare at him some more. Watching him. Not saying anything.

"To rattle me. Right? It's a technique. Right?"

"What's the matter counselor?" asks Monahan. "Did we hit a nerve?"

Jimmy watches how the boys have come to life. Their dull faces are suddenly bright and alert as they lick their lips, smelling blood.

Jason runs his hand through his hair. "Does the receipt have a date?"

"Sometime in March," says Smith.

"What would I be doing with a receipt two months old?"

"How should I know?" says Monahan. "But it's yours. There's no doubt about that."

"If you say so."

Smith caught the tone. "Oh I do say so, counselor," he says pedantically. "I most certainly do say so. It's not me saying these things, it's the evidence. That receipt is in your name and it was at the spot where you took your shot. End of story. I'll get a copy of it for you and you'll see for yourself."

"If you're not the shooter what's it doing there?" said Monahan.

Jason says he doesn't know.

"What does that mean?" says Smith.

Jason can't think of anything to say.

"Why did you kill her?" says Monahan. Not wanting to waste any more time on the niceties.

Jason looks like the stuffing's been knocked out of him.

"C'mon Jason," says Smith. "Tell us what happened."

"That's right," says Monahan. "Make it easy on yourself."

"Maybe you had a good reason," says Smith.

"Extenuating circumstances," says Monahan.

Jason snaps out of it and straightens up. "You're saying," he says deliberately. "I see Sandra Ellison get off the train on my first go round, run home, get my rifle and shoot her, all because she dumped me?" his voice begins to rise. "Is that it? That's how you see it?" He stares hard at Smith. His nostrils flare. Up for the fight now. Angry. Determined.

"Sounds right to me," says Smith.

Monahan nods.

"So where'd the receipt drop from?" Jason wants to know.

"From your pocket," says Smith.

"What pocket?" says Jason. "My shorts don't have pockets."

"Who said you were wearing shorts?" says Monahan.

Jason looks at Jimmy.

"He was wearing them when I saw him last night," says Jimmy.

"Maybe it dropped out of the gun case," says Monahan.

"What gun case?" asks Jason.

"The one you kept the rifle in," says Smith.

"I don't own a rifle," says Jason.

"I think you do," says Smith smirking. "We just found it."

Jason runs his hands through his hair and slumps into one of the chairs. The pudgy lawyer stands dutifully by his side. Sweat beads on his bald head and he fingers his tie speculatively. He's more worried than ever.

"Where'd you buy the rifle?" Monahan wants to know. He and Smith are standing in front of Jason now, crowding in on him.

"I didn't," says Jason.

"It's in your basement," says Smith.

"It's not mine, I keep telling you that."

"Who's is it?" Monahan wants to know.

Jason shakes his head.

"Why'd you kill her?" Monahan asks.

"I didn't."

"And I say you did," says Monahan.

Jason lets out a sigh.

"C'mon Jason, what's going on here?" asks Smith.

It goes on like that for more than an hour even though Jason's clammed up apart from denying everything they throw at him which drives the boys crazy. They keep saying the same things in different ways until even Jimmy is ready to confess. The lawyer keeps raising objections, but doesn't seem to achieve anything on Jason's behalf. Then Smith's cell phone goes off which makes everyone jump. He walks out of the room to take the call. When he comes back he's got the two uniforms with him. He motions to Monahan and whispers something in his ear. They both look at Jason then Monahan moves towards him saying as he does, "The lab says the rifle in the basement is the one used to kill Sandra Ellison." The uniforms follow and stand on either side of Jason and, while Monahan advises him of his rights, Smith cuffs him. Then Monahan, in a voice reflecting the awesome power the state has bestowed on him, charges Jason Friendly with the murder of Sandra Ellison.

Chapter 17

They're lying in bed. Jimmy and Mary Harwood. A flickering candle is their only light. Mary's kid Lucy is having a sleep-over at a friend's, so they've decided to have a sleep-over of their own. At Mary's house. Just the two of them. First a romantic dinner in front of the fire in the living room, then a little dessert. Now it's late, just before going to sleep time. Outside is a full moon, its eerie glow bathes everything in an unworldly luminescence. Shadows dance on the walls. The bottles on her dresser give off twinkley reflections. Jimmy's going over his day. He's telling her about the Skipper's press conference announcing Jason's arrest and how he managed to puff himself up to a size he'd never seen before. "He always looks like he just got a haircut," says Jimmy. "It's a recent thing. And he's got that smell about him too, like he just came from the beauty salon."

"Mmmm," is Mary's only comment.

"He's getting it cut a couple of times a week now. That's what it looks like to me. Is that possible?"

"I'll ask Josephine what's going on," she says thoughtfully.

Josephine runs a beauty salon on Main Street. It's a three chair affair that caters to men and women. She's Mary's best friend. They're kindred spirits almost since the day Mary came to town five years ago. They have a lot in common, these two. The same type of background. Working with the public. Mary waited tables and Josephine's a hairdresser. They're outsiders, these two. Not born here. Newcomers to the community and not part of the crowd.

"You should've seen the look on Jason's face when they carted him off," says Jimmy.

"They?"

"The county guys."

"Laurel and Hardy?"

He gets a kick out of the way she knows who they are. If she saw them she'd really see the funny side of it.

"I guess we shouldn't count on Jason being our next mayor."

"Not this week," says Jimmy and pulls the covers over his shoulders.

She nuzzles into him. "You sound like you feel sorry for him."

"He looked so shell shocked, you know. Like, 'How could this be happening to me?'"

"Oh my."

Ever meet him?"

"Once."

"Where?"

"At that club of theirs."

"Rolling Hills?" He said it like she'd gotten into Aladdin's cave.

"Just the one time. Soon after you closed the case on Thomas. One of them tried to sink his teeth into me and sell me some insurance. He took me there for dinner to show me off. They were nice enough I suppose, but you could tell they were just being polite. I'd catch people staring at me out the corner of my eye, or talking to each other and looking in my direction. It's not a very cozy environment. They've got a definite pecking order there. I'm not sure where my guy fit in, but I don't think he was up there with the big shots. Bringing me there didn't help his situation, and I didn't invite him in when he dropped me off. You should've seen the look on his face. No one had ever done that to him before. Mr. Smooth. There he was suffering the slings and arrows from the members and he got nothing for his trouble. I never heard from him again and that was the end of my country club career. Have you ever been?"

He shakes his head. "Nor likely to the way things are going."

She smiles and touches his face then snuggles in to him under the warm covers. The candle flickers and casts dancing shadows on the white wall. She conjures up Jason's face from that brief encounter and remembers his comfortable arrogance and self-assurance. She matches it to his electioneering pictures pasted all over town and it's the same guy as far as she's concerned. Unchanged. A special type of person untouched by what goes on around him. Cocooned in a social environment centered on the club and all of its machinations. It's all he cares about. Then, and now. "He doesn't seem the type," she says, breaking the silence.

"He doesn't, does he?" he says ruefully. "Then there are these death threats. I told you about that, right?"

She says he did. "Why didn't he report it?"

"He said he didn't want to upset the apple cart."

"What apple cart?"

"The election. His practice. He's got Rolling Hills as a client and lots of the members. He says if they got a whiff of a scandal they'd cut him loose. He couldn't take that chance. And he was sure it was this joker who's been dogging him all this time so he never took it seriously."

"You believe him?"

"Kinda."

They were quiet then. Listening to the noises of the night. The hoot of an owl. The rustling of the undergrowth as a critter makes it's way across the garden. Then Jimmy says, "The boys think they've got him cold."

"And do they?"

"They don't see any connection between Jason's death threats and Sandra Ellison. They say Jason saw her getting off the train, ran home, got the rifle, set up where they found the credit card receipt, shot her, took the rifle home, went out for another run, bumped into Frankie and told him he heard what could've been a shot, and the rest is history."

"What do you think?"

"There's a lot of running around. If he shot her why'd he come out again?

"What about the rifle?"

"I'm tracking it down.

"Prints?"

"No prints. The rifle was wiped clean."

She gets up on one elbow and looks at him. "So what do you think?"

"I don't think he did it is what I think and everything that's turned up so far hasn't changed my mind." He rolls over onto his side and tucks up his knees. Mary spoons into him, squiggling in to make the fit just right. He loves this part of it. It's the best part of the day so far as he's concerned. Better than their love making, though he'd never tell her that. He feels so safe when she wraps herself around him like this. Clinging to him like she'll never let him go. And he, from a place deep inside of himself, feels all warm and toasty. And, for the first time since the last time they did this, secure and content. His eyes begin closing. He's about to drift off when she breaks the silence again. "He doesn't seem the type," she whispers softly in his ear.

Jimmy sighs, "I know," he says. "I know," and wiggles his bottom into her crotch to get even closer, if such a thing is possible.

Friday

Chapter 18

The morning noises at Mary's house are a lot different from the ones at Jimmy's place. Wrens live in the bushes and the shrubs surrounding her home. They rise very early and twitter and chirrup as loud as they are small. It's hard to figure how something so little can make so much noise so early. Like dawn. An hour Jimmy's not seen since the last time he stayed over. Felix, his cat with an attitude, takes care of that problem at his place. No bird would dare set up so close to the house. For a while Jimmy lies on his back looking at the ceiling. Mary's sound asleep. The symphony outside has no effect on her. He's in a twilight zone. Not really awake, but not sleeping either. Dozing. Pictures popping in and out of his head. A newsreel of the story so far. Jason's story. And Jason's eyes. Those eyes. Locking onto his as they drove him away.

After a while Jimmy gets up and tiptoes to the kitchen to make a pot of coffee. He's still thinking about Jason, and the surprise on his face when Monahan read him his rights and Smith cuffed him. How ashamed he looked as they ducked his head and pushed him into the back of their car. Reporters swirling around them. Flashes going off like they were in a war zone. Jimmy sips his coffee and makes a face. It's not the brand he likes, but it'll do. Outside the birds open up a fresh salvo of trilling and shrieks. The backyard is suddenly overrun by blue jays who swoop and screech and make a deafening racket as the sun peeks over the tree line. It's not often Jimmy appreciates the job Felix does for him, but listening to the din outside makes him realize what a good caretaker he is. Between the coffee and the noise outside he's wide awake now and even though it's not yet 7:00 he decides to pay Jason a visit.

Jason is in a holding tank in the basement of the station house. His only company is a snoring drunk in the opposite cell. The walls are cinder block. There are no windows. Each cell has a toilet, a sink and a bunk. There's a strong smell of disinfectant that makes Jason feel sick to his stomach. Light comes from a neon strip in the ceiling of a corridor that runs between the cells. His lawyer brought him some personal stuff after the commotion died down last night. Books, magazines and some toiletries. Then he told Jason, in a voice choked with remorse, he was afraid he couldn't represent him any more. He's out of his depth, he said sadly, and recommended someone he thought could do a better job. "You need a criminal attorney. Contracts and wills are more my speed," is how he put it. The truth of the matter is his clients told him unless he put some distance between Jason and himself, they'd be putting some distance between them and him. Sometimes it's better to look the other way. Jason resisted the temptation to tell his dearest friend to go fuck himself and instead found himself consoling his pal instead of the other way around.

Jimmy finds Jason sitting on the edge of his cot staring vacantly into space. He looks shriveled up inside of himself. He's usually such an imposing figure in his sharp looking suits and shiny shoes, but now his shoulders are slumped and his lithe runner's body looks emaciated and sagging. Gone is the cocky grin and his face is pale and gaunt.

"How's it going, counselor," says Jimmy cheerfully. The guard lets him into the cell. Jimmy hands Jason a paper sack containing a blueberry muffin and a container of coffee he picked up on his way over. He sits down besides him. The gate clangs shut. They look at each other just for a second. Neither mentioning the awful sound the cell door made as it closed behind him.

Jason nods his appreciation for the coffee and says, "I'm being arraigned this afternoon." He stares at Jimmy looking for a reaction.

Jimmy says he knows.

"They really think I did this thing," says Jason like he only just figured it out. That up until that moment he didn't think it was possible. "They're asking for $2 million bail, can you believe it?" he asks incredulously. "$2 million! Like I'm some sort of mass murderer. My problem is that I'm going to have trouble raising that kind of money. It's going to take a few days. I just can't believe this is happening to me. "

"Why's it going to take so long? I always thought you were so well-heeled."

"Mortgages. Investments. It's a long story," he says dully. "The short version is that it's going to take some time."

Jason's coming to terms with now it. The reality. The fact that he's going to jail. You can see it written all over his face. The fear. The uncertainty. Jimmy is sensitive to it, but it doesn't stop him from asking awkward questions.

"Smith and Monahan are going to New York today. They're going to be delving into Sandra Ellison's world to fill out their case on you. They'll be talking to her friends and family. Co-workers. That sort of thing. Anything you want to tell me before they find it out for themselves?"

Jason shakes his head.

"No dirty little secrets?"

Jason says sullenly, "Like what?"

"Sexual persuasions. Drug habits."

"No."

"They found coke in her purse."

"So you told me."

"Was that something you did together?"

"No. You've asked me that already."

"Not even a taste?"

"I told you, no."

"Not even once?"

Jason glares at Jimmy. "Are you deaf?"

"Ever hear of Marc Hilliard?"

Jason gives out with an irritable sigh. "I told you, no."

"He's the guy she gets the coke from."

Jason shakes his head. "We've been through this before."

"She was sleeping with him, did you know that?" says Jimmy.

Jason keeps shaking his head.

"That's who Smith and Monahan are going to see today, Marc Hilliard the drug dealer. The boys are being thorough for a change."

"I don't know him." says Jason wearily.

"It's going to come out."

"What is?"

"Whatever you're not telling me."

Jason chews on a nail. His head is down, saying nothing. An immense snore comes from the drunk in the opposite cell. Neither of them look over.

"Whatever's happened so far Jason is just a taste of things to come," says Jimmy earnestly. "The press are like vultures. Nothing's sacred with those guys. If it's out there they'll find it and use it to crucify you."

Jason picks up a newspaper the guard gave him. He shoves it at Jimmy. The front page is filled with photos of Sandra. "You'd think they'd show her some respect?" he says sadly. "She's dead for chrissakes. Murdered. They make her out to be some sort of drug crazed slut. What must her family think?"

"That's what I'm trying to tell you, Jason. Nothing's sacred, you've been on enough of these deals to know that. 'Course you were on the other side of it, then." As soon as he said it he was sorry. He didn't mean to, it just slipped out. It's like a slap in the face to Jason who suddenly stands up and towers over him. His face is contorted with rage. He enunciates loudly. And slowly. Like Jimmy's deaf. "I Did Not Do This!"

Jimmy blinks.

Jason paces the cell like a caged animal. He's breathing hard and slops coffee on the floor. Finally he calms down, sits next to Jimmy and says earnestly, "That rifle is not mine, Jimmy. I've never owned a gun in my life."

"What about the receipt?"

"Someone put it there."

"Why?"

"Why have I been getting these death threats?"

Jimmy scratches his nose.

"It could be him."

"Who?"

"The guy who's been messing with me."

Jimmy purses his lips. Not sure where this is going. "You're saying?"

"He came to my house, lifted the receipt and left it at the site."

"Why?"

"To implicate me."

"What about the rifle?"

"That too."

"How?"

"He knows how. I told you already, this has been going on for a long time."

Jimmy scratches the back of his neck. "It's a bit thin, Jason" he says skeptically. "If I take it to Smith and Monahan, that's what they're going to say to me. They'll want to know why anyone would live like that? Why you didn't react knowing someone wanted to kill you."

"It's only recently he's talked about killing me."

"So when that started." asks Jimmy. "Why wouldn't you say something then?"

"We've been through this already. I told you I didn't want to mess up the campaign. A whiff of scandal in this town and you're a gonner. Ask my lawyer. He just quit on me because of it. My best friend, can you imagine that? He tells me he thinks he's out of his league and recommended someone else. Bullshit! I'll bet you a million dollars his clients threatened to leave him if he stuck by me. That's what they're like here. You know what

I'm talking about. Any trouble and they run from you like you've got the plague. I figured those threats were from the same guy who's been doing this to me all along. I thought I was safe."

"I still don't get the tie-in with Sandra Ellison. What's her murder got to do with your death threats?"

"Suppose whoever did it wasn't trying to kill her?"

Jimmy raises an eyebrow.

"Suppose he was aiming for someone else?"

"And who would that be?"

"Me."

A show stopper. They sit there looking at each other. The snoring in the other cell offers a distraction while Jimmy thinks it through. Remembering the straight line from the shooter to Jason to Sandra Ellison. He thought it was an odd coincidence then. Now Jason's theory throws a different light on it. If Jason wasn't the shooter then the shooter could have been aiming for Jason, missed him and hit Sandra Ellison by mistake.

Jason watches him mull it over. "Go and look through those things I showed you. They're still on the table. Maybe you'll see something you didn't see before. There's some other stuff in the top drawer of the sideboard. See what you think."

Jimmy doesn't respond. Instead he says, "Hypothetically speaking, do you think it's possible you could have run home, got the rifle, set up where they found the receipt, took your shot, ran home to dump the rifle, gone out again, ran by the library and bumped into Frankie? That seems like an awful lot of running to me."

"It is if it happened that way, only it didn't. I don't own that rifle and I didn't shoot Sandra."

"But it's possible, right. You could've done it?"

"The killing or that amount of running?"

"Both."

Jason looks like he's been kicked in the stomach.

"I'm not saying you did it," says Jimmy trying to placate him. "I'm just looking for holes in the argument."

"My usual running time is twenty minutes. That first time took me twenty four."

"Because?"

"The people from the train held me up. I had to slow down to get through them. Then, when I heard the shot I stopped to look around."

Jimmy writes it all down. "Frankie's got you running into him at about five past nine give or take."

"That would be about right."

"If, and I'm only saying if, you took that shot and did all that running back and forth, how long do you think it would take?"

"Much longer than the twenty four minutes of my first orbit."

"Anyone see you when you left your house?"

"I don't think so. That's why I like to run so late. There's no one around."

"Cars? There must have been cars on the road?"

"I suppose. But even if they saw me do you think they checked the time when they did?"

"You never know. And you're telling me you never heard of Marc Hilliard?"

"Right."

"You never did coke with Sandra?"

"Right."

"Whoever killed Sandra was aiming for you."

Jason nods

"The same guy who's been hassling you since you moved back to Columbia?"

Jason nods again and tells him where to find the key to the house.

Jimmy mulls it over. It's possible. Anything's possible. "I'll check it out," he says and calls for the guard.

There's a rumbling and a grumbling from the opposite cell. Then comes the sounds of someone throwing up and other disgusting noises. Jimmy looks at Jason sympathetically as the guard opens the door. Then the terrible smell hits them. Jimmy covers his nose with a handkerchief. He can hear the guard hurling insults at the drunk as he heads quickly for the street wondering, as he breaks into the fresh air, whose job it is to clear up the mess.

Chapter 19

Jimmy finds the key to Jason's house underneath a big stone by the mail box, and lets himself in. "Anyone home," he calls out. He's standing in the hallway. There's only silence and the smell of lemon scented polish. "Anyone here," he calls again. Something's not right, he can feel it. It's hard to quantify, even harder to explain, but he senses he's not alone. He feels for his revolver. Knowing it's there gives him comfort. He rarely draws it. Back in Brooklyn it was out all the time. Here he can count on his fingers the times he's pulled it, but the instincts don't go away.

He edges into the hallway his hand on the grip, then stands completely still. There's no sound. Not even a creak. He edges further into the house towards the back room then stops. Nothing. He starts forward again, his hand still on the grip. Someone was here, he can see it now as he edges into the back room. Drawers hang open. Things are thrown in a pile on the floor. The coffee table is clean of the letters he came for and the back door is wide open. Jimmy dashes into the yard, but sees no one. There are woods at the edge of the property and Jimmy stands there watching and listening, but there's no movement. He disturbed whoever it was, he's sure of it.

Back inside he takes a look around. Whatever was supposed to be in the sideboard isn't there. Everything is tipped into a pile in the middle of the sun-room floor. There were supposed to be some letters in a bundle, but Jimmy sees no such thing. He gives the house a once over, but no other room seems to have been disturbed. Jimmy rules out robbery, because valuable stuff is lying around in every room. He thinks whoever it was knew what they were looking for. He takes out his cell phone and calls the boys.

Smith picks up.

Jimmy tells him about the break-in and the missing letters.

Smith gets agitated. "What do you think these letters are about, Jimmy? Someone doesn't like him, that's what they're about. Hey, we don't like him. You should hear the stuff we got from Sandra's friends. They don't like him either. They fought like cats and dogs. They broke up because she wanted to see other people. He never told us that, did he? What else isn't he telling us? And what's any of this got to do with Ellison's death anyway? Answer me that, Jimmy."

Jimmy thinks he's not getting the point. "Someone broke into his house and stole evidence. Why would they do that?"

"What evidence?"

"I just told you. The death threats he showed me this morning and some other things he hadn't."

"What other things?"

"Another bundle of letters."

"Saying what?"

"They've been taken so I don't know"

"So?"

"So I don't think we can be so sure he did it."

"On the basis of what?" says Smith. "That he said he had some threatening letters and someone broke into the house and took them. That's it? He's running for office, Jimmy. Politicians get threats in the mail all the time."

"Why would someone come back and steal them?"

"Who says they came back? It could have been anyone. The press. Curiosity seekers."

Jimmy says, "Something doesn't smell right."

"It's him, Jimmy. He doesn't smell right. You've been standing too close to him that's your problem. You've lost your nose for the bad guys."

"I think we should keep looking," says Jimmy. "I don't think he did it."

"Yeah? Well we do!" And that's the end of the conversation.

Jimmy calls up a crime scene crew. They're at Jason's house in half an hour. They find prints all over the back room and a couple of fresh shoe molds outside in the yard. They sweep dust samples from the pile in the middle of the room and vacuum the floor for dirt, hair and dander. Jimmy's still there when Jason's new lawyer shows up. The man has the look of a predator. He's taller than the last one. Thinner too. His handsome, angular face has a hawk-like quality with a high forehead and black hair combed straight back off of his face. He's in his mid -forties and wears a black double breasted suit, a crisp white shirt with a charcoal gray tie and black Oxfords that are shined to perfection. His appearance is elegant. His no-nonsense manner is not. "Who are you?" he says rudely as Jimmy opens the door.

Jimmy flashes his badge.

The lawyer explains who he is. "I hope you've got a warrant," he says and leans forward into Jimmy, his chin thrust out all ready to go.

Jimmy put his hands up. "No need for gun play," he says smiling. "Your client asked me to look at some letters. In any case I'm not sure I need a warrant since your boy's been charged with murder."

There's no smile back. Jimmy tells him about the break-in as he leads him to the sunroom. They survey the mess from the doorway.

A drawer from the coffee table and two from the sideboard were flung across the room. The contents have been emptied in a pile in the middle of the floor. Photos. Receipts. Postcards. Matches. Birthday cards. Letters. Candles. Crap. Rubbish. An accumulation of years of stuff that never got thrown away.

"Could've been anyone," is the lawyer's only comment.

"You sound like Smith and Monahan."

"The county boys?"

Jimmy nods then asks him if he's got any ideas who might've done this.

"How should I know?" says the lawyer. "I just took the case."

Jimmy gives him a look.

The lawyer tones it down. "Souvenir hunters. The press. Like I said, it could've been anyone.

"They knew what they were looking for," says Jimmy.

"Why do you say that?"

"They only went for those three drawers. If it was robbery there's plenty of stuff they could've taken and didn't."

"Maybe you disturbed them," says the lawyer.

"I did, but it looks like they got what they came for anyway."

"What are you, clairvoyant?"

Jimmy gives him a cold stare.

"We need to get Jason here so he can tell us what's missing," says the lawyer.

"I know what's missing, the letters," says Jimmy.

"Letters?"

"Don't you talk to your client?"

The lawyer's jaw juts out again.

"Threatening letters. Death threats. Didn't Jason tell you?"

The lawyer says he knows.

"Well that's what's been taken."

"What else?'

"How should I know," says Jimmy.

"That's why we need Jason."

Jimmy catches the "we." He resents being taken for granted.

"He's being arraigned this afternoon," says the lawyer. "They'll set bail high. He won't be able to raise it. They'll send him to County till the trial. Once he's processed we can check him out, and find out what else they took. If I try to get him out it'll take me a week at the least. You can do it tomorrow. I know this puts you in conflict with Smith and Monahan and your boss, but its got to be done if we want to move quickly."

Jimmy sighs loudly. "I know," he says hearing the "we" again and wondering just how much trouble he's letting himself in for.

Chapter 20

Jimmy stops off at his house before going back to the station. It's the smart thing to do. Felix is already mad at him, he can tell as he walks in the door. He gets a perfunctory meow then the cat runs over to his bowl and sits there staring at it as if the food will appear by magic. There are a few crumbs left in the bowl. Jimmy realizes what a near thing this was. If he'd waited any longer vengeance would be Felix's. That could be anything from peeing on the stove to throwing up on the bed. Or nothing. Sometimes Felix can be forgiving. Right now he looks from the bowl to Jimmy and back to the bowl again while his tail flicks in anger. He's communicating. Telling Jimmy to hurry the fuck up. And don't think Jimmy doesn't. Because he recognizes the signs. So he tickles Felix's ears, and makes a big fuss of him. And pours food in his bowl. And gives him fresh water. And adds a saucer of milk. Sucking up to him now. Trying for grace in the eyes of the Felix. Remembering the bird asylum that was Mary's back yard this morning and grateful for the job Felix does for him.

It's a perfect spring day as Jimmy makes the ten minute drive back to work. The sun shines brightly in the clear blue sky. The buds are ready to burst. They're so fat they change the landscape from a horizon of naked trees to quilts of pastel shades and transparent outlines. Another day of sun and the leaves will set themselves free. Here and there a tree has already done it.

Jimmy can feel the tension as he walks into the station house. It's in the eyes of this man, the desk sergeant, as Jimmy passes him by with his friendly wave and cheery "good afternoon." The sergeant can always be relied upon to reflect the mood of the Skipper. If there's no trouble, Jimmy's good morning is greeted with an enthusiasm that can sometimes appear over the top. It's a good barometer. Like now, for instance, as his greeting is met with a sliding of eyes and a muttered response. Unfazed Jimmy goes to his office and spends some time trying to run down the rifle used in the shooting. A little while later he's summoned to the Skipper's office. Jimmy barely gets inside the door before the bellow comes. "Are you fucking nuts?"

Jimmy gives him the "what me?" look and imagines every ear in the station perking up like deer in the forest when they smell danger. Necks straining. All heads looking in the same direction.

"Who told you you could go to Jason's house?" barks the chief. "I don't remember anyone asking me for my opinion. I thought this was a closed case, right Jimmy? Out of our hands, right? Right? All wrapped up in a neat little package and finished with." He slaps his hands together like a croupier when he's done.

Jimmy stands in front of the Skipper's desk. There's no chair for him now. Or coffee. A measure of the ground he's lost so quickly. The chief glowers at him. He grips his pencil so hard it snaps in two. He looks at the pieces in disgust and hurls them across the room. Jimmy starts to explain, tentatively, how he went to see Jason that morning and how Jason told him there were more letters.

The chief cuts him off. "Again with the letters. I've heard all this before."

"This is a different bunch of letters."

"What do they say?"

"I don't know, they were stolen." Jimmy tells him about the intruder and how he just missed him.

"The place was ransacked?"

"Selectively."

"What's that mean?"

"Three drawers. Nothing else. They knew what they were looking for. I got a crime scene crew there. They got some prints, a shoe mold, and did a lot of that vacuuming and dusting they do. I'll get the report tomorrow." Then he tells him about Jason's theory that the shooter could have been aiming for him and not Sandra Ellison.

The Skipper gives it some thought. "The prints and shoe mold could be anyone's. Enough people have trampled over that place the last couple of days, I can't imagine it'll help your cause."

"That's what Smith and Monahan said."

"And you?"

Jimmy shrugs. "What about Jason's theory that the shooter was aiming for him. Jason didn't know it's a straight line from the shooter, to him to Sandra Ellison. I never told him. "

"And your point?"

"That it's possible. A shooter aiming for Jason could have missed him and hit Sandra."

"What do the boys say?" asks the chief.

"They thought it was a coincidence." Turning their backs on him is what Jimmy remembers happened right then. "They think they've got Jason cold. That's all they care about, closing the case and moving on."

The chief agrees with the boys. You can see it on his face.

"They don't want me making any waves," says Jimmy.

"Me neither."

Jimmy chews the inside of his cheek. Then he tells the Skipper what he's got on the rifle. "I've traced it to a gun show in Pennsylvania two years ago. It's registered to a Mickey Swan. The last address I've got for him is in Syracuse. I put a call in to the cops there and they're tracking him down for me. It'll take a while though."

"Did you tell the boys?"

"Smith. I told Smith. The other one doesn't take calls. Smith's the mouthpiece. He said, and I quote, "They can take all the time they like. That thing belongs to Jason Friendly. We found it in his basement. It's the one used for the shooting and so far as we're concerned, that's all she wrote." Jimmy pauses then says, "I want to take Jason back to his house."

The chief frowns. "Why?"

"To see what's missing from this break-in."

"You know what's missing," the chief says irritably. "Those letters."

"His lawyer thinks something else could've been taken. Only Jason would know what."

"Then let the lawyer do it," says the chief angrily. "What's it got to do with you anyway?"

"It'll take him a week at the least. I can do it after Jason's arraigned."

The Skipper's face turns red. He smolders. He does not want to cross Smith and Monahan and Jimmy's putting him in their line of fire. He retreats into silence while his mind churns through all the bad things they can do to him, hoping Jimmy will help him out here and not poke around any more.

"Suppose these death threats are real?" says Jimmy. "Suppose the shooter really was aiming for Jason?"

The chief's shoulders go up. He can see Jimmy's not going to let it go. "Let the lawyer do it," he growls.

"I can speed this up, Skip."

"Stay out of it."

Jimmy looks pensive.

"What? Spit it out."

"I don't think Jason did it," says Jimmy.

The chief's voice gets loud to emphasize his displeasure. "On the basis of what?"

"All these things I just told you." says Jimmy. His voice rising too.

They glare at each other. It's fortunate the desk is between them otherwise they'd be chin to chin. Then the chief yells at him full throttle,

"Let the fucking lawyer do it!" His face is bright purple and he looks like he's having a heart attack.

Jimmy sees that things aren't going very well here. Not for nothing is he a detective. He lowers his voice and puts a nicer look on his face. "I don't think you're seeing this right, Skip," he says in a voice that drips with concern.

The chief eyes him cautiously. "How so?"

"If Jason didn't kill Sandra Ellison he's definitely gonna be our next mayor."

"What do I care if he wins the election or not. Anyway, he backed out and none of that matters any more. He's going to jail."

"If he didn't do it, he'll jump back in the race again, I can guarantee you that."

The chief looks unhappy. His neat little package is coming undone and things are getting complicated.

Jimmy says, "He can't miss."

"*If* he didn't do it," says the chief.

"He'll win by a landslide."

"If."

"And you'll be his best buddy."

The chief looks like a bull catching his breath after a run at the cape.

"For sticking by him."

The chief's not convinced. He paws the ground and contemplates another charge.

"And getting him out of jail."

The chief's nostrils flare.

"Then you'll be hanging with the big shots all the time at that club of theirs." Jimmy can see a sudden change in the Skipper's eyes. A slight squint as the light of a truth pierces his outer layers and ignites his sensibilities. The chief's never been to Rolling Hills Country Club. In the ten years he's lived and worked in the community he's not received a single invitation. It's a sore point with him. A subtle form of discrimination he chafes at. People he sees every day. Works with. Cooperates with. And not once has the mayor and that bunch ever invited him to the club, not even for a drink. He's just an employee to them, that's how they see him. Him and the fire chief. On the payroll and no one to socialize with.

"This could set you up nicely, Skip" says Jimmy. "You'll never have trouble getting voted in again. They'll be on your side forever after this. Especially the new mayor."

The chief raises an eyebrow.

Jimmy mistakes the eyebrow for scorn, but the chief is only acknowledging the truth of Jimmy's argument. "Supposing you're wrong?" he asks cautiously. "Then I've stuck my neck out for nothing."

"What if this conversation never took place?" says Jimmy. "If I'm wrong, which I don't think I am, you can tell the boys I've been freelancing and you can hang me out to dry."

"You're that sure?" asks the chief, tempted by Jimmy's attractive offer. "Run it by me again."

"I believe Jason when he says he's been dogged for years by some nutcase. Especially because I was on that case when he came back to Columbia. I believe him when he says his life's been threatened because I saw the letters myself. That intruder took them, along with the ones I haven't seen. Whoever did that is the shooter or connected to the shooter. I think Jason was out jogging that night. He heard something that sounded like a shot and reported it. I think that shot was meant for him and missed and hit Sandra Ellison by mistake."

The chief stares into space trying to figure out all the angles. "I'll have to answer for you checking Jason out of jail," he says, thinking out loud. Backpedaling now. Getting cold feet. "Smith and Monahan will find out soon enough then it's my ass that's gonna be in a sling, not yours."

Jimmy holds up two fingers in what looks like a Churchillian salute. "Two days," he says.

"Two days what?'

"Before the paperwork crosses their desk. A third by the time they get to you. Maybe more if we're lucky, they're so lazy. Another day till you track me down and tell me to lay off. Four days. That's more than enough time for me to see if Jason's theory holds water. Who'll do it if we don't, Skip? They've already got the guy tried and convicted and moved on to the next case. Supposing they're wrong? This guy's one of ours. Don't we owe him something? Let me check things out and you can blame me if anything comes your way. I'll take the heat."

The chief takes a pencil from a mug and doodles on the pad in front of him. There's an awkward silence as he absentmindedly shades a graffiti sized J while he figures the odds. And the angles. And the complex machinations that will guarantee his ass is well and truly covered.

Jimmy stands in his bad boy pose waiting for a decision. And looking at the Skipper's hair. And how it looks so freshly cut. Again. And then he sees the little snippets of hair that are sprinkled across his shoulders. And that smell again. That cloying beauty shop fragrance that wafts over to Jimmy's side of the room.

Finally the chief looks up. The J is beautifully shaded. He could be one of those graffiti artists who cover the bridges and subways with their art, it's so good. "Sounds like a plan," he says and gives Jimmy the thinnest of smiles. Then he waves him out of the office in an abrupt dismissal to emphasize the chain of command and let Jimmy know who's in charge here. That even though they've had a conversation that never took place, Jimmy shouldn't think for one moment that they're co-conspirators. Or friends. Or any other such sentimental claptrap.

Chapter 21

Arraignment takes place in the judicial district where the crime occurred. In the *People v. Jason Friendly* that would be the little courthouse in Columbia, in the County of Westchester, in the great state of New York. That's why they ensconced Jason in the holding cell in the station house next door, instead of the County lock up. The tiny courtroom is jammed with reporters. Jason's parents are not in attendance. He didn't want them to be part of a media circus so he told them to stay in Florida. There's only one photographer, a pool guy who shares what he takes with everyone else. He sits behind the DA and keeps taking pictures of everything even though there doesn't seem to be anything to photograph. Jason's case is called after three traffic violations and a creditor suit against a bankrupt with his back to the wall are disposed of. The charges against Jason are then laid out by the DA, and he's asked to enter a plea. After Jason shakily says "Not guilty your Honor," the crusty looking black- robed judge with a shock of unruly white hair announces in a rumbling voice, "Bail is set at $2 million," and bangs his gavel on his desk.

It's a figure impossible for Jason to raise.

Jason's lawyer, smartly attired and sharp of voice, strenuously objects.

The DA, a woman in her mid-thirties in a Donna Karan pant suit and sporting neatly bobbed hair says, without bothering to rise or look in any one's direction, "Flight risk, your Honor."

The judge peers at Jason through rimless spectacles and agrees.

Jason is suddenly surrounded by four burly marshals. They crowd around him so he can't make a fuss and quickly put manacles on his legs, cuff his hands behind his back, and hustle him off to a waiting van to transport him to the County Jail. The procedure takes less than five minutes.

The ride to the lock-up takes half an hour. At the County Jail Jason is processed and put in Area B, a special place away from the main prison population for people who can't make bail, cops in trouble and white collar crimes. Convicted criminals are put somewhere else. Area B has eighteen eight by twelve cells. Each cell has a sink, a commode and one inmate. Nine cells are occupied, ten including Jason's. Lights out is at twelve. During the day Jason can congregate in the rec room and watch TV, or stay in his cell. Once a day he's allowed in the yard for an hour of fresh air. Cells for the main prison population overlook the yard. They hurl catcalls, abuse and wads of wet tissue at the prisoners from Area B.

Jason's lawyer picks Jimmy up at the Columbia Police Station and they drive to the lock-up in his shiny new Lexus. Black, of course. And so elegantly appointed. Full of bells and whistles with a cockpit like a jet fighter. And on the turns, such grace and traction. And that's just the half of it, the lawyer tells Jimmy as he drones on about his marvelous automobile. The lock-up's half an hour away, but it seems to Jimmy to take much longer than that.

Jason's released into Jimmy's custody. They're given a card along with the prisoner. The card is stamped when they take him out and will be stamped again when they bring him back. They're told Jason must be home by ten. It's like a lending library, only for people.

On the ride back to Columbia, Jason doesn't stop talking to them. It makes Jimmy's drive with the lawyer look like a walk in the park. Jason insists on telling them his war stories, gabbling on at them like he's on speed. How he's not slept a wink since this thing started, how bad the food is, how scary the prisoners are and how much he hates his orange jump suit that says COUNTY JAIL on the back. He wears it now. The orange jump suit. On his furlough to find out what the intruder took from his home.

It's almost dark by the time they get there. Jason's glad. He doesn't want his neighbors to see him like this. Jimmy gets out first and scoots up the path to open the front door. Jason and the lawyer quickly follow. Inside Jason's overcome by emotion as familiar sights and smells assault his senses. He touches his furniture reverently and stifles a sob at the reality of his situation. They give him a minute to compose himself then herd him into the sunroom and stand around the heap of stuff the intruder left in the middle of the floor. No one speaks, they all just stare at the pile. Jason breaks the silence. He of the orange jump suit and sallow complexion. The orange suit rustles as he moves. He keeps pulling at parts that irritate him. "These are the drawers where I dump things," he says and squats down to take a closer look. "I kept all the threat stuff in the top one." He points to the sideboard. "There were some other things there I didn't show you."

"Like what?" says Jimmy.

"Apart from the letters there were some cards. Some nails that were scattered in the driveway. Some invoices."

"Are they still there?"

Jason sifts through the pile. "I don't see them." He finds a bunch of papers bound with a rubber band and flips through them.

Jimmy looks expectantly.

Jason shakes his head and tosses them back on the pile and starts to work his way through it. Picking things up and discarding them, moving other things around. Eventually there's just a thin layer of stuff left. Receipts. Slips of paper. The edge of the mess rises up where Jason's thrown everything. It looks like a large crater.

"Do you have the card from the wreaths?" Jimmy asks.

Jason pokes through the mess some more. "Here," he says and hands him a small envelope. "I can see why he missed this one." The envelope is filled with coupons. The card is stuffed inside it.

Jimmy looks at it.

Cut out letters pasted together spell out the message,

> KEEP RUNNING AND YOU'LL DIE
> THIS IS WHAT YOUR FUNERAL
> WILL LOOK LIKE.

The other side is blank. Jimmy puts the card and the envelope into one of the plastic bags he always has with him, then slips it in his pocket. "What about the invoices?" he says. "You got them?"

Jason pokes about some more. "No. They're gone."

Jimmy makes a face. He's anticipating hours on the phone talking to florists trying to track down where the wreaths came from.

"Anyone come to mind who would do this?" asks the lawyer.

Jason says he can't imagine.

"No enemies?" says Jimmy.

"None I can think of."

"A pissed off client?" asks the attorney.

"Maybe."

"What does that mean?" says Jimmy.

"I've spent a lot of time in court. It's possible someone holds a grudge. My secretary's been going through the files."

The lawyer takes an elegant notebook from his inside pocket and makes some notes. He says he'll go over to Jason's office and take a look for himself.

Jason pokes at what's left of the pile.

"What about when you lived here before? Any enemies from back then?" asks Jimmy.

"You mean like high school?"

Jimmy nods.

Jason looks embarrassed. "Could be. "

The lawyer wants to know why.

"It was a small school. The same guys were on all the teams. We ruled. And you could say we weren't very cool about it. " He says it like he wishes he was back there now.

Jimmy says, "You guys were bullies? "

Jason looks uncomfortable. A little squirmy. "You could say that."

"So," says Jimmy, "there could be people from back then that don't like you."

"I suppose so."

"Anyone in particular?"

Jason puffs up his cheeks and blows out the air. "I've got to think about that. It never occurred to me it could be something from when I was a kid. That's a long time ago. There were some guys I had some real run-ins with, but I haven't had anything to do with them for years. I can't imagine it's from that far back, Jimmy. It doesn't make any sense." He pokes around in the mess some more, then gives it up. The only things missing are the letters and the envelope with the nails and cards. Nothing else strikes him.

They check the rest of the house, but Jason says he doesn't think anything's been taken or disturbed. Jimmy's disappointed. He was hoping for a lightening bolt like you see on the TV shows to point him in the right direction. Some fabulous clue that would pave the way to solving the puzzle in ten minutes. Now he's got nothing to show for the stand he took with the Skipper and things don't look good for the home team. The lawyer's disappointed too. He thinks the frame Jason's in will hold up in court and they don't have anything to fight it with. Yet. As they head for the door, a pall of gloom hangs over them. Suddenly Jason grips Jimmy's hand and shakes it profusely while he babbles claims of innocence, slogans of confidence and tearful expressions of gratitude for taking up his cause.

Jimmy's embarrassed by the sudden display of emotion.

The lawyer looks away not wanting to be part of it. Not wanting to get emotionally involved. Or take a liking to his new client. Or feel sorry for him. Or feel anything for him. If you were to ask him why he wanted things this way, he'd say it's how he likes to do business. He'd tell you he needs to stay dispassionate. And unaffected. So he can maintain his perspective and that cool, hard, killer edge he prides himself on. If you were to ask someone else they'll tell you what a cold piece of shit the guy is and count themselves lucky they aren't his wife, or child, or lover, or his friend.

Chapter 22

It's early evening. Getting dark. And cold. Josephine is closing up. Getting ready to leave the salon. She's locked the door and turned out the lights. A man she's never seen before looks in the window. He's smartly dressed in an ankle length cashmere coat with a crisp white shirt and an elegant tie showing. She watches him from inside the shop. Her shop. He sees her and points to his hair, pantomiming a haircut. That's what she does, Josephine. Cuts hair for a living. Here. In her three chair salon on Main Street, in the very center of Columbia. She shakes her head and points to her watch. "It's too late," she mouths so he can read her lips. "I'm closing up."

Josephine is five foot ten. In her mid-thirties. She's got a tight athletic body and works hard to keep it that way. Mounds of curly black hair fall past her shoulders. She has high cheekbones. Perfect lips. Almond eyes. And she's wearing a figure-hugging maroon turtle neck, designer jeans, and plain white sneakers.

The stranger puts his hands together in prayer and mouths "please." He looks like Al Jolson singing "Mammy."

She shakes her head again, but slower this time as she checks him out. He's in his early forties, has a handsome angular face, dark hair, short but not cropped and he's smartly dressed. What's not to like?

He's still begging her. And rolling his eyes. And tugging at his hair. And banging his head against the window. Trying to make her smile. To get her to like him and let him inside.

She looks at him some more and figures why not? What else does she have to do? She primps her hair, fixes her sweater and checks herself in the mirror. Then she switches the lights back on, unlocks the door and lets him in.

The stranger's overcome with gratitude and heaps praise and extravagant compliments on her while she takes his coat. And jacket. And hangs them on the coat rack by the door. Then she helps him into a black cotton robe that ties at the waist, brings him over to the sink and begins to wash his hair.

A shampoo is a special sort of thing. On the one hand it's a functional part of the business, the hair is dirty and it needs to be clean before anyone will touch it. On the other hand a shampoo can be quite a sensual affair. She's caught a lot of guys with the old shampoo trick, gently massaging their scalp and the back of their neck to drive them wild and make them horny, but not this guy. She'll play it straight with him. He's not her type anyway as it turns out. He's an accountant, he tells her as she cleans his hair. He's got a big meeting tomorrow and he wants to look good. He's on his way home from his client. A famous hair salon in New York. He mentions the name. CRIMPERS. He could've gotten his hair cut there, he says, but he got the call about the meeting as he was getting off the Parkway and didn't feel like driving back to town.

After the shampoo she sits him at her station, puts a cape round him and begins to cut his hair with her small scissors. "To go with my tiny hands," she says when he remarks on their size. She snips and carves till she gets the shape she's looking for. She's like a sculptor. Checking the mirror all the time to see how it's going. Bobbing and weaving around the chair like a prize fighter. Putting on a show. Talking all the time as her hands fly about his head in a frenzy of activity. Peppering him with questions about CRIMPERS, the hottest salon in town. Looking for gossip. And dirt. A friend of hers works there, she tells him. "Get your dirt from her," the stranger says with a smile. And the cutting continues. She's giving him her best moves. Her shears fly like she's some crazed sculptor chiseling away at his head. He knows good from bad, this guy, and she wants to show off for him. That's why she's putting on a show. A pride thing. And the fact that her friend works there. At CRIMPERS, the hottest place in town. She wants to show them what she can do, those hairdressers in the City. She's just as good as any one of them, is what she thinks. Even better, maybe.

As she's working and prattling she sees out of the corner of her eye that there's movement taking place under the stranger's cape. It's subtle at first and she thinks no more about it. She continues to talk and cut and dance around the chair, but it persists this movement. It's hard to ignore because now the stranger's hand is going up and down underneath the cape in a most obscene manner. She freezes, but not her brain. Which marches on unhindered. Flashing scenarios one after the other. Each one more terrifying than the last. And still it goes on, this hand of his. Going up and down. Up and down. Underneath the shiny black nylon cape. Slowly and methodically. Until she can't stand it any longer. She draws her hand dryer from its holster like Annie Oakley at a shoot out and smashes the stranger over the head with it. A soft hiss escapes from his lips like air from a punctured balloon. He slumps in the chair. His eyes are closed. His face is peaceful. His head hangs slightly to the right and rests on his shoulder. It looks as though he just nodded off to sleep.

Josephine drops the hand dryer. It lands on the floor with a clatter. Bits of colored plastic break off and fly in different directions. She dashes out the door in a panic and runs up the street screaming for help at the top of her voice. A cop coming out of the diner hears her cries and rushes over to help. People in the street stop to watch what's going on. Small knots gather to stand and stare. She tells the cop about the stranger jerking off in her chair. How she smashed him over the head with a hand dryer and knocked him out. She says she wants him out of her shop. Arrested. And charged with indecent exposure. Then she bursts out crying and starts to tremble.

The cop gets her to calm down and takes her back to the salon.

The stranger is still slumped in the chair sleeping peacefully.

The cop lifts the shiny black cape to see what's going on under there. The stranger's hands are resting in his lap. One hand holds his glasses. The other holds a tissue. "He was cleaning his glasses," says the cop like he thinks she's dumber than a piece of rope.

"You gotta be kidding," says Josephine and stops sniffling and goes over and takes a look for herself. "Can you believe this?" she says and slaps a hand to her forehead. She's already calculating what the law suit's going to cost her. "I can't believe this is happening to me," she mutters and flops down angrily on one of the chairs.

The cop says, "Let's see what he's got to say about it," and gently shakes the stranger's shoulder, "Time to wake up, mister," he says.

The stranger doesn't respond. Instead he slumps down further as a result of the shaking.

The cop looks puzzled and checks the stranger's wrist for a pulse then drops it like it's red hot. He turns to look at her and says with alarm, "He's dead! You've killed him!"

No one moves. For just a second. While their brains digest what they're looking at. And record it. And figure out what to do next. A split second is all it lasts. Then everyone goes about their business and instinct takes over. Josephine's jaw drops. Her eyes open wide in horror. The cop reaches for his cuffs as he walks towards her and slaps them on her wrists while she still sits in her chair. It's so quick Josephine has no idea it's happened until it's done. She looks at her wrists then at him in astonishment. She's about to embark on a tirade of abuse when he starts to read her her rights from a laminated card he's produced from his jacket pocket. She stops in her tracks and instead of cursing listens to what he's saying, responds that she understands when he asks her if she does, then begins to cry softly to herself.

The cop calls the station to make his report and tells them he's bringing her in. The sergeant who takes the call says he'll do no such thing and tells him to sit tight.

Chapter 23

The Columbia Police Station is a block and a half from Josephine's salon. The sergeant tells the chief who grabs his hat and is the first one out the door. The word spreads quickly through the building. Cops pour from the station like a kicked over ant hill and snake their way to her shop in what, from above, must look like a mighty conga line. First comes the chief, then his secretary, and the guy filling the soda machine, cops changing shift, cops hanging around the station, off-duty cops, on duty cops, the janitors. They seem to come from everywhere. Some are Josephine's clients. Some have wives who go to her. Or girlfriends who use the salon. Everyone in town knows who she is except for the cop she bumped into when she was running down the street. Tyree Jones is his name. A rookie. Two weeks in. Who never heard of Josephine Francetti. Or her beauty salon. Him coming from three towns over and all.

Three squad cars already form a perimeter to hold back the onlookers. The chief is the first to pierce the line. He's in a state of high anxiety. His nostrils flare like a wild animal and his eyes are ablaze with a fierce intensity. He barges through a cordon of uniforms and bursts into the shop like the place is on fire. A trail of cops follow like the tail of a comet. "What's going on, Jo?" he says in a voice that oozes with concern. He sounds more like a worried parent than the by-the- book tight ass everyone's come to know and love.

Josephine's perched on the farthest chair, her legs are tucked under her. The patrol car's flashing lights make throbbing kaleidoscopes of color on the walls. Reflections bounce off the ceiling, the bottles of lotions on the styling stations and the sinks. It's like being in a disco without music. She's crying softly to herself. Dabbing her eyes with a bunch of tissues she clutches in her cuffed hands.

Officer Tyree Jones stands next to her. His notebook is in his hand. His pencil is poised as he waits for an answer to the question he's just asked her. His uniform is crisp and clean. Newer than new. His leather belt and holster still have that straight from the factory smell and creak loudly whenever he moves. His pale face is pug nosed and innocent. Everything about him is shiny, and unsoiled, and new.

The dead man's head is covered by the cape Josephine put around him to cut his hair.

Josephine looks at the chief and gives him a hint of a smile. Enough to show she's pleased to see him, then she begins to cry some more. The chief glares at Tyree Jones with a look that says, 'What the fuck is going on?' without actually saying it.

Tyree Jones's stomach churns.

The chief waits for an answer, but not patiently. He hoses the rookie down with a withering stare to convey his pique and irritable state of mind.

Tyree Jones takes a step towards the chief and shows him a particular page of his note book. It's the page that covers the information he's gleaned from Josephine so far. The page where he's written, "she thought the deceased was jerking off in her chair." Tyree Jones is uncomfortable saying "jerking off" in front of Josephine even though it's she who used the term in the first place, and not just once either.

The Skipper snatches the book and reads it greedily. When he's finished he looks over to Josephine with gooey eyes and says sadly, "Oh Jo, this is just awful." He goes over and puts his arms around her to comfort her which turns out to be embarrassing for them both because Josephine's hands are cuffed in front of her. As she stands up to receive the chief's embrace they grind into his crotch. The chief reacts like he's been struck by lightening and arches his nethers out and away from her dangling hands.

The rookie thinks it looks like something from a National Geographic show he once saw.

The chief catches the rookie staring at him and says irritably, "Take her cuffs off. Where do you think she's going?"

Tyree's stomach churns some more. He wants to get away from here. Away from this chief who's been needling him from the day he started. He takes the cuffs off of her and steps back, looking expectantly at the Skipper. Hoping to be dismissed.

It's at this moment that Jimmy makes his appearance. He got the call on his way home from dropping Jason off at the lock-up. He squeezes through the crowd of blues and when he breaks into the clear says to anyone, "What's going on?"

Josephine starts to cry hysterically. They're friends, sort of. Josephine and Jimmy. She's more Mary's friend than his. She cuts his hair every six weeks or so, it's not like he's got that much to cut, and she tells him her troubles. He likes her is the thing, so he listens and tries to nudge her in the right direction. But she's got an albatross around her neck. Things always seem to go wrong for her. Like now, for instance, when she tried to do someone a favor and ended up in handcuffs.

People are still trying to muscle themselves into the salon. The crowd outside is getting bigger. Jimmy looks at the Skipper who seems preoccupied, but gives him the nod, signaling whatever Jimmy wants to do is fine by him. Jimmy puts two fingers in his mouth and gives out with a loud whistle. When he's got their attention he asks everyone to leave except for Brian, the uniform who guarded Jason's gate, who he tells to hold down the door and not let anyone in unless it's the ME or the crime scene people.

After everyone's shuffled out, Jimmy turns to Josephine and the uniform and says, "What happened?"

The rookie starts to speak.

Jimmy cuts him off. "Not you," he says and looks at Josephine

"I thought he was jerking off," she says through sniffles. "His hand was going up and down under the cape. What was I supposed to think? I'm alone with him in the salon and that's going on. What would you do, Jimmy? I'm asking you, what would you do?"

"This was going on while you were cutting his hair?"

"Not to begin with. More like half-way through."

"And?"

"I socked him over the head with the hand dryer." They all look at the dryer lying broken on the floor. "Then I ran outside and bumped into Mr. Sympathetic here." She looks at Tyree Jones like he's gum on her shoe.

"That's it?" says Jimmy. "You thought he was jerking off under the cape so you smashed him over the head."

She nods.

"No chit chat leading up to the fateful moment?"

"Just small talk."

"Not sexy talk?" He knows who he's dealing with here. Josephine likes to get laid.

She gives him a look. "Nothing like that."

"That's all?"

"That's all," she says.

The chief is sitting in the chair between Josephine and the dead guy. He's silent and pensive. Happy to have Jimmy take over.

"And you sir," says Jimmy, addressing the rookie. "What happened then?"

Tyree is frozen like a statue. He stands at an awkward attention over by the sink. His face expresses extreme discomfort "We came back here," he stammers.

"We?" says Jimmy.

"This young lady and myself. She told me what happened and I escorted her back to the shop. I found the guy slumped in that chair. I looked under the cape to see what he was doing. Both hands were in his lap. One hand held his glasses the other held a tissue. I figured he was cleaning his glasses. That's why one hand was going up and down. I tried to wake him up. When he didn't respond, I checked for a pulse and found he was dead. That's when I cuffed the young lady and read her her rights. Then I covered him up and called it in."

"You cuffed her?" asks Jimmy incredulously.

Tyree swallows hard. His Adams apple bobs up and down like a yoyo.

"Where'd you think she was going?"

"I asked him the same thing," says the chief and shakes his head in disbelief.

"What did he say?" asks Jimmy.

"He didn't."

Tyree Jones wants to get out of here in the worst way. It's bad enough the Skipper gave him a hard time, now he's got two of them picking on him.

"And then?" says Jimmy, looking at the rookie again.

"I started to take her statement."

The chief passes Jimmy the rookie's note book.

Jimmy looks at it then hands it back to the rookie. He can see the man is uncomfortable and takes pity on him. "Nice notes," he says, and gives him a wink. Then he says to the chief, "I think we can let him go now Skip, whaddya say?'

The chief nods, glowering at the kid some more.

"Write me up a report," Jimmy says to the rookie. "And I need a copy of your notes. Make sure it's on my desk by the end of your shift."

The rookie moves towards the door.

Jimmy explains to Josephine he's got to keep her under lock and key for a while knowing she isn't going to be able to make bail. That's when she really starts to cry.

The next to enter is the medical examiner. The prissy little man with the narrow point of view and no sense of humor. Tonight he's wearing an old black double breasted pinstripe suit and a thin bow tie no one wears any more. He gives Jimmy a nod, shakes the chief's hand and goes over to the corpse and gets to work. Next comes the crime scene crew with tape measures, cameras, brushes and sprays. After that a reporter tries to get in posing as a delivery man. When Brian determines no one's ordered his coffee and doughnuts, the gig's up and he throws him out. Then the guys from the morgue arrive pushing a gurney and carrying black leather medical bags. There's no room for all these people. Jimmy's getting claustrophobic. Tight spaces and crowds make him feel panicky and nervous. It's a new thing with him. Along with not being able to see so good in the dark and generally feeling like he's a hundred and eight.

He tells the uniform to get a patrol car to take them back to the station house. He tells the Skipper he'll see him back at the ranch, grabs Josephine by the arm and leads her to the waiting black and white. The crowd jostles to get a better look at them. The photographers hold cameras above their heads and keep shooting. Jimmy's amazed that word got around so quickly.

"I never meant to kill him," says Josephine as they're driven off.

"I know that."

"So what am I gonna do?"

"Get a lawyer," Jimmy says sadly.

"Where am I gonna get a lawyer from, Jimmy?"

"They'll get one for you. Didn't you hear what he said when he read you your rights?"

"I don't want some asshole just out of school."

"Don't you have any clients who are attorneys?"

"None that I can think of."

"Who set up your business?"

"I can't go to him."

"Why not?"

"I still owe him money."

"Ahh," says Jimmy. "No one else?"

"Even if I knew someone I couldn't afford it. I'm broke, you know that."

He does. It's all she ever talks about. How every week's a struggle. She owes the rent, the government and everyone else in between. Even though business has picked up lately and she's just taken on another cutter, it's not enough. Her creditors are running out of patience. "I'll make some calls," he says. "Maybe I can call in a favor."

She looks at him gratefully. He wants to put his arms around her, but he doesn't think it's such a good idea with the driver watching in the rear view mirror, hanging onto every word so he can tell his bar buddies when he gets off duty. Instead Jimmy tries to be upbeat. And reassuring. And all that other stuff he comes out with that Mary says is so annoying when your world is falling apart. He was shocked when she told him this. He always thought positive trumped anything, but it seemed it wasn't so. The way Josephine's looking at him now, suggests she feels the same way.

It only takes a minute to get to the station. A lone reporter is waiting when they get there. As they draw up he runs towards them microphone in hand, trying to get an interview. Jimmy pushes Josephine out of the car, shoves the reporter aside, and runs up the steps with her and into the building. He hands her off to Officer Sheila Conners as they get to the desk. Sheila's a client of Josephine's. She was at the salon just this morning. She's wearing a freshly cut bob that Jimmy can't help noticing takes ten years off her. Sheila gives Josephine a reassuring smile and takes her downstairs to be processed.

There's a million things Jimmy's has to do. The crime scene crew discovered who the victim is and now Jimmy's got to track down the next of kin and get it all down on paper. By the time he's done some of it, the Skipper pops his head into Jimmy's office. He's still miffed that the rookie put the cuffs on Josephine. He does a long soliloquy on it including his feeling that Gestapo tactics don't work very well in the suburbs. "What the fuck was that kid thinking?"

Jimmy thinks the chief's a little over the top on this one, but he figures he'll let him blow off some steam and maybe he won't give him such a hard time when he tells him there was nothing else missing from Jason's house.

The chief tells Jimmy he's spoken to the DA about Josephine. "She says it's pretty much an open and shut situation. Accidental manslaughter is the charge. If Josephine pleads guilty she'll probably get a suspended sentence considering the circumstances. The DA sees no malicious intent and is willing to be as lenient as possible. It also didn't hurt that Josephine cut her hair last week."

"How'd you know that?"

"She told me."

"Josephine?"

"The DA."

But that was before they got the autopsy report.

Jason Friendly

Chapter 24

He can't sleep. The cot's lumpy. The one thin blanket he's been issued doesn't keep him warm. There's an episode of shrieking somewhere down the hall, then a crying jag. He can't tell if it's the same person. All he knows is how scared he is. That if things go badly this is the easy part. In this "country club" which is what they call it. In the real prison he won't stand a chance and the way things are looking that's where he'll end up. Another wave of fear washes over him. His mind won't slow down. It jumps from scene to scene. The courthouse. The van. Then processing and being poked and prodded by strangers. Putting their hands on you. In you. Then outside again with Jimmy and the lawyer. To the house. Tears well up as he thinks of the house. His mind travels on like a speeded up movie. Back to jail. Handed in with a card like a library book. Then some banter. Cheerful stuff like, "Don't worry" and "Everything's going to be all right." This from a pudgy detective he hardly knows and a lawyer he's paying every cent he has to. Where are his friends? Who are his friends? Or family for that matter. His parents he told to stay in Florida, but his brother? Cousins? Anyone?

Then there's that mind jarring CLANG he remembers most of all. CLANG. When the cell door closed behind him. CLANG. That awful noise. CLANG. That terrible sound as he walked inside the cell. CLANG. Right behind him. Then the guard's footsteps as he walked away. Almost as bad. Clip clop. Clip clop. Getting fainter. A door opening and closed. And then another CLANG. Softer this time. Not like his. That jarring sound. This one from far away. Not so bad, as bad goes. Everything's bad here, there are just gradations. Then there's the other sounds he hears in the dark. First a snore. Then a cough. Then nothing. Then something else. His ears shoot from one noise to another, turning like radar dishes towards this sound and that, trying to detect where it's coming from and what it is, as if it really matters. They are endless, these sounds. And unfamiliar. And the bed is lumpy. And now he can hear a tap dripping. Or could it be a drain?

Then the fear grips him. It's like a contraction. Doubling him over in his cot. Knees to his chin. More fetal than fetal. He breaks into a cold sweat as his brain marches through the permutations of his demise like a computer on speed. First one scenario. Then another. And another still. All he can do is watch them, lying in the dark on his lumpy bed, as one image after another assaults his mind. There is no window. He has no watch. He has no idea what time it is or how long he's been lying there trying to sleep, tossing and turning in his waking nightmare. It seems like forever. This night. This first night here. How can he do years? It's not possible. He's not capable of such a thing. Fear washes over him like a freezing shower. Someone farts. A mighty roar that makes Jason jump. There are no giggles here. This is no camp. This is Jail. The country club, they call it, but it's no fucking country club. It's a jail pure and simple. And tears course down his cheeks as the word JAIL echoes through his mind. IN JAIL. HE'S IN JAIL. And the way things are going he may never get out.

Chapter 25

His name is Jerry Lewis. The deceased. The dead man in Josephine's chair. The smartly dressed guy she killed in her three-chair salon. It's the same name as the movie star. People are always asking him how the telethon's going, or why he split up with Dean, things like that. He doesn't look like him that's for sure, but on the phone who can tell? Jerry Lewis is a big time accountant. A well connected snappy dresser in Armani suits and crisp white shirts. The meeting he's going to tomorrow, the one he's getting a haircut for, is with one of the owners of CRIMPERS, the beauty salon Josephine admires so much. Where all the stars go, and the models, and all the socialites. The meeting he came from was also at CRIMPERS, the salon Josephine admires so much. Where the partners are splitting up and slogging it out. And Jerry Lewis has taken sides. And done things he's not so proud of. To move the process along. And screw with the other guy. So they can all make a fortune, after he's gone.

Jerry Lewis lives in the newer part of Columbia. The people here don't belong to the Rolling Hills Country Club, their money's too new. They belong to the other golf club in town. The one Jason Friendly lives near. The one that doesn't care whether you're black, blue or yellow so long as you can pay the exorbitant fees the club charges. The houses here are huge and stand on large plots of land. Jerry's got five acres with woods, a lake, sweeping lawns and magnificent views of distant hills. The house is one of those Elizabethan knock-offs with dark wooden beams buried into a stuccoed façade, small paned widows and an occasional turret plunked here and there.

The iron gate to the house is closed but well lit. Jimmy presses the intercom and tells whoever's on the other end who he is. The gate opens slowly and after he's through, closes behind him. A gravely road brings him to a circular driveway in the front of the house. He pulls up to the front door. A maid lets him in and leads him to a cozy study just off the front hallway. Mrs. Lewis is waiting for him there. Jimmy can tell she already knows what's happened to her husband. Her eyes are red rimmed and her makeup is streaked. Two friends are with her, consoling her. Jimmy figures they must be the ones who told her. Word travels fast in a small town.

Mrs. Constance Lewis, or Connie as her friends like to call her, is in her late forties. A photograph on the wall suggests that once upon a time she was thin, but now she's well on her way to obesity. Everything on her five foot seven frame is stretched out. Her surgically altered nose is lost in a sea of pink flesh. A dress she thinks disguises her largeness is betrayed by massive ankles, a thick neck and pudgy arms and fingers. She offers Jimmy a seat and sits down opposite him. The room has flowered wallpaper, matching drapes, thick beige carpeting and deep cushioned chairs that make you want to shuck off your shoes and stretch out for a while.

Jimmy offers her his condolences and tells her all the things you're supposed to say at a moment like this.

Mrs. Lewis thanks him for his consideration.

He tells her what's taken place. Even though she says she knows what's happened, he doesn't know what she knows. It's his job to tell her what happened so he can gauge her reaction. To assess her sorrow. To suspect the very worst that could be happening here and work backwards from there, even though he knows it's Josephine who killed her husband.

When he's finished she says dully, "Cleaning his glasses." It appears she didn't know that little tidbit.

Jimmy gets up to leave having done his duty and not wanting to stay there a second longer than necessary. He gives her his card and tells her to call him if she needs any help.

"What sort of help am I likely to need?" she asks.

"There's a lot of red tape in situations like this," he says kindly. "Sometimes I can speed things up."

She nods like she hadn't thought of that and gives him a grateful smile.

Jimmy makes his goodbyes, gets in his car and heads for home. By the time he crawls in the sack it's 1:00 am. It's his own bed this evening. There's no sleep-over at Mary's tonight, Lucy's back home. Felix is pleased to see him. There's no food in his bowl and he's hungry. To show his displeasure he's thrown up on Jimmy's bed. A pile of still-warm vomit sits in the middle of the comforter. It doesn't stop him from greeting Jimmy with a loud meow and lots of purring and rubbing up against his leg. Cats, it's a well known fact, have no conscience.

Sleep is hard to come by. Two deaths in a week is overkill for a place like Columbia whose last dead body, Mary's husband, was a couple of years ago. Jimmy tosses and turns. His mind is full of thoughts about Jason and Josephine. Then Mary pops into his head and how appalled she was at what happened to Josephine. She's got a good lawyer. She says she'll give him a call. Josephine's getting a suspended sentence, but she still has to plead guilty to accidental manslaughter. Maybe a good lawyer can find another way. It takes Jimmy a long time before he nods off, but even then his peace is accosted by bizarre dreams and strange images.

Saturday

Chapter 26

When he gets up in the morning, Jimmy feels like he's been run over by a truck. A shower doesn't help. Neither does the coffee he brews up. He gets dressed like a drunken man, tops up Felix's bowl, makes sure the toilet seat is down and the cover's up so the cat can drink from the commode and swears he'll be home at a decent hour. Such is the nature of their relationship. Part friend. Part animal. And part enforcer when Jimmy breaks his word.

The lake Jimmy passes on his way to the station house looks like it's on fire. The sun has just broken over the tree line and clouds of steam billow off the water. A breeze catches the mist and swirls it up in long wispy tendrils, and the sun makes eerie shafts of light through the leafing trees.

At the station house he runs into Frankie the Cop, the uniform who brought Jason to him the night of Sandra Ellison's murder. Jimmy doesn't like him very much. Apart from always reminding him he doesn't come from Columbia, Frankie's one of those sharpies who gets off on being a cop. He's perfectly uniformed, has a freshly manicured crew cut and always wears the Ray Bans so you can't see his eyes. There's a way about him that's arrogant and hard-nosed. He's that unforgiving cop you don't want pulling you over for a traffic violation. His pasty round face has a pig-like snout and a thin-lipped mouth that rarely smiles. He likes to roust the kids and give them a hard time. Always looking for a roach or something he can bring them in for. Or write them a ticket. Or give them a warning. Or anything else that allows him to bark in their faces until they piss in their pants. But his numbers are good and you can't fault his devotion. There are plenty of cops out there who are a hell of a lot worse. Jimmy doesn't like them very much either.

"How's it going Frankie?" he says cheerily. He's standing in the hallway in front of his office. Frankie's walking by.

"Fine," says Frankie.

"You see what happened to Jason?"

Frankie shakes his head sadly. "I can't believe it."

"Neither can I," says Jimmy. "They seem in an awful hurry to lock him up."

Frankie agrees.

"They've got him seeing her get off the train, running home to get the rifle, taking the shot from where they found the casing, running home to dump the gun then coming out again and bumping into you."

"Why would he bother coming out again?" asks Frankie.

"Exactly."

"He didn't look like he'd done all of that when I ran into him."

"I didn't think so either," says Jimmy, then he fills Frankie in on the death threats and everything else that's happened to Jason since he came back to Columbia. "Jason thinks whoever's been doing this took a shot at him, missed, and killed Sandra Ellison by mistake. I'm wondering if this could be someone from his past."

Frankie doesn't know what to say.

"You were on the high school football team with him, right?"

Frankie says he was. "Baseball and basketball too."

"You guys were pretty wild then, huh?"

Frankie agrees that they were.

"Any one in particular you remember picking on?"

Frankie bridles. "Hey now, that was a long time ago."

Jimmy gives him a smile to show he means no harm.

Frankie relaxes then and tells him wistfully, "We were so hot back then, y'know."

"Was there someone in particular you liked to pick on?"

Frankie gets all indignant again. "It wasn't like that," he says stiffly. "We were hot is all. We never picked on any one person. We just threw our weight around."

Jimmy scratches his neck. "As a group maybe, but what about individually?"

Frankie gives it some thought then says, "Jason had himself a couple of favorites back then. Kids that pissed him off. He was some angry kid in those days."

Jimmy wonders how many favorites Frankie had. "Any of Jason's favorites still around?"

Frankie can't come up with anything.

"What about when he won the marathon? Did he piss anyone off then?"

"What's the marathon got to do with it?" Frankie wants to know.

"Someone broke into his house after that. Jason says they never took anything. Just moved the trophy and some other things around."

Frankie doesn't get it. "Why would they want to do that?"

"To let him know they were there, I suppose. Some sort of calling card thing."

"Why?"

"That's what we've got to find out." Jimmy lays the "we" out like a worm on a hook.

You can see Frankie working it through. What he'll tell his friends. How he's going to play it. Finally he snaps his fingers. "Errol Jamal, that's someone you might want to talk to. Jason beat him out on the final stretch of the marathon. Errol's someone we drove crazy back in the day. We'd get him so wound up, he'd explode in a frenzy and wave his arms around and try and catch us with this crazed look on his face." He smiles remembering it, but then he sees Jimmy's not seeing the funny side of it so he goes back to being serious again. "I see him around town all the time. He acts like I don't exist." Frankie rests a hand on his holster. "I can't really blame him after all the things we did to him."

"I thought you said you never bullied anyone."

"We never laid a hand on him," says Frankie defensively. "We just teased him a lot is all."

"What does he do now?"

"He's got a candy store on Broadway."

Jimmy says he thinks he knows it. "On the edge of town?"

"That's the one."

"Anyone else?"

Frankie makes a big show of trying to remember. His eyes shoot to the ceiling and his brow is fiercely knit. Jimmy thinks he should give acting lessons. There's another long pause while Frankie goes through the pantomime again then he says dramatically, "You might want to talk to Robbie Jackman. He's got a gas station on Route #35. Not long after Jason came back to Columbia Robbie got drunk one night and said things he shouldn't have. Jason had a special thing going with him the first year of high school. None of us knew what went on, but Jason must have driven him crazy. Robbie said if he ever saw him again he'd beat the shit out of him. Robbie's filled out since we were in school together. He's an amateur wrestler these days. A friend of mine owns the bar where he shot his mouth off. He's the one who told me what went down."

Jimmy writes the names down in his note book. "Anyone else?"

Frankie shakes his head.

Jimmy's face turns glum. "The county boys want to fry Jason's ass, you know that don't you?"

Frankie says that's what he hears, "And you're standing up for him."

Jimmy doesn't see it that way. Standing up suggests a loyalty he doesn't feel. He's doing his job is how he sees it. "What about before high school. Maybe middle school?" he asks. "Any one from then?"

"That far back?"

Jimmy shrugs. "Why not. I've got nothing else to go on."

This time there's no hesitation. "Eighth grade," says Frankie. "Jason had a thing with a kid called Michael Collis. I'm not sure what happened, but I know the parents got involved. It went on for quite a while, then Jason stopped talking about it and left the kid alone."

"Where do I find him?"

"He hasn't lived here for years."

"Maybe you could give me a hand here Frankie, whaddya think?"

Frankie's tail begins to wag.

"Maybe you could ask around for me. The old school crowd, people like that. See if anyone's heard anything. Maybe someone saw Collis recently. They've got a pretty tight case on our boy. They've already got him strapped to the gurney."

That gets Frankie's attention.

"We're all he's got and look what we've got to go on," says Jimmy frustratedly. "Nothing." He writes his cell phone number on a card and gives it to Frankie. "Call me if you hear something, I don't care if it's four in the morning. Time's getting short."

Frankie gives him a mock salute and swaggers down the hallway. He's thrilled at the way things have turned out. His head is up, his chin thrust out. Already, in his own mind, he's bucking for Jimmy's job.

Jimmy watches him saunter away and hopes he hasn't created a monster.

Chapter 27

A little while later, Jimmy gets word that the ME has called a meeting in the chief's office. When he gets there the ME's in a froth. Jimmy's never seen the man so discombobulated, but here he is now, this normally ice cold fish, spouting and burbling in a most uncharacteristic manner.

The chief sits bolt upright behind his desk. He gleams in his spotless uniform and shiny buttons. His square jaw is set. His deep blue eyes stare impassively, but there's something about his manner that Jimmy doesn't recognize. A preoccupation. A sense that he's not quite with them. The Skipper's hands give him away. They keep moving around his desk touching things. Twiddling a paper clip. Doodling on his pad.

Jimmy and the ME sit opposite him. Everyone has coffee thanks to the chief's secretary. In cups and saucers this time instead of cardboard or mugs. Some sort of etiquette thing Jimmy doesn't understand. To impress the ME he supposes. Jimmy's glad he's with in crowd again. Sitting down and having coffee like the good old days when Smith and Monahan were around.

The ME sits primly on his chair. His saucer balances on one knee. He takes the cup handle between his finger and thumb, pinkie extended, raises it to his thin lips and takes a sip. He's wearing an old fashioned blue serge suit, a white shirt and a striped blue bow tie. He looks like something from the forties. Especially with his razor sharp side part and his round steel glasses. "Here's the thing," he says excitedly.

His reedy voice grinds through Jimmy's brain. The Skipper's too. Their brows furrow in an attempt to fend off the annoying noise.

"As far as the autopsy's concerned," the ME looks at the chief ignoring Jimmy completely, "we've had a bit of a surprise."

"A bit of a surprise," the chief mimics not rudely, but not kindly either. He looks up from his doodle. "How so?"

"It wasn't a blow to the head that killed Mr. Lewis."

The chief cocks an inquisitive eyebrow. "What did?"

The ME gets a puffed up look about him like he could well be the smartest man in the world. "He was poisoned," he says and triumph floods his mean little face.

The chief's expression is priceless.

Jimmy's too. "You mean Josephine didn't kill him?" he asks incredulously, leaning into the ME. Making sure he's got it right and not misheard, or got the wrong end of the stick.

The ME's mean face returns in an instant. He doesn't like repeating himself, he's got a thing about it, and now Jimmy's face is in his. "It would appear not," he says stiffly,

"So what happened?" the chief asks, equally amazed.

"I just told you," the ME snaps, forgetting who he was talking to for a moment. "Someone poisoned him."

The chief glares at him.

The ME looks away and takes a nervous sip of coffee. The cup rattles as he puts it back on the saucer.

"Let me get this straight," says Jimmy. "You're telling us Josephine's innocent?"

The ME's jaw tightens. He doesn't answer. Instead he says to the chief, "It's an arsenic derivative, the poison that killed him. It takes about two or three hours to work it's way through the system depending on the weight of the victim, then death is instantaneous. Nothing happens before. There are no ill effects, symptoms or tell tale signs. You just keel over and die. That's what this guy did," he looks at his notes, "sometime between the time Josephine slugged him and the officer took his pulse. But two to three hours is long before she met him. She couldn't possibly have poisoned him."

It takes a second for it to sink in, then the Skipper's eyes light up like he just won the lottery. "So Jo's innocent," he says gleefully. "That's what you're telling me, she's innocent?" He too wants to make sure he's not misheard. Or jumped to conclusions. Or got the wrong end of the stick.

The ME wonders if they're both deaf. "Yes she's innocent," he says frostily. Pissed off now.

"Thank the Lord," exclaims the chief.

Jimmy's surprised at the Skipper's reaction.

So is the ME

Jimmy's surprised the chief called Josephine "Jo."

So is the ME, who continues to burble specifics and details in a vain attempt to get their attention back.

The chief's not listening to him any more. He picks up the phone and tells the sergeant to generate the paperwork for Josephine's release. "All charges are dropped," he barks into the mouthpiece. "There's been a mistake. I'll be down as soon as I'm finished here." He puts down the phone and looks at the ME. Waiting. Expecting. Hoping the ME's done, but the ME doesn't get the hint. There's a look of sufferance on his hollow-cheeked face as he drones on in that reedy voice of his about bone densities, fat content and blood sugar levels. The chief can't take any more of it and cuts him short. "Is that it?" he wants to know. "Lewis was poisoned by person or persons unknown and Josephine's innocent. That's the story right?" He's already standing up.

The ME stutters to a halt.

The chief heads for the door.

The ME's flabbergasted. He thought he'd get a better reaction than this. Now there's this curt dismissal like he's some sort of errand boy and this sudden preoccupation with Josephine. It's all too confusing. He sits with his cup in his hand not knowing what to do.

"Get the report to me as soon as you can," says the chief over his shoulder. "Then we'll figure out whose case it is." He's already out the door and half way down the corridor.

Jimmy turns to the ME and gives him a wink.

The ME shudders.

Jimmy follows the Skipper down the hall.

The ME stands up and puts his cup on the chief's desk. He shakes his head in frustration, mutters something obscene and walks out of the empty room.

Jimmy hurries after the chief. He gets to the cells just as they're bringing Josephine out. Officer Conner, she of the freshly bobbed hair, has Josephine by the arm. Josephine looks dazed and unsteady. Her face is pale. Her eyes are red rimmed. She's wearing the same clothes she wore yesterday only they're crumpled now like they've been slept in, which they were. When she sees the chief her face lights up and she runs into his arms.

The Skipper is caught off guard.

So is Officer Conner.

And the sergeant who's just arrived with Josephine's release papers and personal belongings.

Josephine whimpers, "Oh Stanley" and she drapes herself around him. Clinging to him tightly and burying her head deep into his shoulder.

The chief is embarrassed. He doesn't know what to do. He's standing in the middle of the room in his spotless uniform and gleaming black shoes with a blank look on his face and Josephine wrapped tightly around him. Feelings of affection and tenderness wash over him, drowning out his natural caution and good sense. Slowly he puts his arms around her. And holds her tight. And tells her everything's going to be all right in a voice no one's ever heard before. Soft. And soothing. And full of concern.

The sergeant's mouth drops open.

So does Jimmy's.

And Officer Conner's.

And still the Skipper holds onto Josephine tightly. Stroking her hair now. Telling her how sorry he is as she softly weeps into his shoulder.

Jimmy's seen this before. Been here before. At a moment like this that comes out of nowhere and changes your life forever. It happened to him. Sixteen years ago when he found his best friend screwing his wife in his bed. Their bed. A wild card no one expected. Not him. Not them. And nothing was ever the same again. So here now is the Skipper, in that same sort of fix, or so it seems to Jimmy, where a truth is exposed when you least expect it and all hell can break loose. The Skipper has a wife and family. He can get hurt from this. His life can fall apart from this. So Jimmy steps in now to try and help him out. He peels Josephine off of him and, using the same tone the chief was using, says the same comforting things to her. Talking softly to her and stroking her hair which makes her cry all the more. And wrap herself tightly around him. And bury her head deep into his shoulder. Then Jimmy slowly puts his arms around her and holds her tight. To comfort her. And take the heat off the Skipper.

The chief realizes what he's done. That he let himself go, if only for a second, while people were watching. But now, stepping back and away from Josephine and Jimmy, he rallies under the cover of Jimmy's grand gesture and straightens his back. And sets his jaw tightly. And acts as if nothing's happened. Silently giving thanks to Jimmy's kind favor.

Jimmy says he'll take Josephine home.

The sergeant hands Jimmy the release paper and a large manila envelope containing Josephine's things.

Jimmy hustles Josephine up the stairs and out of the back door to his car.

"You think they figured it out?" she says as they drive off.

"That you're screwing the chief?"

She shoots him a look.

"For a moment they did," he says. "We all did. Some of us still do."

She smiles and says gratefully, "Then you stepped in and saved the day."

He dips his head graciously.

"I recovered quickly, don't you think?"

He shrugs.

"Clung to you like I did to him."

"Maybe they bought it. Who knows?" but he doesn't sound too convinced.

"Stanley recovered quickly."

Jimmy grins. Stanley. He never heard anyone call the chief that before. "He's good at that," he says, then his face turns serious. "The Skipper could've messed up real bad here, Jo. Put his whole life in jeopardy. The man's got a family and everything. What were you thinking, draping yourself around him like that?"

"I never spent a night in jail before, Jimmy. Not ever. It's not nice, you know what I mean? When I saw him I just lost it, that's all. I just lost it."

Jimmy curses as a car pulls out in front of him and never speeds up. "Look at this guy," he says irritably. "Can you believe it? Not a single car behind me. You'd think he'd wait if this is how fast he wants to go."

She agrees with him. How could she not? Then she says, "They both come in to the salon." She's talking about the sergeant and Sheila Conner.

"I wouldn't count on it buying you any loyalty."

Josephine knows it to be true. Folks are more likely to spread ugly rumors than to stand up for you is her experience.

"How come you let that guy in last night?" he asks.

"He looked nice."

"Someone else you could screw?"

"Hey," she says. "I thought we were friends."

Jimmy stares ahead and grips the steering wheel tightly.

"I know you're not jealous" she says. "What is it then?"

He tells her to forget it.

"C'mon Jimmy. What's with you?"

He's silent while he gathers his thoughts then tells her reluctantly, "You're always putting yourself in the line of fire."

She snorts indignantly, "Like I knew that guy was gonna jerk himself off in my chair."

"Not that," says Jimmy. "Screwing the chief."

"Yeah. Well," she answers. "That's got nothing to do with you, has it."

"And that man was not jerking himself off in your chair," says Jimmy. "He was cleaning his glasses."

"That's right," she shouts. "And, as it turns out, I'm not the one who killed him either, so lets drop it shall we. No more daddy talk, all right?"

Jimmy chews on his cheek. The car in front is still crawling along. There's a line of cars behind him now. He figures the driver must be ninety-five. Why else would you drive so slowly? "I think you should stay at Mary's for a few days," he says .

"Why?"

"The press are going to drive you crazy. This way they won't know where you are. It'll give you some privacy and some time to sort yourself out."

Josephine thinks it's a good idea. "I'll have to borrow some of Mary's stuff. I'm not intruding on you two, am I?"

"Nah," he says. "When the kid's around I stay at my place anyway."

"When are you gonna move in?"

He chuckles, but not really. "We can't talk about you screwing the chief, but it's all right for you to organize my life for me."

It's Josephine's turn to make a face.

Jimmy goes back to last night. "So you let him in. Then what?"

"We made some small talk. I hung up his coat."

"Did he say where he'd been?"

"New York. At a place called CRIMPERS. It's a beauty salon. They're his client."

"Why didn't he get his hair cut there?"

"He got the call about a meeting as he got off the Parkway. He said he didn't feel like driving back."

"What else did he say?"

"Nothing."

"Why's that?"

"Because that's when I slugged him."

Chapter 28

Jimmy calls Mary, tells her the plan and drops Josephine off at the house. They're good friends, Mary and Josephine, and Mary's happy to help out. She says a sleep-over sounds like fun. A bottle of wine. Maybe a movie and some popcorn. It turns out she knew all about Josephine's affair with the Skipper. That's what friends are for, she tells Jimmy. She didn't say anything about it to him because it was a confidence. He's got to admire her for that, but it still pisses him off that she has secrets.

After he's got Josephine settled, he drives over to Mrs. Lewis's house to give her the news : the person they arrested for killing her husband didn't kill him and has been released; her husband died of poisoning, not from being bludgeoned to death with a hand dryer; and the poisoning probably took place in New York, in which case the NYPD will probably be handling the investigation. When he's finished telling her all this, Mrs. Lewis faints dead away. She's lucky Jimmy's there to catch her, she could have hurt herself. Jimmy's not so fortunate. She must weigh more than a ton. He feels something pull as he hands her off to her friends, the ones who were there last night. They take her to a different part of the house and leave Jimmy to let himself out.

On the way back to the station Jimmy stops off at Errol Jamal's candy store. Errol's the guy Frankie the Cop said he should take a look at. The one he and Jason drove crazy when they were kids. The store is on Broadway in a five shop mini mall on the outskirts of town. The shop isn't Jamal's, it belongs to his parents. They live above the store. Jamal's got an apartment over by the river. They're kind of partners. Him, mom and dad. He does all the work and they take all the money. Jamal's a skinny thirty five, six feet tall and all arms and legs. He's got a thin pale face and long sandy hair that keeps falling in his eyes. He's wearing sneakers, jeans and a denim shirt with a white tee shirt underneath. His clothes are rumpled and well-worn. So is he.

Jimmy catches him as he's about to close up.

Errol tenses as Jimmy walks in the door. He thinks he's going to be robbed. It's all he ever thinks about when he's closing up the store. Every night at closing time he turns into Walter Mitty, deflecting a robber's gun with one slick move and beating him senseless with a combination of punches and chops to the back of the neck. That's the 'A' fantasy. The 'B' one has him handing over the money and begging for mercy in sniveling disarray and shameless cowardice.

Jimmy shows him his badge.

Errol tells him why he's so pleased to see him. How it's like a vacation having on the spot protection like this. "No need to worry boys," he says in a W.C. Fields imitation. "Cavalry's here! Smoke em if ya got em. Ah yessss. Ahhhhhh yessssss."

Jimmy smiles.

"What's up?" Errol wants to know.

"It's about Jason Friendly."

"I hate the fucker," says Errol with a scowl.

"That's what I wanted to talk to you about."

Errol locks the door and flips the open sign to closed. His impersonator's face is replaced by something not so nice.

"You know he's been accused of murder?" says Jimmy.

Errol says he does.

"Think he did it?"

"How should I know?"

"C'mon Mr. Jamal, you've known him all your life. You think Jason Friendly's capable of such a thing?"

Errol's back behind the counter now and begins to play with a book of matches.

"We went to school together if that's what you mean." He flicks the hair out of his eyes with a twitch of his head. "I wouldn't say I know him."

"Not a friend, then."

"Hardly."

"Ever cross paths with him these days?"

"I see him around."

"No conversation though?"

"No."

Jimmy looks around the shop. It's a dusty affair. There's an old glass counter that Errol must spend twelve hours a day behind. Inside its sliding doors are boxes of baseball cards, some open, some still sealed. Lighters and pipes are there too. Shelves full of magazines and candy line the walls. Smokes are behind Errol in big stacks. Displays of gum and Tic-Tacs in cardboard boxes couch the old fashioned register. There's a rubberized mat where the money changes hands. It's blackened and worn, but you can still make out the 'Marlboro Man,' astride his horse, with a cigarette in the corner of his mouth. "Didn't he beat you in the marathon?" he says.

Errol laughs at that. "Yes he did," he says using the W.C. voice again. "Yes he did."

"What's so funny," asks Jimmy.

"Son of a bitch beat me at everything."

"Not this week he didn't."

Errol appreciates the irony. "How's he doing?"

"Not so good."

Errol grins. Pleased at the come-uppance of his nemesis.

Jimmy explains the reason for the visit, that he's doing some deep background on Jason's past. "Your name came up," he says.

"Who brought it up?"

"Someone said you didn't like him."

"So what? I told you that myself. Who brought my name up?"

"It's not important," says Jimmy.

"It is to me. Next thing I know I'll be reading it in the papers. I know how these things work."

Jimmy tries to steer it back on track. "Why don't you like him?"

Errol's pacing behind the counter.

"I heard he gave you a hard time in high school."

Errol is astonished. "That's how far back you're going? You must be pretty desperate for background. Don't forget kindergarten. All sorts of terrible things went down there." Errol stops his pacing and looks at Jimmy who is not seeing the funny side of this. "That bunch thought they were such hot shit in those days," he says bitterly. "They took it out on us something awful. It drove my old man mad. He went to speak to the principal about it. He even went over to Jason's house to try and get it to stop."

"Who's us?"

"Anyone who wasn't on one of their teams."

"Anyone still around?"

"I suppose."

"Anyone you think I should talk to?"

Errol looks at him dead pan. "Like I'm gonna tell you."

Jimmy moves to leave, then stops and says, "You're not still pissed he won the marathon, are you?"

Errol purses his lips. "Sure I am. I trained hard for that thing and the bastard still beat me. So what?" His voice begins to rise. "What's that got to do with anything? You come here asking your background questions. Who cares about what happened back then? Maybe there's something here you're not telling me?"

Jimmy blinks.

Errol's eyes are bugging out of his head. He's beginning to look like Jack Nicholson in The Shining. "Well, is there?" he shouts, then marches to the door, unlocks it, holds it open and tilts his head towards the street.

Jimmy heads for the door saddened by his failure to make any progress. As he steps outside he asks him, "Do you own a rifle, Mr. Jamal?"

Errol sniffs the air like there's a foul odor. "I ain't telling you nothing," he says petulantly. "You're the detective, find out for yourself." Then he slams the door in Jimmy's face and clicks the lock so he can't get back inside.

Back at the office Jimmy's about to place a call to Jason at the lock-up, a procedure that can take as long as an hour, when Frankie the Cop swaggers in and plops himself down on one of Jimmy's chairs. "That guy I told you about. The one Jason had problems with in middle school."

"Michael Collis?" says Jimmy hopefully.

"That's him," says Frankie. "No one's seen him in years."

Jimmy's face falls.

"His dad lives in Hillsdale."

"In Putnam County?"

Frankie nods. "He's a janitor at the middle school there. They moved away a long time ago. Long before you got here. He was a lawyer when we were in school with Michael, then something went wrong. Somebody said the father was a boozer. Someone else said his wife left him. No one's sure when it happened, here, or after he moved. I barely remember Michael myself. I don't think he was with us in high school. I figure the family must have left when we graduated middle school."

Jimmy thinks it sounds like a wild goose chase. "I drew a blank with Errol Jamal," he says dejectedly. "He doesn't own a rifle, I checked. Not legally, at least. He didn't look like he was hiding anything either. He looked like he was just plain mad. That's a whole different thing."

"Will you see Michael's old man?"

Jimmy's not very enthusiastic. "You got anything else?"

Frankie doesn't.

"No one hear anything?"

"Not so far."

"You think you could get me the school records on Michael Collis?"

Jimmy's chubby face looks droopy and sad. "Smith and Monahan are pissed with me because I'm not with the program. The chief's gonna cut me loose any time now and I've got nothing to help Jason out. Not a thing. Not even a hint. Everything's going just perfectly."

Frankie's eyes widen. Stories like this are worth a lot of drinks with the people he hangs out with.

"I was about to call Jason," says Jimmy. "Anything you want me to tell him?"

"Yeah," says Frankie. "Wish him good luck," and he turns to go.

"It doesn't look good for our side," says Jimmy to his retreating back. Then he picks up the phone to try Jason again.

Chapter 29

The chief doesn't look very happy as Jimmy walks into his office. He's sitting at a messy desk in his shirtsleeves. Papers and files cover most of the surface. It's a far cry from the morning's spotless display for the ME. Two empty coffee cups and a bunch of screwed up papers are in a pile on the corner of the desk. The top button of his shirt is open, his tie is undone and his wide forehead crinkles in a scowl. He has no friendly greeting for Jimmy this afternoon. "What's going on," he growls, looking up from the printout he's reading.

Jimmy tells him how he stashed Josephine over at Mary's house, away from the prying eye of the press.

The chief responds with a grunt. He's decided to continue with his charade that nothing's going on between him and Josephine. That nothing happened in that jail room downstairs and anyone who thinks it did must be mistaken. So there's no small talk between the two of them about what took place down there. No knowing grins to show that they're on the same page here. Or the fact that Jimmy saved his ass and "thanks very much for the effort." There's none of that. It's business as usual. It's the best way, the chief rationalizes, to preserve the chain of command and his dignity.

"Jerry Lewis," he says now, referring to the dead man in Josephine's chair, "that's an NYPD responsibility. Two or three hours from the approximate time of death places him in New York at a beauty salon on Madison and 65th St. called CRIMPERS. That's the 23rd Precinct's territory. Detective Morgan Flynn has the case. I said we'd be happy to cooperate with him and sent him all the paperwork we had on the thing. Anything else you think we should do?"

Jimmy says he can't think of a thing. The chief's manner doesn't surprise him. It's not the first time he's been exposed to it. He tells him about his visit with Mrs. Lewis and how she passed out on him. "But not," he says, "before I told her that her husband had been poisoned, not beaten to death with a hand dryer."

"You'll have to go and see her again when Flynn wants to interview her," gruffs the chief. "Smith and Monahan worked with him when they thought that coke dealer Marc Hilliard might have something to do with Sandra Ellison's death. Turns out Hilliard had a pretty good alibi. He was locked up at the time of the shooting."

Jimmy knows all about it. Marc Hilliard was the first place he looked when he got the Skipper's green light to check things out.

"You'll be getting a call from Flynn soon, so be nice to him. What's happening with Jason?" The chief looks hopeful.

Jimmy says he doesn't have anything.

"All that fuss about taking him to his house and you got nothing?"

Jimmy squirms a little then tells him he's still tracking down the rifle but hasn't heard from the Syracuse police yet.

The chief is not pleased. Smith and Monahan have already been on at him for Jimmy's lack of loyalty, and, by inference, his own as well. It turns out the paperwork for Jason's trip home traveled quicker than Jimmy said it would. And here's Jimmy now saying for all his putting his neck on the line, he's got nothing to show for it. "What the hell, Jimmy," he says, rubbing a hand over his face. "I want to see the right person go down for this thing as much as you do, but damn it all I can't believe you've got nothing."

Jimmy stands at the edge of the desk. A hang dog expression covers his face. He's not invited to sit. Or offered coffee. Again.

"Well?" says the Skipper. "Nothing to say? No great insight? No hopeful stratagems"

Jimmy tells him about Michael Collis and how he's going to Hillsdale tomorrow to talk to his father. How he thinks everything that's happened to Jason might be linked to his past.

"It's a bit thin, don't you think and what the fuck does it have to do with Sandra Ellison any way?"

Jimmy agrees that it is a bit thin. What else was he going to say?

"I hate those screwballs as much as you do, Jimmy," says the chief, talking about Smith and Monahan. "But if they've got a case, they've got a case. You know what I mean?"

Jimmy says he knows what he means. He also knows the Skipper's trying to be nice here. That if Jimmy hadn't pulled his chips out of the fire this morning he'd be yelling and screaming at him by now. "I don't think he did it is all I'm saying. "

"So you say," says the Skipper, "but that's all you say. You've got no evidence, no clues. Nothing. You're putting me in the middle of these guys Jimmy, and I don't like being there. And guess what? They don't like it either."

Jimmy apologizes, but, he says, it doesn't change the way he feels.

"They're coming here Monday morning," says the chief like the end of the world is on its way.

Jimmy says he knows. He tells the chief Frankie Harlan's been helping him out.

The Skipper gives him a baleful stare. "S'okay by me," he says magnanimously, "but those county boys are gonna run your ass ragged. So don't be looking to me for any cover, you know what I'm saying here? I've stuck my neck out far enough for you. Anyway, you said I could hang you out to dry if things didn't work out. Well I got news for you, they didn't."

Jimmy gives him a thin smile.

"But you know," says the Skipper, as he stretches and yawns like everything's wearing him out, "I agree with you. Jason doesn't seem the type to kill someone.

Chapter 30

It's dinner time. Jimmy, Mary and Lucy are at the pizza parlor in the middle of town. They're sitting at a corner table by the window looking onto Main Street eating slices and drinking sodas off a red checkered table cloth and paper plates. The place is jammed. All the tables are taken. Everyone is talking loudly. There's a cacophony of laughter and shouting and the jangling of crockery and silverware being set down or cleared away. A bunch of people crowd the front counter waiting for pies to take home. There's a cozy warmth to the place. A mingling aroma of garlic and onion, marinara sauce and freshly baked bread that embraces the senses like a welcoming blanket. A gentle drizzle sparkles in the outside street lights. Headlights throw reflections off the shiny road. A few brave souls with umbrellas scurry by. The girls are all wound up about Josephine staying with them. She didn't join them at the pizza parlor for fear of being recognized and hounded by the press. "It's like having someone on the run hiding out with us," says Lucy excitedly, which reminds Mary to order a pie to take back for their fugitive.

"She took the longest shower," says Lucy. "Then she just curled up on the couch and went to sleep."

"She's all beat up," says Mary.

"What's the story there?" Jimmy wants to know. He's talking about the chief.

"She says it just happened."

Jimmy's aghast, "Just happened?"

"What just happened?" asks Lucy.

Jimmy and Mary look at each other. Jimmy reaches over and gives Lucy a handful of quarters for the video games. It's a new thing they put in the back room of the restaurant. The grown-ups get some time to themselves and the management makes some more money off the kids. Lucy grins and slides out of the booth not waiting for an answer. Mary goes on talking. "You know how much Jo likes her exercise?"

Jimmy says he does. Everyone does. Josephine loves her sex and that bit of information is all over town.

"One day the chief comes into the salon late," says Mary, "and there's no one else around. Need I say more?"

"He's got kids."

"What's that got to do with it?"

Jimmy makes a helpless gesture. "I always thought that counted for something."

She looks at him like he's crazy.

Jimmy changes the subject. "Wanna know what the chief said to me when I got back to the office?"

She waits. And waits. When he doesn't say anything she gets the point and squawks, "Nothing? That son of a bitch said nothing. Not even a thank you?"

Jimmy shrugs. What's there to say? Then he tells her about his encounter with Errol Jamal. "He went from doing W.C. Fields to showing me the door in five minutes, whaddya think of that?"

Mary says she doesn't know what to think. Neither does she know who W.C. Fields is.

"An old time movie star who's got a distinctive voice."

She wrinkles her nose. "So why'd he use it on you?"

"It's probably a thing with him. Anyhow, one minute he's doing W.C. the next he's showing me the door."

"Because you accused him of murder?" asks Mary with her mouth full.

"I did no such thing."

"I bet that's what he thought."

"He was more concerned about not seeing his name in the papers. Anyway," he says trying to explain his interviewing technique, "you want them to make a mistake. The only way to do that is to ask them a lot of questions."

"So did he?" Mary takes a slug of soda.

"What?"

"Make a mistake?"

"Of course not."

She smiles mischievously. "Sharper than you, then?"

"Not necessarily."

"How so?"

"He probably didn't do it."

"Oh that!" says Mary and they break up laughing.

Lucy comes back for more quarters. Mary fishes in her bag. Jimmy's got a couple left in his pocket. Between them they come up with six. Lucy takes a chomp on a slice and disappears again.

"Then I get a call from Smith and Monahan," Jimmy goes on. "Actually it's Smith. He's the one who makes the calls. The other one doesn't know how to work the machinery. Smith says how come I'm not helping them with Jason? Instead, he hears, I'm trying to get him off. Then we get into an argument where I say I am helping them by making sure they get the right guy. Smith says they've got the right guy, Jason fucking Friendly. And if I want to play on their team I better get with the program, because with what they've got on him, Jason's going down for this particular crime. Can you believe that's what he said to me? 'This particular crime.' Who talks like that? Any cop show you saw did you ever hear someone say, 'this particular crime?' And the tone he used on me. Like he's the smartest guy in the world."

"What did you say?"

Their heads are barely an inch apart across the table.

"I told them I thought they were making a big mistake."

"And he said?"

"I was the one making the big mistake, then he hung up on me."

She cuts another slice from the tin tray and puts it on his plate.

"After that I went to see this other guy who owns a gas station on #35. I'm telling you, Mary. This has been one helluva day. This is someone who shot his mouth off in a bar four years ago about how much he hates Jason."

"Four years? Who told you this?"

"Same guy who gave me Errol."

"That cop you don't like?"

Jimmy nods.

"Do you trust him?"

"He and Jason go way back. I really think he wants to help."

"What did the man at the gas station say?"

"Robbie Jackman, that's his name. Big guy. Some sort of amateur wrestler. Another one Jason gave a hard time to when they were kids. Robbie wasn't so big back then. He says he hates Jason with a passion. Says everyone knows how he feels and he's never tried to hide it and if I think he tried to kill him I should show him some evidence or get the fuck out of his garage." Jimmy takes a slurp of his Coke. "He looked like he was going to pick me up and throw me in the car."

She looks doubtful. "You think he'd have done it?"

"I wasn't going to wait and find out."

Mary picks up a crust and begins to gnaw on it.

"What are you going to do?" she asks him.

"I'm still working on tracing the rifle. The cops up in Syracuse are checking out this guy Mickey Swan for me. He's the last person there's a record for. No luck so far. The lab boys found lots of prints in Jason's house. They're sorting them out, but it's slow going. The footprint in the back yard is from a size ten pair of Nikes you can buy anywhere. None of it means shit. The next thing, I suppose, is to find more people Jason went to school with and see where that takes me. Not much is it?"

She agrees. It's not.

Then he says mournfully, "They're coming back Monday."

"Laurel and Hardy?"

He nods.

"When?"

"The morning sometime."

She squinches up her face.

"I've got twenty four hours or so to come up with something before they close me down for good and I can't count on the Skipper. I said he could hang me out to dry if things didn't work out. This afternoon he told me he's taking me up on my offer."

"Why did you do that?"

"To buy some time."

"You really think Jason didn't do it?"

"I do. He was out jogging. He heard a noise that sounded like a gunshot. He came forward, told us about it and got put in a box by Smith and Monahan for his trouble. Somebody framed him."

"Who?"

"That's what I need more time for. To ask around and nose about. If there's anything out there that's the only way it's going to shake loose."

"What if you don't find anything?"

"I'll be very upset. This guy did not do this. There's not a doubt in my mind."

"How long do you need?"

"Another couple of days."

She licks some sauce of her fingers, cocks her head to one side and says, "So fuck 'em!" and leans over and gives him a kiss on his chubby cheek.

It's what he loves most about her. The clarity she brings to all problems.

Monday

Chapter 31

The phone rings. It seems like it's part of the dream. Bells jangle. Cell doors clank. But it' not a dream. It's the phone. Jimmy's eyes begin to slowly open. First one. Then the other. He reaches over and grabs the receiver. He looks at the clock and croaks, "It's 6:30. This better be good."

Detective Morgan Flynn of the NYPD identifies himself. He offers no apologies for the earliness of the hour. He says he'd like to see Mrs. Lewis today if it's convenient.

Jimmy yawns and scratches his head and says he'll try to set it up. They agree to meet at the diner in the middle of town at 10:00 unless Morgan hears otherwise. He gives him directions, hangs up the phone and goes back to sleep. Felix snuggles into Jimmy's spine and goes back to sleep too.

Later Jimmy and Morgan are huddled in a booth in the rear of the Columbia Diner hunched over coffees. Morgan's talking. Jimmy's sipping. Morgan takes a call on his cell phone, says thank you a lot but doesn't look very happy as he snaps the phone shut and fixes it back on his belt. "I'm running seven cases," he says, explaining the call. "Can you imagine?"

Jimmy says he can't. He's worn out working one.

Morgan Flynn is in his thirties. He's a tall man, even sitting down you can see that, and sleek and quite handsome. His black hair is gelled and slicked back, his sensitive face has a fashionable two day stubble and his brown eyes are sharp and piercing. He's wearing a tailor made dark blue suit that gives him the look of a model. He's a no-nonsense kind of man who's serious about what he does and prides himself on the results he consistently achieves. He signals the waitress he'd like a refill.

She wanders over, fills their cups and gives Jimmy a wink. Then she wanders off again.

Morgan raises an eyebrow.

Jimmy doesn't blush, but he feels a soft warmth rising under his collar. He's wearing his blue suit fresh from the cleaners, a white shirt and a blue striped tie. He looks shabby next to Morgan, but sharper than he usually does. That's probably what the wink was for.

Morgan asks him about his time with the NYPD.

"How'd you know about that?" says Jimmy.

"I asked around," says Morgan. "Then I pulled your file."

Jimmy asks him why.

Morgan says, "I like to know who I'm working with."

Jimmy shrugs. What difference did it make?

"You were pretty good back then."

"Till the end," says Jimmy.

"What happened?"

"What does the file say?"

Morgan grins. "That your boss had a soft spot for you."

"What's that mean?"

"All the shit's missing."

"Just as well," Jimmy says and grins.

"So what happened?" Morgan asks him again.

Jimmy shifts in his seat.

Morgan waits.

Jimmy sips his coffee.

Morgan sees he's not going to get an answer. "My father was a cop in Brooklyn," he says, changing the subject.

Jimmy raises an eyebrow.

"A beat cop. He never got a shield. He didn't want one is what he told us. He liked to walk the streets swinging that night stick of his. He drove the kids wild twisting it around and bouncing it off the pavement. They looked at him like he was some sort of saint. Maybe you knew him, you were around in those days."

Jimmy says he knew a lot of cops called Flynn.

"That's my stepfather's name," says Morgan. "McLernon's my dad's name. James McLernon. Big guy. Six feet tall. Worked out of Park Slope."

Jimmy actually flinches. James McLernon was a good friend of his in those days. "No kidding," he says, remembering all the bars they used to hang out at and all the liquor they drank. "How's he doing?"

"He died last year of a heart attack."

Jimmy's stunned. James is dead? How is that possible, he only just found him again. "Your dad was a rare breed," he says sadly. Picturing them staggering down the street together, holding each other up. James mumbling terrible things about Morgan. This Morgan. "It's all he ever talked about," he says shaking his head. "How the two of you didn't get along."

"I thought you could be the guy. Your file doesn't say where you went, but I heard it was Westchester some place.

"Your dad and I were pretty close," says Jimmy. They were. Like brothers.

Morgan listens transfixed as Jimmy tells him stories he never heard before. About his father. James Mc Lernon. The cop. The drunk. Who walked out on him and his mother. But now here's a different tale. Of bravery and a loyalty to the boys in blue.

Morgan drinks some coffee. Finally he says, "When we got back together again dad talked a lot about you. It's so strange to finally meet you. He never understood why you just upped and left. One day you were there, the next you were gone and you never came back. Not even a phone call. He never understood that."

"I was in some mess back then."

"So you ran away to Columbia."

"That was after, when I'd sorted myself out. And I wouldn't call it running away," says Jimmy. "Reinventing myself is how I see it."

"Me and Dad got back together when I joined the force. They came to him to check me out. That's how he heard about me. One day he called me up. We had a nice talk and bit by bit we got to be friends. It took a while, but it turned out to be a nice thing."

He takes another gulp of coffee then gets down to business. "The way we see it Jerry Lewis was poisoned while he was at a business meeting at CRIMPERS, that's a beauty salon on Madison at 65th . It's very fancy. The two partners are fighting. One wants to split up, the other wants to be paid more than he's been offered. Jerry Lewis took sides. He favored William, the partner that wants to split up. The other partner's name is Daniel Phillips."

"William?" asks Jimmy. "No last name?"

"Just William. He's a difficult type. Thinks he's hot shit. We spoke to everyone working in the salon the day Lewis was there. Nobody saw anything. Nobody heard anything. Mostly they all seemed worried. The fight between the partners is hitting them pretty hard money-wise. This should kill business altogether. Ooops. Sorry. Poor choice of word."

On the drive over to Jerry Lewis's house, Morgan tells Jimmy another small world thing. "Sandra Ellison got her hair cut at CRIMPERS. So does her boy friend Marc Hilliard. He's back on the street by the way. They could only hold him for so long. It's a ticketable offence, a couple of joints. No coke, can you believe it? The guy sells coke for a living, but they can't find any on him or in his car. He doesn't sell weed, but that's what they get him on."

Jimmy tells him his about his troubles with Smith and Monahan.

"We think they're morons at the precinct house," says Morgan. "No one takes them very seriously."

"Well they're big shots where I come from and they drive everyone crazy."

By then they're at the Lewis house. Constance Lewis answers the door. There's no maid today, she sent her home. Neither did she call the lawyer her brother suggested, or ask her friends to be with her. It's no one's business, is how she sees it. Murder's a private matter. So here she is facing the police by herself. Her bleached blonde hair is teased up in a timeless beehive, her makeup is heavily applied and her fluffy pink dress makes her look even bigger than she is. There's a Miss Piggy feel about her, even to the way she walks.

Jimmy makes the introductions.

Morgan shakes her fleshy hand and shows her his ID.

She invites them inside to the room off the hallway and asks them to sit down.

Morgan makes some small talk about how nice the room is. How sorry he is for her loss. Then he leads her gently into his questions. About their lives, and their friends lives, and who might want to do such a terrible thing to her husband. Using one thing to get to the other. To get her permission to go through her husband's things. Voluntarily. Without having to get a warrant. He slips it in at the end of a long list of questions. "Does your husband have an office in the house?" he asks.

She says he does.

"Is there a safe by any chance?"

She says there is.

"Could we take a look inside?"

She says she has no objection and leads them downstairs to her husband's office.

The office takes up most of what used to be the basement. It's plushly carpeted with modern furniture and a magnificent oak desk that takes up the center of the room. An entire wall is filled with a floor to ceiling bookcase stuffed with books on accounting and law. A couple of elegant filing cabinets stand against another wall and four comfy looking armchairs face the desk. Art covers all the wall surfaces. Modern stuff Jimmy doesn't understand. There are no windows. Mrs. Lewis goes over to a picture, a large garish thing with big splashes of color, and takes it down. Behind it is a safe. A large gun metal affair with fancy looking tumblers and a shiny black handle.

Morgan asks her for the combination.

Mrs. Lewis rattles off the numbers.

Jimmy writes them down.

Mrs. Lewis waddles over to an armchair and sits down.

Morgan takes out a pair of white rubber gloves and snaps them on.

Jimmy does the same, then reads out the numbers for the safe.

Morgan turns the dials.

There's a clunk as the cylinders disengage and the door pops open. There are three shelves inside. The bottom one has various files of legal documents, eight one-ounce bags of marijuana triple bagged so the smell doesn't permeate anything else, and a dozen glassine envelopes of a white powdery substance that looks like cocaine or heroin.

Morgan takes out a digital camera and photographs everything.

Jimmy puts the drugs in plastic evidence bags and places them on the desk.

Mrs. Lewis gets up and goes to take a look.

Jimmy watches her reaction.

Morgan too.

She stares at the bagged drugs seemingly in a trance.

Jimmy's sure she's clean. He feels sorry for her is the thing. It's bad enough her husband's been murdered, now they're going to drag him through the mud.

On the middle shelf, Morgan finds a collection of stock certificates, ten thousand dollars in hundred dollar bills, the deed to the house, birth certificates and a large stack of incredibly explicit pornographic eight by tens.

Jimmy puts them face down on the desk with the other discoveries.

Mrs. Lewis reaches out for one.

Jimmy asks her not to. "Fingerprints," he explains.

She's embarrassed. And shocked. And completely bewildered.

The top shelf is crammed full of files, documents and legal papers.

After Morgan takes everything out he finds a small bottle with an eyedropper top, half-filled with liquid. The label says POISON in large capital letters. He takes a picture of it while it's still in the safe, then he bags it and puts it on the desk with the rest of the haul.

"Oh my Lord," is all Mrs. Lewis can say when she sees what Morgan's found. She's trying hard to hold back the tears, not wanting to fall apart in front of these strangers.

Morgan asks her gently, "Have you been in here since your husband died?"

She says she hasn't.

"What about before?"

"I never intruded in here unless he needed me."

"What about to clean the place?" Morgan asks.

"The maid does that."

"You never went inside the safe?"

"Never."

"What about now?" asks Morgan.

"I just told you no," she says with some irritation. "I couldn't bring myself to." She wipes the corner of her eye. "I just couldn't."

They give the office a quick once over so they can get out of there. Out of this poor lady's unhappy face. They check the rooms and the garage, but there's nothing else to find. She gives them permission to take Mr. Lewis's laptop, his address book and an old Rolodex Morgan found in his desk drawer. Jimmy compiles an inventory of the things they're taking, signs it, has Morgan sign it, has Mrs. Lewis sign it and leaves her a copy and a receipt.

Mrs. Lewis sits in the armchair staring straight ahead, the receipt is clutched in her hand. The house is quiet. Not even a clock ticks. They leave her like that. Feeling like they stole the light from whatever's left of her sad life.

Back in the car Morgan wants to know what Jimmy thinks about the poison. Jimmy says he doesn't know. Neither does Morgan. "And the dope?" he asks.

"I think," says Jimmy, "that Jerry Lewis wasn't such a good boy." He's moved by Mrs. Lewis's predicament and feels sorry for her. It's hard to come back from a thing like this. Not just losing your husband, but finding out he's not who you thought he was. He's struck by her innocence and vulnerability and acutely sensitive to what she's going through. "Every time you found something, it blew her mind. I watched her. I can't imagine she was putting it on. No one's that good."

Morgan grunts. He's not so impressed. Not when you're juggling seven cases, each one with its own set of sad faces. "Why didn't she check the safe?" he wonders aloud. "Everyone checks the safe when somebody dies."

"Everyone?"

"Everyone who's got a safe."

"She couldn't go in the office let alone the safe, that's what she said," says Jimmy. "I can understand that."

They toss it backwards and forwards for a while, then Morgan asks Jimmy if he could check Jerry Lewis out for him. "Friends, neighbors, that sort of thing."

Jimmy says he'd be glad to.

They're at Morgan's car now. He shakes Jimmy's hand and thanks him for his help. "I'll call you," he says and gets out of Jimmy's car and into his own.

Chapter 32

After leaving Morgan Flynn, Jimmy takes off for Hillsdale Middle School to talk to Harvey Collis, Michael Collis's father. It's a nice, twenty-minute drive through rolling hills and pretty countryside. More trees have popped their leaves, but not enough to create a solid canopy. Instead the landscape is a patchwork quilt that looks like it's seen better days with holes and bare spots and bits with just a hint of faded green.

Jimmy opens the window wide to clear his head so he can think straight and maybe come up with something, but the more he thinks about it the more complicated it seems to get. There's Morgan Flynn mentioning Marc Hilliard, Sandra Ellison's drug-dealer boyfriend. And then this odd tie to CRIMPERS where both Hilliard and Sandra get their hair cut and Jerry Lewis got himself poisoned.

Hillsdale Middle School was built in the mid-sixties. It takes a lot of effort to keep it going. There are leaks and overloads, rodent infestations, inefficient wiring, and, in the winter, the constant battle to keep the place warm. Harvey Collis runs a crew of three men. Between them they cover everything from plumbing to electrical work. Something big is taken care of by outside contractors, but they're able to keep on top of the small stuff, which usually keeps the building going fairly well.

Jimmy finds Collis in his office in a corner of the basement, going through a bunch of invoices. He's in his mid-fifties and wears blue denim overalls with a bib front and large clumpy work boots. He's a big man. Not fat, just big. Six feet four and built like an ox. His melon-like face has thick lips and a large flat nose with flared nostrils. The top of his large head has the same three day growth as his face, but it's easy to see that the balding process is well under way. A large circle in the center of his scalp is as clean as white tile. His office is really a large cubicle with shelves and filing cabinets that take up most of the space. A gray metal desk that looks as old as the building takes up what's left. There's room for only one chair and Collis is sitting in it. He looks up as Jimmy raps on the glass. Jimmy stands in the doorway.

"Whaddya want?" snarls Collis.

Jimmy shows him his badge.

Collis examines the tin. "Out of your jurisdiction, aren't you?"

Jimmy agrees that he is. "I'm trying to find your son," he says.

"Is he lost?" Collis wants to know.

Jimmy says not so far as he knows.

Collis puts down the invoices and stares at Jimmy in a most unfriendly manner. "What do you want with him?"

Jimmy tries an explanation. Telling him about Jason Friendly and Sandra Ellison's murder. "We're doing some deep background on Jason's past. A number of things have come up that point to some inconsistencies in the case we've been building against him."

"He did it, didn't he?"

"It certainly looks that way, but there've been some incidents that might have a bearing on the case."

"Like what?" Collis wants to know.

"Well sir, I'd rather not go into it. That's the reason I'd like to speak to your son."

Collis looks at him skeptically. "A man's been accused of murder and you want to speak to my son about it?"

"I didn't say that, Mr. Collis."

"What did you say?"

"I said I wanted to talk to him about Jason's past."

Collis humphed. "This sounds like the biggest load of bullshit I've ever heard."

Jimmy clears his throat and tries again. "We've been speaking to number of Jason's old school friends to try and fill out his past. It turns out he was quite a bully back then."

"Yeah. So. What's that got to do with him killing that woman?"

"Well," says Jimmy, feeling more and more like he's climbing up a melting rope. "Like I said, these incidents might have a bearing on things."

"What incidents?"

"As I said Mr. Collis, I'd rather not go into that."

"You think my boy's been involved in these so called incidents?"

Jimmy says not exactly.

"Then what do you want with him?"

Jimmy says he's following up every possibility.

"And what possibility does my son fall in to?"

Jimmy's getting nowhere. "I'm looking for people who can help me with this line of inquiry. Do you know where I can reach him, Mr. Collis?"

"What line of inquiry?"

Jimmy looks at him.

"You just said you were looking for people that can help you with this line of inquiry," says Collis. "I'm asking you what that line of inquiry is?"

"These things that have happened to Mr. Friendly."

Collis looks angry. "You think this crap your talking about is gonna get him off? Is that what's going on here?"

"No sir. Not at all. Like I said, this is just deep background we're working on. Tying up all the loose ends. All murder inquiries go this way. You check out every detail and make sure you've covered every base. That's why I need to speak to your boy. Maybe he remembers something, some obscure fact that could help us tie up this loose end."

"What loose end?"

Jimmy was having a hard time keeping cool. "I just told you, Mr. Collis. These incidents."

Collis shakes his melon-like head slowly like he thinks the whole world's gone mad. He picks up the invoices again and scans them. Then, without looking up he says reflectively, "I haven't spoken to Michael in a long time. We had a bust up some years ago. Since then we don't talk very much." It was sad the way he said it.

"An address?"

This seems to be a painful subject for Collis. Gone is the angry giant. Here now is someone who looks like he's lost just about everything. "Last place I know of is Albany. That was about a year ago," he says sadly. He writes the address on a scrap of paper and hands it to Jimmy and waits impatiently for the next question.

Jimmy can't help noticing he's got the same look on his face that Errol Jamal and Robbie Jackman had when he finished talking to them. Pissed off and angry is what they looked like. This guy looks the same way. Jimmy figures he's lucky to have gotten what he's got. He gives Collis a wan smile, thanks him for his help, hands him his card and says goodbye.

Chapter 33

Jimmy's sitting in his office leaning back in his chair. His feet are on the desk, there's a mug of coffee in one hand and the phone in the other. He's just put a call in to Jason and it hasn't come through yet. They're telling him on the other end to be patient. They're busy, they say, as if he's not. Now he's talking to Jason's lawyer who's called to tell him he can't find anything in Jason's former case files that lends itself to grudges or murder. Jimmy's surprised. He wonders if he should take a look himself. "Not one thing?" he asks.

"It's all nickel and dime stuff," says the lawyer. "I can't see anyone wanting to kill him over any of it. The biggest thing he's had in a while is this deal with Sandra Ellison. Other than that it's wills, closings, and things of that sort. The court stuff is minor, kids mostly, for drugs and traffic violations."

Jimmy tells him about Collis, Jamal, and Jackman, and asks him to check their names against the files. "It's an outside shot," he says, "but you never know. Maybe he did some work for them."

"And?"

"And nothing," says Jimmy. "They looked clean to me, but maybe you'll find something different."

The lawyer says he'll look into it.

Jimmy says, "Smith and Monahan have got Jason doing a lot of running around that night. It doesn't make sense to me. You might want to put some posters up in the neighborhood asking if anyone saw him. It would be great if we could find a witness to corroborate his version of things."

The lawyer thinks it's a good idea. "I'm on it," he says and hangs up.

After that Jimmy speaks to the Syracuse Police Department who tell him Mickey Swan, the owner of the rifle that killed Sandra Ellison, was no longer at the address Jimmy gave them. To their credit they didn't leave it at that. They sought out the landlord and got a new address in Hyde Park, Dutchess County, NY. That's where the trail went cold. There's no Mickey Swan there now, neither is there a forwarding address. The information on the form Mr. Swan filled out when he bought the rifle gave a social security number but the numbers are written so softly there are a number of variables. A six could be an eight. A five could be a six. "This is going to take some time," Jimmy grumbles and makes a few calls to get the ball rolling.

Then he tries running down Michael Collis. The address his father gave him is a dead end. The college Michael went to has no information about him. He's not in the New York State database. Or Connecticut. Or New Jersey. Or the Feds. The social security number Jimmy got from Michael's school records doesn't help. The IRS says he hasn't filed a return in last ten years and all their warnings and threats of levees come back with 'addressee unknown' stamped on them. He never registered with the draft board. "The guy's probably in Canada," Jimmy mutters.

Frankie the Cop knocks on the door and pops his head inside. When he sees Jimmy's not on the phone and there's no one else around he asks, "Who you talking to?"

Jimmy ignores him.

Frankie says he's reporting in. He's got nothing to report, but he's reporting in just the same. He's gone before Jimmy can ask him a question. He stares at the door and runs his hands through his hair, imagining the meal Laurel and Hardy are going to make out of him. A little while later he's not disappointed as he stands in front of the Chief's desk. Again. With no coffee. Again. While they all sip theirs.

The boys yell and curse at him in a skillful duet of accusatory venom. Smith calls him a, "Judas," spitting out the word like it's a poisonous bile.

Monahan ask him sarcastically, "You want all our other cases so you can fuck them up too?"

The chief says nothing, not wanting to get any of the same treatment.

The boys dress Jimmy up, down and sideways. They pound him with insults and work themselves up into a frenzy of angry abuse till they get to the climax. The finale. Where they scowl. And grimace. And grunt and groan. While they tell him in angry tones and hostile stares that they're taking him off the case and he should, "Get the fuck out of here."

The chief nods in fervent agreement while smiling his smarmy smile at the boys.

Back in his office, after kicking a hole in the wall and punching a dent in his filing cabinet, Jimmy's call to Jason finally comes through. There are clicks and buzzes and long periods of silence as he's connected first to the warden's office, then the visitors area and then finally to the special prisoner unit. A subdued Jason gets on the phone.

"How ya doing?" asks Jimmy.

Jason mumbles a reply.

Jimmy says, "You don't sound so good, Jason."

Jason's voice quivers. "If you knew what I'm going through you wouldn't sound so good either."

Jimmy says he can only imagine. "Any more thoughts on people I should look at?"

Jason says he hasn't come up with anyone.

Jimmy tells him who he's been to see. "Errol Jamal, Robbie Jackman and Harvey Collis."

"Why Collis?"

"I was looking for his son."

Jason says dully, "You think it's one of them?"

Jimmy says he doesn't.

"So why'd you go and see them?"

"Frankie Harlan said you hassled them in school. It was an outside shot."

Jason's got nothing to say.

"No one else you can think of?"

Jason says he can't.

Jimmy tells him Frankie Harlan's been helping out. "He wishes you luck."

Jason's not impressed.

Jimmy tells him he's been kicked off the case.

Jason doesn't seem to care.

Jimmy talks about the weather.

Jason shows no interest.

Jimmy can hear what's going on here. He's been through this himself and recognizes the signs. Where depression takes over and you start to spiral down. "You're not going to beat this thing this way," Jimmy says sternly. "A jury's only got to see your face to figure you did it for sure. You're miserable and depressed? You've got every right to be. You think you got a raw deal? Absolutely. You think you're never gonna get out of this mess? You're damn right if you keep on this way. We've seen this before, you and I. An innocent man's found guilty and ends up in jail forever. Wanna know what helped put him there? Depression. He wrapped himself up in it and wouldn't fight. His defense figures if he won't help himself, why should they? The jury, who sees everything, thinks if his defense isn't putting up a good fight he must be guilty. Hasn't it happened to you? A client folds before you even get going. That's what you're doing now Jason, folding. I can hear it in your voice, and so can your lawyer. Turn it around my friend, before it's too late. Depression does bad things to you. I know. I've been there. It's like a lead overcoat. Once you put it on, it's hard to get off. Get yourself a regimen. Lift some weights. Find a chess partner. They play chess there don't they?"

Jason says they do.

"Keep your mind active, that's the key. You could be there for a while so you better get your head around it. Study a subject. They've got a library don't they? How about writing? Get it all down on paper. You might even have a best seller by the time you're finished, but you've got to do something. One more week like this and you're done for."

Jason didn't realize how far down he'd gone. He thanks Jimmy for the pep talk and says he'll try harder and that ends their conversation.

Chapter 34

When Jimmy gets home there's a message from Jason's lawyer on his answering machine saying Jason's had some thoughts on the names Jimmy mentioned. Jimmy calls the lawyer back, but no one picks up. He leaves a message of his own, then he heads for the kitchen. Felix trots behind him. His tail points skyward. He's pleased to see him, hence the erect tail and he brushes himself up against Jimmy's leg in a frenzy of nuzzled affection. Jimmy tops up the cat's bowl, then does some chores. He washes the dishes that have accumulated in the sink over the past week. A curd of grease and soapsuds sits on top of the cold water they've been soaking in. He hates this part of the routine. Plunging his arm through the scum to find the stopper and let the water out. The curd sticks to his arm like a blanket of crud. Every week he does the same thing and reacts in the same way. You'd think he'd change the routine is Mary's point here. To which Jimmy, of course, has no answer.

After the dishes, he changes Felix's litter box not that the cat uses it all the time. But sometimes if he's left indoors too long and he's not pissed off, he'll do his business there. The phone rings as Jimmy is trying to maneuver a garbage bag over the end of the tray. He turns his head and holds his breath to avoid the foul smelling dust that rises up as the stuff pours into the bag, and he curses out loud as the phone continues to jangle. He's rushing now. Not wanting to miss the call. Which throws off his timing. And his aim. And dried lumps of cat shit and clumps of sodden litter cascade onto the floor. Jimmy lets out a stream of invective, then picks up the phone and says "Hello" in a calm voice, like nothing's happened.

"What did you say to Jason?" says Jason's lawyer.

"I gave him a pep talk."

"That's a different person I just came from."

Jimmy's says he's pleased to hear it.

"I heard you got kicked off the case."

"Internal politics," says Jimmy. "No one wants me to make waves. "

The lawyer commiserates with him then says, "Jason's got someone for you look at. A guy named Ted Butler. He says you might want to run him down."

"What for?"

"He thought it might be a good idea."

"Why?"

No answer.

"That's it?" says Jimmy. "Just the name?"

"The guy's got something to do with the Club."

"Rolling Hills?"

"I think so."

"He didn't say why?" asks Jimmy.

"No."

"And he didn't give you any more information?"

The lawyer says that's all he knows.

Jimmy mumbles something incoherent.

"Another thing," says the lawyer. "Jason wanted to know where Michael Collis's father is practicing."

"Practicing?"

"I assume he meant the law. The man's an attorney isn't he?"

"Not any more," says Jimmy and tells the lawyer how he went to see the father to track down the son and how the son, Michael, is nowhere to be found.

"The father's a janitor?"

"A janitor," repeats Jimmy.

"What happened?"

Jimmy's tell him what Frankie Harlan said. That it was a long time ago, but there were rumors of alcohol. "Why's Jason asking about Collis's father?"

"I don't know."

"Didn't you ask?"

"No."

"Weren't you curious?"

No answer.

"And you didn't ask him anything about this Ted Butler?"

Nothing.

"Weren't you interested?"

Still no answer.

"I don't understand why you wouldn't want to know," says Jimmy. "Why wouldn't you be interested in anything Jason has to say?"

More silence.

"Unless you're not putting your best foot forward. Is that what's going on here, counselor?" Jimmy's right. He knows it. The lawyer's dragging his feet. "You don't think he stands a chance, do you? You think they've got him cold."

The lawyer doesn't say anything.

"You should be ashamed of yourself," says Jimmy with disgust. "Jason's no more guilty than you are."

"I know that," says the lawyer defensively,

"Then what is it?" Jimmy wants to know. "Why this sudden lack of energy?" He hates this type of attorney. A gunslinger who's only out for himself. With no morals or ethics. Only greed and ego and selfishness. "You don't think you can win, do you? That's it, isn't it? That's what's going on here."

Silence.

"You'll take his money and go through the motions, but you've got bigger fish to fry, isn't that right counselor? You got your fifteen minutes of fame and some new clients because of it, and there's only so much of you to go around, isn't that what's going on here? You put your energy where it does you the most good. That's how it works in your world, doesn't it? Our Jason's the guy they made up that term for. You know the one. When you put something on the back burner. Isn't that what you're doing here, counselor? Putting Jason on the back burner."

There's another long pause, then the lawyer says dryly, "My word detective, two speeches in one day. You must be up for some kind of award."

Jimmy ignores the sarcasm. "Don't give up on him is all I'm saying."

The lawyer goes for indignation. "I have no intention of doing any such thing, And what about you?" says the pit bull. "Are you giving up on him now you're off the case?"

Jimmy let it go. He'd made his point and there was no sense in having a fight with the man. "Just let me know what Jason says about Michael Collis's old man," he says and puts down the phone.

Chapter 35

They're invited to Josephine's, Jimmy and Mary, for a little get together to celebrate her release from the clutches of the law. She lives in a medium-sized apartment complex on the outskirts of town. One of those community affairs with a pool, tennis courts and perfectly manicured grounds. There are eight two-story buildings clustered around the amenities. Josephine lives on the second floor of one of them. They can hear her and someone whose voice they don't recognize in the middle of a heated exchange from the parking lot. They can hear them clearer in the hallway as they walk up the stairs to the apartment. And clearer still when Josephine flings opens the door to let them in and returns to her discussion with the stranger without missing a beat.

The girl's name is Mitchiko, but they only find that out later. Mitchiko was born in Los Angeles of Japanese descent. She's twenty-seven, tops, with a nose ring that Jimmy can't stop staring at. She has a Modigliani-shaped face, perfectly bobbed black hair and the smoothest skin Jimmy's ever seen. She's wearing skin tight jeans and an equally tight tee shirt that shows quite clearly she's not wearing a bra. Her black leather jacket is draped over a chair. She wants Josephine to go into business with her is the point of the discussion. In Scarsdale. Closer to the City. A much bigger place than she has now. Grander. More elegant. "She's lost here," says Mitchiko at the end of a long soliloquy about the wonderful possibilities the two of them could achieve together. She looks at Jimmy and Mary and smiles a hello, expecting them to agree.

"What does 'lost' mean?" Mary wants to know.

Mitchiko takes a deep breath, then launches into a seminar on what a great talent Josephine is and how hard it is for her to be creative stuck out here in the sticks. When Mitchiko sees Mary's frown, she quickly explains she didn't mean it as a Columbia put down. "I'm an artist," she says vehemently. "So is Josephine, otherwise I wouldn't want to go into business with her. The people we hire will be artists too. Scarsdale's got lots of beauty salons, but none of them are dedicated to fashion and art. That's our hook. Our work will compete with the top salons in the City. Our message will be, 'Why schlep to New York, pay city prices, travel costs and maybe a sitter, not to mention the time factor, when you can get the same fashionable haircut here in Scarsdale for half the price?" She takes a gulp of air and charges on. "It's hard to create that type of atmosphere in a three-chair salon anywhere, not just Columbia. There's no juice in an environment like that. No clash of creative talents where one person feeds off another and everyone moves forward."

Jimmy hangs his coat on the rack by the door and does the same for Mary. He has no idea what Mitchiko's talking about. He's not so crazy about her either. She's skinny and pierced and a little too over-the-top for his liking.

Josephine's one bedroom apartment is small. The living area and kitchen are one space. A large window overlooks a building that looks just like hers. She's made it cute, though. The furniture is draped with quilts and blankets. Candles are everywhere. And the walls are covered with photographs of hairstyles and her publicity.

Josephine is busying herself in the kitchen laying out some treats for everyone. Crunchy chicken strips, deep fried wings, coleslaw and the like. She nods at the food. "Help yourselves," she says and goes back to making her point to Mitchiko that since the Dead Man in the Chair episode, business has never been better. "People are showing up I haven't seen for years. The book is full two weeks in advance."

"C'mon Jo," says Mitchiko. "We're talking about a big salon here. Thirty-five hundred square feet and a full basement. Room for a spa, maybe. Won't you come and look at it, puleeeeeze." Then her tone suddenly changes and she throws down the gauntlet. It's like someone waved a wand and someone else showed up. She's opening the place with or without Josephine, she says abruptly. She's got an investor and some money of her own and she's all ready to go. Things are bad where she is and she can't wait to get out of there, so she's doing it anyway. That's the point she's making here. She's going to do it with or without Josephine.

Josephine won't be rushed. She says she needs more time to think about it, then she introduces everybody officially, grinning slyly at Jimmy as she drops her first bombshell.

"Mitchiko works at CRIMPERS," she says with a flourish and a curtsy and a flick of her head.

Then another bombshell. She asks Jimmy to guess whose hair Mitchiko cuts. It reminds him of a "Saturday Night Live" skit where they ask a contestant, "Who's behind the curtain?" The contestant says it could be anyone. Jimmy's got the same look on his face.

Mitchiko says, "Sandra Ellison."

Jimmy chuckles. Josephine's always coming up with surprises.

Mary fills a plate with food and sits down, enjoying the drama.

Jimmy asks Mitchiko, "Did Sandra ever say anything to you about Jason Friendly?"

Mitchiko smiles. "Only what an asshole she thought he was."

"No sense she was scared of him?"

She shakes her head.

"Or that he threatened her?"

"Nah," says Mitchiko. "Nothing like that."

"What about Marc Hilliard? You cut his hair too?"

"Oh no," says Mitchiko, giggling. "He's William's client."

"Why the laugh?"

"I'm sure you know what Mr. Hilliard does for a living. Well our William likes to stay close to his drugs. I think they trade services."

It's Jimmy's turn to smile.

"He's who Sandra should've been afraid of," says Mitchiko.

"Hilliard?"

She nods.

"Because?"

Mitchiko snorts, "Because of the business he's in. Duh?"

But Jimmy's checked him out already. Marc Hilliard was busted by the NYPD the night Sandra got shot. No way could he have done it. Morgan Flynn checked him out too. "And you hate working at CRIMPERS now?" he asks.

"I do," she sighs. "It's just awful."

"Mr. Lewis being murdered, or the fight with the partners?"

The question flusters her. "Well," she says quickly, "of course Mr. Lewis getting......" she's having trouble coming up with the right word, "getting, ah, ah, killed. Of course it's a terrible thing."

Everyone agrees on this point and clucks about it for a little while. Then Mitchiko goes on to say what a nice guy Mr. Lewis was and how the whole salon was shocked by what happened to him. But it wasn't what she meant when she said working there was awful.

"Mr. Lewis's, ah, ah, death happened the other day and it's surely a terrible thing, but this fight between the partners, William and Daniel, has been going on forever. You can't imagine what it's like working in a situation like that. Long faces. Thick tension. It's just so depressing." She lights up a cigarette and sucks in the smoke then blows it out dramatically. "We used to be the hottest place in town, you know. All the stars used to come in, and the top models. It was the greatest place to work in. The most fabulous creative environment ever put together, that's how good it was." She takes another angry puff. "Now all we do is stand around with our thumbs up our asses while the two of them slog it out."

Jimmy says it sounds terrible.

"Who knew it would go on for so long? One guy wants to buy the other out, you make him an offer and work out a deal. It's not that hard, is it? Isn't that how it's supposed to be done? But oh no, not this bunch. William thinks he can wait Daniel out while he grinds him down and tries to ruin him. It turns out William's a greedy bastard as well as a prima donna. Who knew? He's got new backers is what's going on here. A money's no object situation. 'Get rid of Daniel,' is what they've told him, 'and we'll do the rest.' A product line, more salons. The sky's the limit. You'd think William would want to pay Daniel off quickly so he can look good to his new best friends, wouldn't you?"

Jimmy says there's no figuring people when it comes to money. "They do the most amazing things for it. You think William or Daniel could have poisoned Mr. Lewis?"

Mitchiko scowls at him. "Why would they want to do that? He's their accountant for chrissakes." She takes another violent pull on the cigarette.

"Morgan Flynn thinks Lewis took sides and annoyed the other guy. You think something like that's possible?"

"Who's Morgan Flynn?"

"The cop handling the case."

"What do you mean by other guy?"

"The partner Jerry Lewis didn't side with."

"Which one didn't he side with, William or Daniel?"

Jimmy says he doesn't know.

She sounds incredulous. "So they killed him?"

Jimmy says, "It's just a theory."

Mitchiko stares at him. It's plain she can't make up her mind about something. Neither can she stand still. She fidgets and touches things and nervously smoothes her hair down and sucks on her cigarette. She looks twitchy and uncomfortable.

"I hear Daniel's having a hard time of it," says Jimmy. Trying to keep it going. "He's got his back to the wall."

Mitchiko says she heard about it. She says her heart goes out to him and tells him Daniel was the one who trained her and gave her clients when she started there as a stylist. Without him she would've been no place. "Not that other one," she grumbles. "William wouldn't help a blind man cross the street." She stops fidgeting and gives Jimmy another hard look. Then she says, "It's all we ever talk about at the salon. You know that, don't you?"

"I can just imagine," say Jimmy. "So what do they say?"

She cocks an eye at him and gets that thoughtful look on her face again, then she seems to make up her mind. "That maybe one of them was trying to kill the other."

Jimmy purses his lips. This is getting good. "Daniel and William?" he says, just to be sure.

She nods and viciously spikes out her cigarette in an ashtray. Then it suddenly pours out of her in an uncontrollable froth, everything they talk about in that little staff room of theirs. The theories and the gossip. All of it. Climaxing, after covering every possible eventuality, in the group's ultimate conclusion.

"There was a meeting that day between all of them, right? Daniel, William, and Mr. Lewis."

Jimmy nods

"Supposing," she says, moving to the conspiratorial, "When the maid brought them in their coffees and teas, Mr. Lewis picked up the wrong cup and got poisoned by mistake?"

Jimmy gives it some thought. "Took the coffee meant for someone else, you mean?"

"Right."

It's certainly a possibility. "Who's using the poison?"

"Could be either of them."

"Yeah," he says. "But you must have a favorite?"

Mitchiko chews on her lip. It's all they ever talk about, didn't she just tell him that? Of course they have a favorite. "William," she says softly. "Everyone thinks it's William."

"No dissenters?"

"Only to keep the discussion going, but we all think it's William. He's the one with more to lose. Maybe his backers are getting antsy and threatening to walk away. It's been going on for a long time now, I told you that. William must be looking like an asshole to these guys. He must've said at the beginning Daniel would be gone in a couple of weeks and what do you know? The guy's still standing there nine months later."

"And not Daniel?"

"Nah," she shakes her head. "No one thinks Daniel's got the balls."

"What about you?"

"I can't see him doing it either."

"And William?"

"In a New York minute."

"What makes you so sure?"

"He's that type. He's one of those people that pretends he's all moral and upstanding, but he'd steal the clothes off your back if you're not looking."

Jimmy raises his eyebrows.

"I also heard him threaten Daniel. He's some piece of work this guy. That's another reason I want to get out of the place. I can't stand the sight of him."

"Threaten?"

"'I know people who can take care of people like you.' That's a threat, isn't it?"

Jimmy says it sounds like one to him. "Where did this happen?"

"On the stairs in the salon."

"When?"

"Last week. I'm going up behind Daniel. William's coming down. Daniel makes like he's going to hit William only he isn't, he's just messing with him. William moves to defend himself and Daniel continues going up the stairs like nothing's happened. "

Jimmy has no idea what she's talking about.

Mitchiko tries again. "When we were kids you'd walk past someone and pretend to make a move, sudden like. But then, instead of doing that you'd smooth your hair, or scratch your neck and keep going. If the other guy falls for it, you make him look like an idiot."

Now he gets it.

Mitchiko laughs. "Daniel got William good on that one. William puts his guard up like a boxer and looks like a complete moron in front of all those people watching. Oh yes, there was a big audience for this one. That's when he said it, hissed it more like, like some creepy gangster. I'm not sure other people heard it, but I did. I was close, see, right there behind Daniel. That's when William whispers to him in this creepy voice, 'I know people who can take care of people like you.'"

"Think he meant it?"

"If you saw the look in his eyes you wouldn't ask. They used to be friends, these two. Can you believe that?"

"What kind of friends?"

"Trained together. Roommates when they first got here. That sort of friends."

"What went wrong?"

"They got hot, that's what went wrong."

Jimmy doesn't understand.

"William became a big celebrity. Hairdresser to the stars. TV shoots. Magazine spreads. That sort of hot."

"So?"

"He can't handle it, or maybe he can. Maybe this is what you do when you get so popular."

"How's that?" asks Jimmy.

"You throw your weight around and screw everyone in sight because all you want, once you've had a taste of it, is more. That's what's happened to that one. The more PR he gets the harder he is to deal with. When I first met him he was as nice as pie, now he'd kill his own grandmother for a nickel or a headline."

"And Daniel?"

"A nice guy."

"Nice guys finish last," says Jimmy and thinks of Jason Friendly.

"You're right," she says sadly. "You should see what William's only doing to him. Paying the receptionists not to book him clients. Messing with his appointment book. Squeezing him. Pushing him. Trying to break him down."

"What's he done to stop them?"

"Nothing. He can't do a thing. If he says something, they deny it. I've seen it happen. These receptionists will do anything for some extra money. William's promised them big bonuses when it's all over. It's really quite disgusting."

Jimmy agrees. "Sounds like some fight."

"Down and dirty," says Mitchiko. "And all because Daniel won't take William's puny offer. Daniel says he's just as responsible for the success of CRIMPERS as William and wants to be paid accordingly. William says the business is losing money and it's not worth what Daniel wants. That's probably true by now, because William's not been pulling his weight for a while and done all sorts of things to sabotage the place. As soon as Daniel's gone the backers will pump in more money and they'll all go to the moon on the back of Daniel's hard work. That's why he hangs on. He's got 50% of what they want. It's a branding thing. The name CRIMPERS is still quite strong in the industry. As soon as they get Daniel out of the way they'll make themselves a fortune. The longer he lasts the worse things get for us, but I don't care any more. I found this place in Scarsdale. It's absolutely perfect and doesn't need to be fixed up. It'll take me two more weeks to get the legal stuff taken care of, then I'm out of there." She looks at Josephine fondly. "And I really want you to come in with me on this."

Jimmy double checks again. "You're saying the people at the salon think William was trying to poison Daniel and Jerry Lewis picked up the wrong cup by mistake. That's what you're telling me?"

"You didn't hear it from me," says Mitchiko. "I'm no snitch."

Jimmy says it's not snitching. "Someone's been murdered and you're helping me with the investigation, what's wrong with that? That's what you're supposed to do." He sounds so responsible and old he wants to throw up. "How come you didn't tell the cops any of this?"

"They didn't interview me."

That's a surprise. "Why not?"

"They only talked to the people who worked in the salon that day."

Jimmy can't wait to call Morgan Flynn and tell him what he's found out.

Chapter 36

After the "Jimmy and Mitchiko Show," they open up another bottle of wine and the talk moves on to Josephine and what she wants to do with her life. By the end of the third bottle, Mary's committed herself to backing Jo in the Scarsdale endeavor. Mitchiko has to be restrained from jumping up and down in a most extraordinary victory celebration and the downstairs neighbors are spared the torment of having their living room ceiling come crashing down on them. After that there's endless chatter about the decor, another bottle of wine is opened, and then, as the evening draws to a close, the new partners have dreamy conversations about the possibility of making tons of money. Then Mitchiko says she has to be at work early and breaks up the party. "Sorry to be the pooper," she says, "but the drive to Brooklyn takes over an hour." She slugs down a cup of black coffee, fills a traveling mug with the stuff and says her goodbyes with a sudden breathless urgency. Jimmy and Mary leave with her. They part company in the parking lot after receiving Mitchiko's hugs and kisses, on both cheeks please like the French do, and her babbling gratitude for Mary's involvement in the project.

Mary's driving. She's the designated driver. Jimmy's been drinking wine. Red wine. Not a lot, but more than he should have. He shouldn't be drinking at all, but every now and then at a restaurant he'll have a glass. Or at a party. It's been going on a while, this drinking. Three or four months, she thinks, but this is the first time he's let her drive. "Have a nice time?" she asks him.

Jimmy twists towards her, restrained by his seat belt. "I want you to get a nose ring," he says slyly.

"And burn my bras."

"If you like," he says and takes out his cell phone to call Morgan.

Mary points out the lateness of the hour.

Jimmy tells her how early Morgan called yesterday, "Payback's a beautiful thing," he says and punches out his number. "6.30 and not a word of apology."

"Everyone's up by then."

"Well I wasn't."

Morgan answers the phone like he's still going strong. "How's it going, Jimmy?" he says full of vigor.

Jimmy feels tired all of a sudden. The wine has taken its toll and his voice doesn't match Morgan's perkiness. "It's good," he says trying to muster some energy.

Mary's amused.

"Everything all right?" Morgan wants to know. "You don't sound so good."

"I'm fine," says Jimmy. He's thinking payback's not what it used to be. Then he tells Morgan everything Mitchiko just told him. When he's finished there's a pause while Morgan makes some notes. Finally Morgan says, "That's a new one on me. None of our interviews turned up anything like that. How come we never spoke to her?"

"She says you only interviewed people that worked the day of the murder."

Jimmy can hear Morgan leafing through his notes.

"Yep," says Morgan. "We got her name along with a bunch of other people who weren't there. We should've talked to everyone. There's a bug running through the station, half the squad is out sick. We're all doing double duty." He sighs. "It should've been done before. I'll get to it."

Jimmy mumbles something sympathetic.

"This is good stuff," says Morgan. "Thanks for the heads up. On another subject, we got the lab report from the things we found in Jerry Lewis's safe. You'll never guess what the liquid in the bottle marked poison was? Water."

"Water? Why would you put water in a safe?"

"Why mark it poison when it's water?" says Morgan. "None of it makes any sense."

They chew it over for a while then Jimmy says, "What about the dope?"

"Ah yes, the dope. Coke and marijuana. Lewis's prints are all over the bags and another set. Unidentified. They got a partial on the bottle marked poison that matches the unidentified ones on the bags of dope. Same goes for the porno. The unidentified person touched everything. Must be the person who got him the stuff, that's what I think. By the way, didn't you think they were the most amazing pictures?"

Jimmy says he did and gives Mary a sideways glance. "And they're not Hilliard's prints?"

"They are not."

They toss that around then Morgan says, "How's your thing going with the mayor?"

Jimmy chuckles. "He's not the mayor. He was running for mayor."

"Yeah? Well what happened?"

"He's not running for mayor any more, that's for sure." Then Jimmy tells him what's going on.

"Wow," says Morgan when he finished. "And you've got nothing to show for your trouble?"

"Jack shit."

"'No tie with Hilliard?"

"None that I can make," says Jimmy. "Hilliard's alibi is rock solid. You guys had him around the time of death on a drug charge, and the train stopping at Columbia was a random thing. He could never have planned for that."

"So your guy's going down. What's his name? Jason Friendly. He's going down, right?"

Jimmy says sadly, "Looks like."

They go through a few more niceties then Morgan says, "I gotta go," and hangs up.

Jimmy tells Mary the story so far.

Mary's driving. She's got nothing to say.

Jimmy says, "It doesn't make sense," talking about the bottle marked poison being water.

Mary agrees. It doesn't make sense, but she still doesn't have anything to say. Not about that anyway. But she does about the wine. "What's with the drinking?" she asks him.

"Mmmmmm," says Jimmy, and slumps down in the seat.

"Well?" she asks.

"I'm not drunk, if that's what you're asking."

"No one's accusing you of that."

"Mmmmmm," says Jimmy again.

She knows what the "mmmmm" means. He only uses it when she catches him doing something he's not supposed to, and he doesn't know how to answer without giving some improbable explanation that most people call lying. "C'mon," she says. "What's going on?"

That's when the conversation turns to him moving in with her.

Tuesday

Chapter 37

The next morning finds Jimmy with a touch of embarrassment and a slight headache. Red wine does that to him. It's got something to do with the nitrates. It was like that when he was a boozer. People get migraines from the stuff, so he figures he's getting off easy. He pops a couple of Tylenol and puts up the coffee. In the shower his mind settles on his embarrassment. Mary calling him on the wine. "What's with the drinking?" she wanted to know. Point blank. Right between the eyes. And quite rightly. He's an ex-drunk drinking. Hello? What's wrong with this picture? She poked at him and prodded at him, and wheedled reluctant responses out of him, never letting him off the hook. The "talking cure" Freud called it. Get it all out. That's what she can do, Mary. Get it all out. It's from years of waiting tables and listening to people's problems, she'll tell you. So they talked, Jimmy and Mary, while she drove him home. She poking at him and listening till finally, after they peeled back all the layers, they got to the nub of the thing. That first taste. That sip. At Julliani's. Their favorite restaurant. On the outskirts of town. Just before Christmas. When the talk began about him moving into her place.

One of her friends brought it up, Mary said with a smirk. She thought it was funny, that's what the smirk was all about. "Listen to this," she says over the Crème Brule, "Marnie wants to know when you're moving in." That's when he took that first sip. He remembers it quite clearly. Reaching for the glass like it was the most natural thing in the world to do. Only it wasn't so natural. It was his first sip in fifteen years. She didn't notice, is what he thinks. Is what he wanted to think.

They kept on yapping about him moving in with her, but the alcohol zoomed in on his brain and lifted him to fuzz-land like a rocket ship blast off. Just a sip mind you, but off he went. On the elevator. Higher. And higher still as Mary jabbered on. Making her points that he was going to hear again and again. About how cool it would be. On and on she goes, but now he's welcomely buzzed. Fudging the edges of her harsh talk. Softening the frame of the reality she kept hurling at him. It didn't last for long, this buzz. How high can one sip take you? But after that first time, when ever conversation gets intense, the softer edges make it easier to deal with, this new mantra of hers. Because now she never lets it go, the moving in thing. How much Lucy likes him. How much easier things would be for them. More and more they're having these conversations. Popping up when he least expects them. Like burps or farts. It's beginning to prey on his mind and spoil his nice time.

He tells her all of this in response to her relentless prodding during the drive home from Josephine's. There's no eye contact when he says these things. He stares straight ahead through the windshield as it tumbles from his mouth. Getting it all out like the poison from a sting. "It's the moving in that's getting me down," he tells her forlornly. He says he doesn't think it's such a good idea. "Maybe later," he says unhappily, but right now he thinks he likes things the way they are. He hopes this doesn't sound selfish. Selfish? Who's he kidding? It's the ultimate in selfishness, but as much as he loves her, he can't see them living together. Being on top of each other. Using the same john. Peeing in the middle of the night, or worse. Burping, farting and who knows what else. It doesn't happen on his overnights, these things. But if he's there permanently it would be just a matter of time, and then what? All of them under one roof. Sleeping in Mary's bed in front of Lucy. They don't do that now. And Lucy, with that look on her face. The "I know what you and my mom are doing" look.

All these thoughts swirl around his brain as he tells her why he doesn't want to move in. "I'm just not ready for it," he says sadly. His chubby face is flush and the folds of his jowls hang down like a bloodhound. "I hope," he says earnestly, "I haven't blown it and fucked up our relationship. Or pushed you away. Or been too honest. Or any other stupid thing I'm capable of doing."

He misreads how she's looking at him. That glance of hers. He thinks he's going to get an earful, but all she does is laugh. Then she pulls the car to the side of the road and leans over and hugs him. And kisses him. And tells him whatever he wants to do is fine with her. That he's the nicest, kindest, most wonderful man she's ever known and she loves him dearly for it. That she's happy to go along with anything he wants to do so long as he promises never to leave her. "Never to leave her'" that's what she said. He always thought it would be the other way round. That she'd tire of him and find someone younger. After all, he's no George Clooney. "But if I ever see you take another drink," she says seductively. "I'll never go to bed with you again."

Relief is what he feels as he looks at himself in the mirror. Like he's been reprieved. The embarrassment is gone. So has his headache. And that nagging backache he's had since catching Mrs. Lewis as she fell to the floor. He hums the Alka Seltza commercial. "Plop, plop. Fizz, fizz. Oh what a relief it is," and after toweling off and dressing, a blue suit today with a white shirt and no tie, he puts in a "Priority" call to the county jail to speak to Jason. A "Priority" wipes thirty minutes off the hour long procedure, if you're lucky. It takes Jimmy fifteen minutes to get to the office, and, fifteen minutes after he's settled at his desk his "Priority," call to Jason comes through. And, just like his lawyer said, Jason sounds much better than the last time they spoke. Jimmy gets straight to it and says, "What's with Ted Butler."

"This is a guy I had some problems with at the club."

"When?"

"The one time I took Sandra there. He came on to her. I called him on it and we got into a scuffle outside the club."

"What does that mean, 'came on to her?' "

"He tried to grab her hand. I saw it clearly."

"Then what happened?"

"I followed him outside and after some words I took a swing at him. People held us back and that was the end of it. He went home. We stayed. I haven't seen him since."

"Ever have trouble with him before?"

"Never."

"But he's not from your past?"

"No."

"So he couldn't be the one doing all this stuff to you. Unless, of course, it's more than one person. Did this happen before or after you threw your hat in the ring?"

"After."

"It doesn't sound right to me, but I'll talk to him anyway and see what he's got to say, you never know." He tells Jason where he's gotten with the rifle. "Mickey Swan moved to Hyde Park two years ago. After that no one knows where he went. I've got a social security number with two of the numbers difficult to read. He had to support himself, so he's got to be on record someplace. It'll take a while, but I'll find him."

Jason's got nothing to say except "thank you."

"What about Michael Collis?" Jimmy asks. "You think this is worthwhile pursuing? This guy's really gone. I mean everyone's looking for him, including the IRS."

"It was so long ago," Jason sighs. "I can't imagine this goes that far back. Where's his father's practicing?"

"He's not."

"Why not?" asks Jason.

"Beats me. He's a janitor at the middle school in Hillsdale."

"A janitor?"

"He doesn't speak to his son," says Jimmy. "That's what he told me. He hasn't seen him in years."

"A janitor?" Jason's stunned.

"Rumors of alcoholism. Also divorce."

"Incredible."

"He doesn't seem like such a nice guy."

"He isn't."

Jimmy sighs. "Another dead end."

"Not necessarily."

"What's that mean?"

"In my bedroom," says Jason. "In the bedside table on the right-hand side, bottom drawer, there's a file marked Collis. Read it first, then we'll talk."

"You think that file's still there?"

"Why not?"

"Did you look for it when we checked out the rest of the house the other day."

"I never gave it a thought."

"Mmmmm," says Jimmy.

Chapter 38

A little while later Eddie Smith shows up. He pokes his head around the door of Jimmy's office with a big grin on his face. Eddie's the same age as Jimmy with a little more hair and a much bigger gut. He's taller too, with more of an "In The Heat of the Night," Rod Steiger look to him. He's messy and paunchy and likes to wear his hat on the back of his head. Eddie used to play the line in Brooklyn from eighth grade through high school, holding back opposing defenses so Jimmy could run through them and break all those records. That's how long they've known each other, these two. They both went into the NYPD only at different times. Jimmy's star rose quicker than Eddie's. Eddie never got out of the ranks on account of him not being so smart. He joined the Columbia force three years after Jimmy, not knowing Jimmy was there. How small a world is that? He's still a uniform and, every now and again, helps Jimmy out on an investigation.

He's Jimmy's only real friend apart from Mary. Columbia doesn't take too kindly to strangers. Everyone's polite and sociable, after all it's not such a big place that you don't bump into the same people all the time. But there's always that thing that creeps into the conversation, that feeling of not belonging. Of being reminded, from time to time, that you're not from there. It's not just the Rolling Hills crowd that does it, it's everyone. Mary feels it too. If you're not from Columbia you're a bit of an oddity. Something different. Not like them. An amusement, even. With a different way of talking. Of thinking. Of background. Not aliens, but pretty close. People to be polite to, and indulged, but not taken too seriously.

"Where've you been?" Jimmy asks Eddie.

"Vacation. I told you I was taking some time off."

"It's been busy," grumps Jimmy. "I'm sorry. I forgot." They spend a little time talking about Eddie's trip and when he's finished Jimmy says, "but I'm glad you're back. There's work to be done."

Eddie glows. It's what he likes doing best of all. Being Jimmy's sidekick. He flops down on one of the chairs and stretches his legs out in front of him.

Jimmy brings him up to speed. What's happened to Jason Friendly. The search for the owner of the rifle that killed Sandra Ellison. How he thinks Jason's being framed and how he's been looking for someone with a grudge against Jason from way back.

"Why?" asks Eddie.

"Nothing recent shows up, but he was a bully back then. He even admits it."

Eddie looks skeptical.

"I know. It's not much," says Jimmy, agreeing with him, "but it's all I can come up with. This guy Michael Collis pops up as a maybe but he's nowhere to be found. Even his father doesn't know where he is." Then he tells him about the new name Jason's given him. Ted Butler. "The guy belongs to Rolling Hills and lives in Chappaqua. They had words at the club. Jason thought Butler was coming on to Sandra Ellison so he took a swing at him. He thinks maybe it's Butler who framed him."

Eddie's giving him the "you gotta be kidding me" look again.

"I know," says Jimmy. "It's all very thin." Then he fills him in on the Jerry Lewis poisoning.

"Jesus," says Eddie. "I've only been away for a week and look what I missed."

Jimmy says it's a tough break, but he's got something nice for him to do. "I told Morgan Flynn I'd check Jerry Lewis out. Background stuff. Friends. Family. That sort of thing. Go up to Rolling Hills and ask around about Lewis. He wasn't a member, but maybe someone knows him. It'll give you an excuse to talk to people. Slip Butler into the conversation and see what comes up."

"All these years I've been here," says Eddie, "and I never once got inside that place."

"So now's your chance. Put on some nice clothes," he says eying Eddie's sloppy uniform, "and knock yourself out."

"I thought you were off the Friendly case."

"I am."

"But?"

"But 'leave no stone unturned' is my motto. And who else is gonna do it? Everyone's got Jason strapped to the gurney already. Make sure you tell the sarge you're working on the Jerry Lewis background stuff for me. And do *not* mention Ted Butler's name."

Eddie gives him that look again. Like give me a break.

"I know," says Jimmy. "I know. I'm sorry. No offense."

"None taken," says Eddie and gets up and leaves the room.

Chapter 39

Jimmy checks the patrol schedule. If he's going to Jason's house to look for the Collis folder he doesn't want to be there when a black and white goes by. Everyone knows he's off the case and they all know what his car looks like, so there's no point looking for trouble. Some people don't like him, surprise, surprise, and they'd be only too pleased to get an opportunity to slip the knife in. There's an hour window before someone passes the house. Jimmy drives over, retrieves the key from under the stone and lets himself in. The house has been closed up. Now it's got that stale musty smell about it. Even Jimmy's "eau de Felix" drenched home smells nicer. He undoes the catch of his holster and puts a hand around the grip and stands perfectly still, but there's nothing to hear. Or feel. Not like the last time. Today everything's dusty and undisturbed.

He goes upstairs, a hand still on the grip, and checks all the rooms, but no one's around. He goes back to Jason's bedroom, over to the bedside table, and opens the bottom drawer. There's no file. He checks the upper drawers and the table on the other side of the bed, but there's nothing to be found. On the way back to the station house he puts in another priority call to Jason. He figures it'll come through by the time he returns the way it worked this morning, but the operator brings him up short. She says the paper work on Jason has just been updated.

"I'm sorry detective. We've been told you're no longer on this case. You're denied access to Mr. Friendly." Then she lowers her voice and says, "Why don't you leave it alone, Jimmy."

Jimmy's known her for years. Margie's her name. Just on the phone though. He's never met her in person. "These are bad boys," she says in a whisper. She means Smith and Monahan.

Jimmy thinks she's been watching too many westerns

"They do mean things to people."

"I know," says Jimmy, "I know."

His next call is to Jason's lawyer who picks up on the first ring. Jimmy tells him what's happened. "The Collis file's missing from the house and now, because I'm off the case, I can't get access to Jason."

"I'll set up a meeting," says the lawyer. "Call you back in five."

He calls Jimmy back in ten and tells him to meet him in front of the lockup after lunch. Jimmy figures the guy for a cheapskate. All the things he's done for his client, you'd think he could spring for a lunch.

Later Jimmy and the lawyer are in the visiting room for special prisoners at the Westchester County Jail. The lawyer shines in his black mohair suit, crisp white shirt and charcoal tie. There's a look on his face Jimmy's not seen before. Energized? Enthusiastic? Something along those lines. Jimmy looks dog eared next to him. His hair is untidy, his blue suit is dusty from traipsing around Jason's house and his shoes were not so clean in the first place.

The visiting room is a windowless space of whitewashed cinder block. In the center is a steel table bolted to the floor with an iron ring in the middle of it. Four metal chairs are arranged haphazardly around it. A fluorescent light blazes from above. Jason, clad in his orange jump suit, is led in by a burly guard. His thin frame seems lost in the bulky prison garb. There are black circles under his eyes. His hair is lank and greasy. He looks like he's disappearing, that if he stays in this place much longer there'll be nothing left of him.

"The folder's gone," says Jimmy wasting no time.

Jason runs a hand through his hair. "Who would've thought it was Collis?"

"Who says it is?" says Jimmy.

"Who else would take the file?"

"Enough people have traipsed through there it could be anyone. A reporter. A souvenir hunter."

The lawyer agrees.

"It's annoying, I know" says Jimmy seeing the disappointment on Jason's face. "They said the same things to me when I disturbed that guy the first time I went to your house, only not so polite. But it's a valid point just the same. It could be anyone. What's in the folder?"

"Everything to do with the Collis affair," says Jason.

"And what's the, 'Collis affair?'" asks Jimmy.

So Jason tells them.

The Collis Affair

Chapter 40

They're twelve years old. Jason Friendly and Michael Collis. Eighth graders. Michael wants to be friends. Jason doesn't. Michael keeps doing dumb things to get Jason's attention. Jason doesn't appreciate it and reacts badly. Violently. Spitefully. This goes on for some time. Michael's parents are a mixed marriage. She's Thai, he's white American. They're always looking for trouble, these two. Perceived slights. Prejudicial treatment. Racial insults. All that chip on the shoulder stuff that most of the time isn't so. Like the time when the Michael thought he heard someone call him a "gook" in an altercation with Jason's crew. Actually they called him a "geek", but when you're looking for trouble you only hear what you want to. Mrs. Collis was outraged and whipped herself up into a briny froth. Then there's the other thing. The sports thing. Michael's father is jealous of Jason. Jealous of the way things always fall in for him. Jealous of how he hits a ball. And throws it. And catches it. Any ball. In any game. Jason's always better than Michael, no matter how hard Mr. Collis works with him. And coaches him. And attends every game to cheer him on and record his stats.

Harvey Collis is an attorney at Harrison Kegly, one of New York's oldest and most prestigious law firms. He's in his mid-forties and still an associate. He should be a partner. He's way behind schedule for a Yalie. The company's taking a wait and see attitude with him. They're not sure what they've got here with Mr. Collis. There's a feeling among the partners that something's not quite right about him.

The boys get into another fight at school. Ink is spilled on Michael's sweatshirt. Some pushing and shoving occurs and maybe a swing or two. When the Collis's hear about it they stir themselves up into a frenzy of righteous indignation and decide that now's the time to take a stand. They compose a malicious missive on Harrison Kegly stationary to cow the Friendlys into submission and bring them into line. Harrison Kegly stationary is a weighty bit of business with an embossed coat of arms,

156

the company name in raised gold lettering, and a whole lot of other stuff designed to project money, power and influence. Pleased with their efforts, Mrs. Collis types up the letter and Harvey Collis rushes over to the Friendly's to make his pitch.

It's 8:30 at night and dark outside. He's tall this Harvey Collis. And large. When Jason's father opens the door, Collis fills up the entire doorway blocking out the porch light like an ugly shadow. He introduces himself and says he has something important to say and can he come inside. Mr. Friendly invites him in. He and his wife stand in the foyer waiting to hear what Collis wants. Jason is upstairs in his room. Collis gets to the point. He tells them he has this letter. The letter he and his wife have just concocted. The one they wrote on Harrison Kegly stationery. In this letter, he says waving it at them like McCarthy with his list of communists, there are a series of accusations regarding Jason and his dealings with his son – everything from deliberately spilling ink on his expensive sweat shirt, to tripping him up in the hallways and harassing him on a constant basis. When Collis has finished listing his complaints, he says the letter will be distributed to the following people and straightens up to his full height for this final piece of theater and intones, "The school superintendent, The chief of police. Every member of the school board. The school principal. Unless...."

The Friendlys hear the 'unless' and seize upon it, "What's the unless?" they want to know. Hoping there's an easy way out here.

Collis hands the letter to Mr. Friendly so he can see he's not bluffing, then says, "We want to be reimbursed for the sweat shirt and I want an apology from Jason to my son with the understanding that this harassment ends now."

Mr. Friendly sees nothing wrong with these terms and, using some frothy language of his own to soften the situation, agrees. He hands the letter to his wife and goes upstairs to get Jason who's been listening to the proceedings from the landing. Mr. Friendly hasn't read the letter, he doesn't want to. He only knows he's got a deal on the table and wants to put it to bed before anyone changes their mind.

Mrs. Friendly is a gentle soul, slow to anger and quick to smile. While Mr. Friendly is upstairs she reads the letter. A venomous missive designed to hurt and maim. Written on Harrison Kegly stationary for maximum effect. About her son. The one she loves so dearly. Described in this letter as a "Nazi." And a "storm-trooper." And "vermin from which the world should be spared."

Mr. Friendly tells Jason the deal. Jason balks. "Michael's been asking for it," he says and won't go along.

Mr. Friendly says the alternative, the distribution of the letter, will do him a great deal of harm. It would be better for all concerned if he says sorry and shakes the kid's hand. That would make the thing go away, something he and his mother would like very much because, as he tells Jason with a great deal of passion, he needs this situation like he needs a hole in the head.

Jason relents and heads for the stairs, ready to bite the bullet and take what he considers to be an unjustified hit.

Mrs. Friendly is reading the letter for the second time to make sure she's got everything clear.

Harvey Collis stands in the foyer. No one's invited him to sit. His hands are clasped in front of him. His head is bowed. He looks like a bouncer with nothing to do. He's thinking to himself how great things are going. How much he's enjoying the Friendlys' discomfort and trying to remember every detail so his wife can enjoy it too.

Jason comes down the stairs looking unhappy, but unbowed.

He's followed swiftly by his father whose face is a mask of neutrality.

Mrs. Friendly finishes reading the letter for the second time. There's a moment of silence as she digests the contents. Then she looks up and glares at Mr. Collis with a look of withering scorn. Her face twists into an angry mask and she explodes in an outraged fury. "Nazi? You call my son a Nazi? Are you mad? Are you crazy? Get out of my house," she screams and she pushes and shoves the startled Harvey towards the front door.

Collis opens the door himself. He has to otherwise he'd be trapped by the oncoming demon who's swatting at him with the letter. His letter. On Harrison Kegly stationary. Pushing at him. Shoving at him. Screaming at him like a tribal banshee. "You son of a bitch," she shrieks. "Get out of my house you disgusting bastard. Get out!" Her spittle flies in his direction like a sudden rain squall.

Collis tumbles out of the house and onto the front lawn. He turns to face his attacker who stands in the doorway, her arms folded across her chest and her scornful face full of venom and hate.

Mr. Friendly stands by her side not quite sure what to make of the situation.

Jason ogles from over his parents' shoulders.

They all watch with amusement as Collis tries to muster some dignity and make his way to his car.

The Friendlys think Collis will send the ugly letter out to all the people mentioned in the list. Why would they think otherwise? So does their attorney, a dear and wonderful friend, who advises them to see the people and try and head things off at the pass. After reading a fax of the letter, he tells them Collis had no right using Harrison Kegly stationary for personal matters, especially as it's clear it's meant to intimidate them. He has friends there. Senior partners. He'll make some calls, he tells them, so they know what Collis has done.

"What happened?" says Jimmy.

"Nothing," says Jason. "We went around and saw all those people he said he was going to send the letter to. I got a slap on the wrist. I apologized to the kid, then it was the end of the school year. They moved away after that and I never saw them again."

"Well he's not a lawyer any more," says Jimmy. "I wonder if this is what brought him down."

Jason's attorney says he'll see what he can find out. "That could've ruined his whole career. It's a very dumb thing to do."

"My parents weren't supposed to keep the letter," says Jason. "It was just a threat. Collis didn't know mom was going to go crazy on him and hold on to it. It was quite funny, really. It's kept us laughing for years. How she exploded and went after him. She says if she had a knife, she could've killed him. The look on Collis's face was priceless. He never sent the letter out, but we didn't know it at the time. We took the threat seriously, how could you not? In the end our lawyer got Collis's firm to write a disclaimer and send it to all the people on the list. It must've been a massive a black eye for Collis."

"If this is what brought him down you can see where he might be bitter towards you," says Jimmy.

"Who'd have thought?" says Jason, bowled over by the idea.

"Let's see if we can match his prints to anything before we jump to any conclusions," says Jimmy. "A tech guy owes me a favor. I'll have him dust the rest of your house. We only did the back where the break-in took place the last time. We'll need a set of Collis's prints for comparison. He's not in the system, I checked already."

"How will you get them?" asks the lawyer.

"I'm working an investigation about pilfering from the high school. It's a pattern that covers a number of Westchester schools. There's a couple of people they have their eye on. I'll see Collis on this issue. Tell him it's got nothing to do with his son, it's just an odd coincidence that I'm seeing him again. Then I'll show him the photos of the suspects and see if he IDs them. He'll leave his prints on the pictures. We'll see if they match up with what my guy gets from the house."

"And if not?" Jason wants to know.

Jimmy gives him a wry smile and says, "One step at a time counselor. One step at a time," and gets up to leave.

Chapter 41

A little while later Jimmy finds Eddie by the station house coffee machine holding court with some of the younger guys, regaling them with stories of when he was a cop in Brooklyn. Cops in the suburbs see the NYPD as the big time. They're like ball players who say that playing in the majors is "going to the show." Anyone who's worked in the City has gone to the show. They're heroes to these guys, especially someone like Eddie who blows off more hot air than a steam vent. He sees Jimmy and gives him the nod, signaling he's got something for him, and follows him back to his office.

"Boy that Rolling Hills is a trip," he says flopping down on a chair and assuming his usual position. His legs out stretched and his belly sticking up like a burial mound. "What a bunch of assholes."

"I wouldn't know," says Jimmy. "I've never been there. Whatcha get?"

"Anyone who knew anything about Lewis only says nice things about him. No hint of scandal or bad boy stuff. Always available for charity work and quick with a donation. Everyone I spoke to knew something about the Butler incident with Jason. Butler doesn't sound like he's that far up the food chain there. No one gave off a warm and fuzzy when they talked about him, and the consensus was they wished Jason had beaten him to a pulp."

"That popular?"

Eddie nods.

"Anything else?"

"I called a buddy in the Chappaqua Police Department. He's a sergeant down there. He says Butler doesn't even have a parking ticket outstanding."

"Mmmm," says Jimmy. "Let's go and see him anyway, just to make sure."

"Now?" Eddie brightens up. His tail suddenly begins to wag and his eyes are sharp with anticipation.

"Why not?" says Jimmy and punches out Butler's telephone number. "What else have I got going?"

Butler picks up.

Jimmy explains who he is, but doesn't tell him what it's about. Just that he's working on the Jason Friendly investigation and needs to ask him a few questions. He'll be there in half an hour.

Butler's voice quivers. "What's this about?"

Jimmy says he'll tell him when he gets there.

Butler bleats, "Should I get a lawyer?"

"You can get the attorney general for all I care," says Jimmy. "Just make sure you're there when I get there, I'd hate to drive all that way for nothing."

Butler splutters and stutters and complains that he doesn't understand the need for the visit, but in end he says he'll be waiting. And he is. Half an hour later, as Eddie and Jimmy knock on his front door.

There's something about Ted Butler that's got snake-oil salesman written all over him. A smarminess. An obsequiousness. He's an insurance broker. His clients are rich and he belongs to the County's toniest club, but none of it has had any effect on his oiliness. He gives off the smell of someone who'd do anything for a sale. He's pudgy and round and dressed in a loud sport jacket, open-necked blue shirt and lint covered maroon knit pants. He's got a round face, beady eyes and a pencil thin mustache that lives below a featureless nose.

Butler leads the two policemen down some stairs to a nicely done office in the basement of the house. There's a plush carpet. Expensive art on the walls. A nice oak desk, and two very comfy chairs that face it.

Eddie and Jimmy lower themselves into the chairs.

Butler frowns and goes behind his desk. After sitting down he nervously picks the lint off of his trousers like a pigeon pecking at the dirt.

Jimmy says, "I understand you had a fight with Jason Friendly at the Rolling Hills Country Club not long ago."

"Yeah, so what. Is that a crime or something? Don't tell me he's pressing charges."

"He says you were coming on to his date. Sandra Ellison."

Butler looks puzzled. "Who's Sandra Ellison?"

"C'mon, Mr. Butler. A man of your stature must read the newspapers. Sandra Ellison got shot in Columbia a couple of days ago. She got off a train and never got back on. They're holding Jason Friendly, a fellow club member, for the crime. Remember now?"

"That's Sandra Ellison?" He says he didn't realize she was the same person. His complexion is pasty. Beads of sweat appear on his forehead. He dabs at them with a handkerchief he's pulled from his trouser pocket. "Is this what you came here for?"

Jimmy nods.

"It was a misunderstanding. That's all."

"You didn't come on to her?"

"I did not."

"So why'd Jason take a swing at you?"

"He thought I did."

"Why would he think that?"

"You got me."

"He says you touched her hand."

"I did no such thing."

"What happened after the fight?"

"I went home."

"And that's it?"

"That's it," says Butler.

"Ever have trouble with Jason before?"

"Never."

Jimmy rattles off a bunch of questions without making any headway, then he says, "I'm sorry to have to ask you this Mr. Butler, but can you tell me where you were last Wednesday night around 8.30 or 9 o'clock?"

"The night of the murder?"

"Right."

"I thought you had Jason for that."

"We do, but in a case like this we've got to check out every detail no matter how obscure."

Butler takes out a small pocket diary and leafs through it. "Last Wednesday night I was making a pitch to some guys at the Rotary Club in Dobbs Ferry."

Eddie's making notes.

"Anyone we can call to verify?" asks Jimmy.

Butler gives him a couple of names, but he's not pleased about it. "I'd be grateful if you'd go gently when you speak to these guys. They went for my pitch, but it doesn't mean they still can't cancel the policy."

Jimmy says he'll be the soul of discretion.

After that there's not much to talk about. Jimmy thanks him for his cooperation and says they're sorry to have bothered him.

Later, in the car, Jimmy tells Eddie to run a check on Butler and see if he's in the system. "And see if we can get a set of his prints. Maybe he was in the service, something like that. Also, see if you can get pictures of him and Harvey Collis from the DMV and find out what cars they drive. The DMV should have all…"

Eddie gives him a look that says, 'It's not my first day.'

Jimmy stops with the instructions, acknowledges the mistake and apologizes. Then he asks Eddie if his patrol route covers the strip mall where the shooter stood when Sandra Ellison was murdered.

Eddie says it does.

"Show the pictures of Collis and Butler around there. Maybe someone saw one of them."

Then they're back at the station house.

Chapter 42

Smith and Monahan think the case on Jason's a slam dunk. So does the DA and the chief. And anyone else who's involved in the thing including the media. No one's taken Jason's side and there's a strong guilty bias to all of the reporting. It's just too good a story to expect anyone to buy into Jason as an innocent bystander. You've got your drugs. Your sex. And your rock and roll. And there's good-looking Jason Friendly to play the bad guy for you. It's the stuff of movies. The poor guy doesn't stand a chance. No one believes he's innocent except for Jimmy. He's the odd man out. The fly in the ointment. The stone in everyone's shoe. The last time Smith and Monahan rubbed Jimmy the wrong way they ended up with egg all over their faces. That's when Jimmy discovered who killed Mary's husband and they didn't. Not that they think that can happen this time. This is an open and shut case they've got here, but they like to leave them laughing if they can so they reach out to Jimmy now and include him in the latest turn of events. Smith calls him later in the morning and, after a frosty minuet, fills him in on what's been going on.

"Last night," he says. "The NYPD arrested Marc Hilliard, Sandra Ellison's boy friend. They've got him on possession. Again. They must be on this guy like flies on cow shit to get him twice in one week. This time they found dime bags of pot in his car. The cop we're working with, Morgan Flynn, says that what they've heard from her friends is that Sandra Ellison liked her cocaine very much. Lots of it, is what they say. It's why she dumped Jason. Apart from being dull and boring, he didn't do coke. Marc Hilliard did. And sold it. The perfect play if you like that sort of thing." His voice becomes conspiratorial. "Flynn says Hilliard told him she was quite the gal at the parties. He would have people over, get her juiced up and turn her loose. He says there's nothing she wouldn't do for another line.

"Anyhow, I digress. Here's the new thing that's cropped up. They found Ted Butler's number on Hilliard's speed dial. It's a Westchester number so that's why we came into the picture. And Ted Butler, we've been hearing, is someone you've been checking up on, even though you're not supposed to. My oh my, what a coincidence."

Jimmy's not surprised they know. The station is like a sieve. There are no secrets there. Once he set Eddie in motion it was just a matter of time before it would seep out. Or maybe it was someone at the club who said

165

something. Either way they knew so what's the difference? "How'd you know it's the same guy?" Jimmy asks. Offering no apologies.

Smith says, "It's a Chappaqua address, we checked. It's the same guy all right, so now we've got Butler's connection to Hilliard to be worked through. It's like that AT&T commercial says, they're all connected. Since you've just been to see the guy who better to follow this up for us, so we're putting you back on the case. Not," he says sarcastically, "like you were ever off it. Either way we think this is a better use of your time. So does everyone else."

Jimmy takes that to mean the chief.

"Anyhow," says Smith cheerily, "they've got Hilliard locked up at the 23rd Precinct. We're going down there to talk to him about Butler. Like, is Butler a buyer or a seller, that sort of thing. And what's the deal between Butler and Sandra Ellison. Maybe he knows something about that situation we don't. Wanna come along?"

"Sure," says Jimmy, surprised at the turn of events.

They drive to the City in the boys unmarked Crown Vic. Jimmy's in the back. Smith and Monahan are in front. Smith's driving. Smith and Monahan barely say a word to each other or to Jimmy for that matter. It's not a hostile thing. It's just that no one's got anything to say. Instead they listen to News 88 and stare out the window.

The 23rd precinct house sits between Amsterdam and Columbus on 91st St. The street is cluttered with a hodgepodge of parked patrol cars, vans and scooters. Auto wrecks take up valuable parking spaces. The building is part old part new. The new, late fifties is plunked onto the side of the old, late twenties, with no regard to the style of the original structure. The only thing contiguous is the height. One side is glass and chrome, the other is granite and turrets. Inside is the same no matter what side of the building you're in. Organized chaos. Too much humanity in too small a space. Corridors are full of people, stairways are jammed with bodies and the elevators are packed like sardines. It's been a long time since Jimmy's been in an NYPD precinct house. It's not like he's missed it, but it feels good to be around it again. He soaks up the atmosphere. Absorbing the hustle and bustle. And the noise. And that smell of fear and authority that mingles so perfectly you can't tell which is which.

The boys puff themselves up and present themselves to the desk sergeant like they're visiting potentates. They expect the same kind of treatment they get in the suburbs only this isn't the 'burbs and the sergeant doesn't seem very impressed with them. He cocks an insolent eyebrow and gives the lads a look that says, "what the fuck do you want?"

Jimmy remembers it being like this in Brooklyn when a cop from the suburbs showed up. They got two or three murders a week in those days and he's sure it's not much different now. Smith and Monahan handle a murder a month, maybe. How good do you have to be to stay on top of a murder a month? The City cops look down on them. You can see it on the face of this desk sergeant. And the uniform who checks their IDs, takes their weapons, pats them down and explains each action to them like a proctologist doing an internal. He's polite and business-like and very loud so everyone can hear him. And enjoy the show. And shake their heads in wonderment at the boys. The rubes. The kids from out of town. Today's entertainment.

The uniform deposits Jimmy in an office where he can watch the proceedings through a two-way mirror. The boys are in a windowless interview room next door where Hilliard and his lawyer are waiting for them. The walls are a dirty gray and covered with scuff marks and coffee stains. The mirror Jimmy sits behind covers half a wall. Metal folding chairs are situated around a green metal table. Marc Hilliard sits next to his lawyer, a weasely looking character with fox-like features and beady eyes wearing a shiny gray mohair suit that reminds Jimmy very much of Jason Friendly's attorney. The lawyer sits straight-faced and stiff-backed with one sharply creased leg crossed daintily over the other. His Gucci briefcase sits open by his chair. A yellow legal pad is on the desk in front of him. A closed gold Mont Blanc pen lies on top of it.

Smith and Monahan remain standing. After the introductions and handshakes Smith throws the first punch. "Why'd you want Sandra Ellison dead?" he asks Hilliard.

Hilliard's handsome features are a mask of indifference.

"How come you had her hit?" asks Monahan.

Hilliard continues to stare.

"C'mon man," says Smith. "Don't waste our time."

Hilliard screws up his face.

"Why'd the two of you wanna whack her" says Smith.

"What did she do?" says Monahan.

"What did she know?" says Smith.

"What did she see?" says Monahan like he just had an epiphany.

"Right," says Smith, agreeing. "She must have seen something the two of you were cooking up."

Hilliard looks at them disdainfully.

Monahan says, "She saw you and Butler doing a deal."

"That's it," says Smith. "That's what she saw. The two of you cooking up a deal."

"You guys are crazy," says Hilliard and cracks up in their faces.

Morgan Flynn comes into Jimmy's room and sits next to him. He's his usual spiffy self in a blue three-piece pinstripe suit, crisp white shirt and black silk tie. His cologne wafts lightly through the room. He makes Jimmy look like the janitor.

"I'm working the Hilliard case with the boys here," he says like they've been sitting together for hours. "What a pair of crack pots. They think they walk on water when they can barely take themselves to the bathroom."

Jimmy chuckles.

Morgan says, "Hilliard's saying he doesn't know anything about Sandra Ellison's death. The dime bags aren't his. Someone planted them. They had no probable cause to search him or his car and they didn't read him his rights. He's screaming police brutality to anyone who'll listen, but no one's listening. The boys are on an ass covering mission is what's going on here. They still think your guy the mayor killed Sandra Ellison, but they're covering all the bases. It shows they're not entirely brain dead. Nice they brought you along for the field trip though. You get a packed lunch?"

"Not yet," says Jimmy.

The boys are getting mad. "Whaddya laughing at?" Smith asks Hilliard.

Hilliard shakes his head like he can't believe they're so dumb.

No one says anything for a while then Hilliard pipes up. "Ted Butler turns up on my auto dial. Butler had some doings with Jason Friendly and Sandra Ellison. You want to know what the tie is, that's what my lawyer's telling me."

"That," says Monahan. "And why you had her killed."

"I keep telling you," he starts laughing again. "I've got nothing to do with that."

The boys believe him. Monahan's just trying it on for size. For form's sake. Part of the routine. The show. They're sure Jason Friendly murdered Sandra Ellison, end of story.

"Tell us about Butler," says Smith.

"What do I get for telling you?" asks Hilliard.

"What do they have on you?"

It's a moment of truth for Hilliard. If he tells them what he knows about Butler, he's making a confession of sorts. If he doesn't, they won't deal with him and he might miss a move. Things don't look good for him right now and he needs all the help he can get. He chews on a fingernail and confers with his lawyer. His arm is draped around the laywer's shoulder. He whispers in his ear. The lawyer whispers back. This goes on for some time.

Then Hilliard finally says, "Someone planted weed in my car. The weed gets the cops into my apartment. Need I say more." He needn't. The search warrant would yield them his cocaine stash and that would put him in the system for more years than he can imagine.

"What do you want?" says Smith.

"I want these bullshit charges dropped," says Hilliard.

The boys tell him they'll see what they can do.

Jimmy thinks Hilliard will be lucky if they can get him a cup of coffee.

Hilliard starts to talk. "Ted Butler belongs to that country club they've got up there. Happy Hills? Something like that. This I know because every now and then Ted sells a couple of grams to his co-members. When he does this, I'm the one who gets it for him. I'm not saying I sell it to him, are you listening to me here? I'm saying when he wants some, I get it for him."

Smith doesn't believe what he's hearing "You're saying you give it to him for free?"

"That's all I'm saying about it," says Hilliard.

Monahan looks at him in amazement. "You're asking us to believe you give Ted Butler free coke?"

"I just told you," says Hilliard. "I'm not talking about that any more." He looks at his lawyer.

The lawyer says, "If this is what you want to talk about the interview's over."

It's the first time the lawyer's spoken. The boys take the threat seriously.

Smith says they'd like to hear what he knows about Butler and Ellison.

"One time Sandy's up there with the creep."

"Creep?" says Smith.

"Jason Friendly," says Hilliard. "Sandy thought he was a creep."

Smith asks, "Where's this taking place?"

"Columbia. Jason took her to that club."

"Rolling Hills?" says Monahan.

"That's the one. Sandy told me all about that place. All stuck up and full of themselves. One Jew, one Nigger and a Spic's on the waiting list. Anyway, she's up there having a miserable time and out of coke, so she calls me. Can I do something for her?"

"Your girl friend's with another guy," says Monahan, "and you don't care?"

"Who says she's my girl friend? She's someone I was sleeping with. What's that got to do with anything anyway? You wanna hear the story or not?"

They say they do.

"So I tell Sandy I'll get Teddy to slip her some.'"

"Ted Butler?" says Smith.

"Ted Butler," sighs Marc like they're beginning to get on his nerves.

Smith says, "Ted passed coke to Sandra Ellison at the Rolling Hills Country Club the night she was there with Jason Friendly, that's what you're telling us?"

Hilliard says he is.

"As a favor to you," says Smith.

"Right."

"Nothing else?" asks Monahan.

Hilliard asks, "Like what?"

Monahan says, "Like Teddy wouldn't mind whacking her for you."

"Why would I want him to do that?"

"Because she saw you doing something," says Smith.

"Or overheard something," says Monahan.

Hilliard laughs. "You ever see Ted Butler?"

The boys shake their heads.

"The guy can barely cross the road by himself. He's a shlub. A loser. Of no account. A little man who likes his coke and did me a favor. The rest of it, all this bullshit you keep talking about whacking Sandy is make believe."

They toss it around for a little while longer, but the boys believe him. They believed him before they even got there. They wish him luck and tell the guard they're done.

But Marc Hilliard is by no means in the clear. His problems with the NYPD are a different matter entirely. Finding the dime bags in his car got them a search warrant. The search yielded enough coke to put him in the system for the rest of his life. Marc was right about one thing though. Someone did plant the weed in his car, but it didn't have to be the cops. More likely a rival. Someone who wanted his spot. They planted the dope and called the cops on him, that's how the business works. Now the cops have something on him they can get their teeth into, so he lets them flip him. What choice does he have? It's either that or getting fucked up the ass for the rest of his life in Sing Sing. So he wears a wire for them and goes about his business. Hanging with the big shots and making his deals. A few month later they find him naked and dead in a dumpster on 100th St. and

Riverside Drive with the recording device stuffed down his throat and the little plastic microphone jammed up his ass. But that was all in future.

Chapter 43

Outside on the street the wind's picked up. People hunch their shoulders and lean into it as they walk. It's early spring and there's a bite in the air. Smith and Monahan turn up the collars of their raincoats and revert to form. There's only so long they can be nice to someone they think is beneath them. They tell Jimmy they're not driving back to Columbia with him.

"We got something to do in Jersey," Smith says tersely.

"You'll have to find your own way home," Monahan says in a flat tone.

"Go and see Butler and clear this business up for us." says Smith. "What's he doing with the drugs? What's the story with him and Sandra Ellison?"

"It doesn't sound like anything that'll help your buddy Jason," says Monahan.

"But you never know," says Smith.

"So she liked her coke," says Monahan, "big deal. Jason say anything about this when you saw him?"

Jimmy says he didn't. "Just that he thought Butler was coming on to Sandra. That's why he wanted me to go and see him. He thought maybe Butler's the one that framed him."

"Here we go with the framing thing again," says Monahan, getting worked up.

Smith says, "Jason probably eyeballed them when he handed her the stuff."

Jimmy agrees that it sounded like that.

"Butler doesn't sound like any framer to me," says Monahan. "This boy sounds like an old-fashioned dealer. And don't you be counting on any collar here."

"Butler's ours no matter what," says Smith. Then they break out a song and dance routine, going on at him with a series of instructions that seems to go on forever. There's a line from one and then a follow up from the other like they're talking to a moron. Jimmy never says a word. What's the point? The boys are just trying to assert their authority over him and make sure he understands the rules of the game. That nothing's changed here. That even though he's back on the case they're still in charge, and Jason Friendly, so far as they're concerned, is guilty. End of story. When they finished their duet they walk away from him shoulder to shoulder, leaning into the stiff breeze. "Stay in touch," says Smith without turning around. And then they're gone.

Jimmy's about to hail a cab when Morgan appears by his side. "The girls dump you?" he asks watching Smith and Monahan disappear onto Amsterdam.

Jimmy chuckles.

"Wanna get something to eat?"

Jimmy says he's starving.

"Deli?"

"I can taste it," says Jimmy.

They end up in a booth in Bloom's on Broadway. It's been a while since Jimmy's had Jewish food. He's almost delirious with anticipation. An exaggeration, but you get the idea. He doesn't get into the City much any more. Some dinners with Mary once in a while, but nothing like this. Being back in a station house and now a deli? For a moment it feels like the old days. Like he's stepped into some sort of time warp. A deja-vu situation. And for just a moment it's like he never left.

"You can't get this stuff up there," he tells Morgan, "There's not a Jewish deli for miles." He orders matzo ball soup, corn beef on rye with mustard and an orange soda from a pretty young waitress who's on them the minute they sit down.

Morgan says he'll have the same. "Lunch is on me," he says with a smile. "That stuff you gave me about CRIMPERS was a big help on the Lewis case."

Jimmy nods an acknowledgement.

Morgan asks, "You think Mitchiko's a dyke?"

Jimmy says he doesn't know. Then he wonders about Josephine. That maybe the two of them are an item. But then he dismisses it because all Jo ever talks about is guys, although these days that doesn't mean anything. And what about her banging the chief? "Mitchiko's a feisty little thing, don't you think?"

"She's not my type," says Morgan.

"Was she wearing a bra?" asks Jimmy.

"What difference," says Morgan. "There's nothing to see anyway. She looks like a guy she's so flat-chested."

Jimmy has to agree. "What did Mitchiko tell you?"

"That there's some kind of connection between Jerry Lewis and a kid called Julio Perez. There's also a tie between Julio and Marc Hilliard."

"Who is this kid?"

"He's an assistant at CRIMPERS. Mitchiko and a couple of others there identify him as the salon go-to guy."

The soup arrives along with pickles, coleslaw and crackers. Jimmy slurps it up like someone's taking it away from him.

"Julio Perez, they say," says Morgan, "can get you anything you want. Coke, weed, special requests from hookers, things that fall off the backs of trucks. Marc Hilliard, it turns out, is Julio's coke supplier. This we learned from more than one member of the staff. We've got witnesses who saw Hilliard give Julio a package. Some people say there's something going on between Julio and Jerry Lewis, but I can't get a handle on that one yet."

Jimmy picks his head up from the bowl, "What does that mean?"

"People have seen Julio and Jerry Lewis talking in the salon. No long conversations or anything like that. No arguments. No passing things to one another. Just a few words here and there. Whispers. Like on the quiet. Someone thinks he saw them at the Penthouse Club. Julio denies it. He says he doesn't even know who Jerry Lewis is. We took Julio in based on the witness statements that he sells drugs in the salon and got warrants to search his home and his locker at CRIMPERS. The locker gave up traces of the poison that killed Jerry Lewis." Morgan watches Jimmy stuffing his face. "You think you can make a little less noise, I'm trying to talk here."

Jimmy's eyes twinkle as he slams another chunk of matzo ball into his mouth.

"Julio's apartment also yielded traces of the poison that killed Jerry Lewis. And traces of cocaine, heroin, pills and weed. We've got Julio locked up in Brooklyn. He lives in Park Slope. The not so good part. He blames everything on his cousin Hernando Perez who lived with him and also worked at CRIMPERS. According to Julio, whatever we found in his apartment belongs to Hernando. Hernando left town right after Jerry Lewis's death. According to Julio, he stole all his money and some jewelry and hasn't been seen since."

The sandwiches arrive. The waitress takes Jimmy's empty soup bowl. Morgan tells her to take his too.

"You're not going to eat that?"

Morgan pushes the bowl over.

The waitress smiles, hands Jimmy back his spoon and goes away.

Jimmy starts a fresh bout of spooning.

Morgan stares at him. "When was the last time you ate?"

Jimmy keeps slurping, savoring every drop. Vowing he and Mary would spend more time in the City starting now, this minute, so he can have this delicious food all of the time. He looks up at Morgan. Waiting for more.

"The prints on the stuff we got from Lewis's safe are Julio's. His prints are on the bottle marked poison, the drugs , and the porno."

Jimmy stops spooning to stifle a burp, then takes a bite of his corned beef sandwich. Flecks of mustard gather in the corners of his mouth. "It looks like you got your guy," he says.

"Not so," sighs Morgan disgustedly. "The DA says we've got a problem. Since the stuff in the poison bottle in Lewis's safe was water we've got no case against Julio on that issue."

"And the drugs?"

"Just because Julio's prints are on the bags, doesn't mean he sold them to Lewis. We've got no witnesses and Jerry Lewis is dead so he can't tell us what happened there. A defense lawyer can punch holes through the whole thing with no trouble at all."

"What about his locker?"

"He says everything is cousin Hernando's."

"What's that story?"

"We can't find him."

"And so?"

"Until we find Hernando and get his side of things, we've got nothing. There's a Missing Persons out on him. We found pictures of him when we searched Julio's place. They're being distributed as we speak."

"Meanwhile?" asks Jimmy.

"We gottta turn Julio loose. I'm gonna have another go at him before we do. Wanna come along?"

"How's that going to square with your boss?"

"I told you about the bug sweeping the station? Everyone's got it. I don't feel so good myself. I told him you were working the case from the Columbia end. He's happy you're here. My partner's out sick. Now he doesn't have to find me another one. What do you say?"

"Sure," says Jimmy and takes another bite of his sandwich.

Julio Perez is being held at the Williamsburg precinct house in Brooklyn. They take the subway. "There's too much traffic this time of the day to drive," explains Morgan. "This'll take us ten minutes."

And it does. They even get a seat. Jimmy can't remember the last time he was on the subway. He used to do it all the time.

Chapter 44

The Williamsburg precinct house is where Morgan Flynn began his career as a rookie. There are plenty of people there who still remember him. When they walk in the door he's greeted with friendly jeers, boos and catcalls that he fends off with a cheeky grin and some sharp quips of his own. Jimmy finds himself with uniforms on either side of him who begin to nudge him towards the processing unit till Morgan explains he's with him. Jimmy figures it's because he looks so shabby next to Morgan's rock star appearance and doesn't take offense. After some more banter they're taken to the interview room where Julio Perez is waiting for them. Jimmy sits in the adjoining room and watches through the glass again. The interview room looks like the one they just left. Windowless. Same sort of furniture. Same iron ring in middle of the table. And a two way mirror covering half of one wall.

Julio Perez is a short wiry Mexican. He's twenty-one with jet black hair, a rat-like pockmarked face and sharp eyes that never stop moving around the room. He wears the uniform of an assistant, black slacks and black tee shirt with CRIMPERS written in bold white lettering across the chest, but he doesn't have the manner. There's no eager to please look on this young man's face. Pride and anger is what you see in Julio Perez's eyes. This is someone, Jimmy thinks, who's not willing to play by the rules.

Julio scowls around the room particularly at the two-way mirror. He flops down on a chair and sullenly waits for whatever's coming next. A uniform stands by the door.

Morgan enters with a flourish. Morgan the Powerful. Morgan the Magnificent with his Ray Ban sun glasses so Julio can't see his eyes. Morgan with a yellow pad and pen and a file tucked under his arm. He nods to the uniform who nods back, but says nothing. Morgan sits down at the table, pinching his trousers at the knees to preserve his crease. He scans through the file looking for something in particular, finds it, then looks up at Julio. "I hear you're the go-to guy at CRIMPERS," he says to Julio, going straight at him.

Julio frowns. "Que? he asks. Innocent as a babe.

"The go-to guy," says Morgan. "You know, like I need some weed, you're the guy I go to. The go-to guy. Get it?"

Julio shakes his head. He did not get it.

"Coke!" says Morgan. "I'd go to you for coke. That's what they'd tell me if I was a new guy at CRIMPERS and looking for a little something. Go to Julio, they'd tell me. He'll get it for you. There it is again. Go to. I'd go to you, Julio. Now do you get it? You're the go-to guy."

Julio's looking for a hook. Something to talk about, but so far the cop's only shown him what he knows, not what he wants. Julio figures he must want something. Everyone wants something. That's why they come to him in the first place. He's the go-to guy, isn't that what the cop just called him. And you know what? He's right. You want something you come to Julio. So he waits. Knowing it'll take a while. That the slick one wants to put on a show for his friend behind the mirror, whoever that is, and that will take some time.

Morgan continues his rambling. "What if I want some pills?" he asks Julio.

Julio doesn't answer. He stares at some invisible spot on the wall. Looking in Morgan's direction, but not at him. Passed him. Like he's not there. Soon now, Julio figures. Soon the cop will get to it.

Morgan flusters and blusters then goes off on a tirade, but still Julio won't talk to him. Morgan's worn himself out with all these pyrotechnics, so he slips it in after a particularly arduous segment of stomping around the room and banging things down. He grabs the back of Julio's chair and leans in close. Nose to nose. Eyeball to eyeball. "But if I wanted a little poison, you could get that for me couldn't you?" Then he steps back to watch the reaction.

A surprise. Julio didn't think they'd figure out the poison so fast. He thought the smokescreen cousin Hernando gave him had worked, but now that he knows what they want he sees his way clearly.

Morgan's watching him.

Julio doesn't move a muscle.

Morgan's beginning to feel the first pangs of defeat, but then Julio opens up a little. He finally focuses his attention on Morgan and says softly, "Is that what this is all about?"

Jimmy, watching through the window, smiles. He's good, this Julio. Especially for such a young kid. He taps the glass. A prearranged signal for a confab. Morgan's pleased for the break.

"He threw you a bone," says Jimmy when they're together in the next room.

"I know," says Morgan.

"He'll say Hernando told him who he sold the poison to. That he had nothing to do with it or anything else."

"So why's his print on the bottle?"

"He gave the bottle to Hernando not knowing what he wanted it for. That's what he'll say."

Morgan agrees, that's what he'll say. "I'll tell him about the witnesses who saw him selling drugs in CRIMPERS."

Jimmy shakes his head. "No one's gonna testify about something so small. Everyone's got too much to lose. You get them on the stand they'll make up all sorts of stories about how you got them to sign those statements. It'll be a disaster."

Morgan agrees. He raises his eyebrows and gives Jimmy a rueful smile.

Jimmy looks at him expectantly.

"What?" says Morgan.

"He's gonna say you've got nothing on him, blame everything on Hernando and not tell us a thing."

"And so?"

"Let me do the good cop thing."

Morgan makes a mocking bow.

Jimmy's out the door before Morgan can change his mind. More and more Jimmy's feels like he's stepped into a time warp. Like he's a kid again back in Brooklyn.

Julio's pleased to see him, whoever he is. "Hey, the good cop's here," he says, and gives Jimmy a welcoming smile. Everybody knows the good cop/bad cop routine. He appraises the way Jimmy's dressed and can't help comparing him to the other one. The bad cop. So slick in his Ray Bans and designer suit. This guy, thinks Julio, looks like he slept in the clothes he's wearing.

Jimmy smiles back and sits down.

They look at each other. Each appraising the other. Like gladiators. Circling.

Then Julio says, "No one's going to testify against me you know that don you? They've all got too much to lose. I'll keep saying it's Hernando's fault and until you talk to him, you can't prove me wrong. You got nothin on me boss. You're gonna have to let me go."

Jimmy keeps smiling. That's what good cops do. Smile. It's the bad cops who do all the scowling. "I've got two good witnesses," says Jimmy.

"Who?" demands Julio. Suddenly sitting up straight. "Tell me who it is? It's a goddamn lie."

"My witnesses says they saw you doing business at CRIMPERS."

"So what, man," says Julio. "It's their word against mine. Don't mean nothin. Like I said, you got nothin on me."

"C'mon Julio," says Jimmy. "Don't take that attitude with me. I'm the good cop, remember? Save that drama for my partner, he expects it. All I want is for all of us to get what we want out of this"

"And what do I want, Mr. Good Cop?"

Jimmy keeps smiling. "Not to spend another minute behind bars. That's what I'd want."

"And how do I achieve that?" asks Julio.

"By telling me what I want to know."

"And that is?"

Jimmy's smile fades. "C'mon Julio. Cut the crap. Tell me who the poison was for."

"And I get?"

"Probably a year at the most."

The blood drains from Julio's face. "Whaddya mean, a year at the most?"

"If you're lucky you'll get off with six months and probation."

Julio's angry. "For what?" he roars.

"Possession. Something minor, but you'll have to go into the system."

"Fuck the system," says Julio. "I ain't goin nowhere."

Jimmy makes a face.

Julio sits quietly, thinking things through. Then he says, "This is how it's gonna go down, Mr. Good Cop. I tell you who my cousin Hernando told me the poison was for and you let me go." He glares at Jimmy. Then he glares at the mirror. "I done nothin wrong here and you can't prove otherwise."

Jimmy makes a face then says, "We'll say we found some stuff on you, coke or something. That'll put a couple more years on your tab, who's to say anything different? You see where this is going, Julio?"

"I'm not tellin you nothin if I'm goin inside."

Jimmy stands up to stretch his legs. His back is kicking in again. Not for the first time does he wish he let the large Mrs. Lewis fall to the ground.

"I'll talk, then I'll walk," says Julio.

"Listen to the poet," says Jimmy.

"Well?" says Julio.

"Well what?"

"Do we have a deal?"

He says he's got to talk it over with his partner and walks out of the room. "What do you think?" says Jimmy when he gets next door. "I told you that's what he'd say."

"So you're clairvoyant," says Morgan, "you any good with numbers?"

Jimmy waits

Morgan grins. "So what do you think now, Carnac?"

Jimmy looks through the window at a cool Julio sitting with his eyes closed, taking a nap. "I think he'll tell us what we want."

Julio smirks at them when Jimmy and Morgan walk into the room together. He tells them who his cousin Hernando said he sold the poison to. He signs an affidavit to that effect and gives them a signed statement, but it still blows their minds when he tells them it's Jerry Lewis who bought the poison from cousin Hernando. It's not what they expected to hear. Their faces fall and they think they're back to square one. But then Julio throws them another bone, because they're such good guys and it looks like he's going to pull this off. So he tells them who asked Jerry Lewis to buy the poison for him. And watches as their faces light up when he gives them William. The one everyone thought was trying to kill his partner and killed Jerry Lewis by mistake.

Hernando Perez

Chapter 45

Hernando Perez, Julio Perez's cousin, comes from the bad part of Mexico City. One morning before the sun had risen, he kissed his mother on the forehead while she slept, slipped out of the shack they shared with another family on the outskirts of town, and headed north towards the United States. That was two years ago when he was nineteen. He scrubbed floors and washed dishes in a bunch of cantinas all the time moving closer and closer to the border. He was waiting tables in a cafe ten miles from Arizona on the Mexican side when three burly men with mean, unshaven faces came in and sat down at the corner booth. They hunched over the table and talked in hushed tones stopping only when Hernando took their order, but not when he brought them their food.

From what he could hear it was plain they were smugglers. They came in a lot after that and Hernando always waited on them. They liked him. He took their orders and brought them their food without saying a word. It's what they liked most about him. They liked to carry on their scheming uninterrupted. Eventually, in their way, they became friends. And soon after that, for $500 of the $900 Hernando managed to save, they said they could get him across the border. They had someone on the other side to help him get situated, they said, because they liked him so much and they'd all become such good friends. Not long after that on a moonless night Hernando and his guide crossed the desert into America and met up with the contact, a mean-looking man with unruly black hair and an angry scar from his temple to his throat. He was nice enough till the guide left. Then he pulled out a gun, took what was left of Hernando's money, cold-cocked him and left him to die in the Arizona desert.

But Hernando was lucky. He was found by a border patrol guard who discovered a green card glued to the sole of his foot. The card had cost Hernando a lot of money. He bought it so he could get a job in America. He knew no one would hire him without it. He was less sure the card would hold up with the immigration authorities. It's why he chose not to risk it and got into America the back way. He stuck the green card to his foot so no one would find it like they did his money. The green card passed inspection. Hernando heaved a sigh of relief. It took him a year to save for it and he was never sure he hadn't been taken for a ride. Now it was worth every penny. After the INS let him go, he began to work his way across the country. Hooking up with the Latin community wherever he went and always moving on after a score. Like a house. Or a mugging. Once even a small time dealer. Heading east man, always east to New York City where cousin Julio lives and all that pussy he likes to brag about.

Cousin Julio was an assistant at CRIMPERS, a hot beauty salon in New York. He washed people's hair for a living, swept the floor and ate people's shit with a big smile stuck on his rat-like face. He also did $1,500 a month out of the place between the weed, the coke and the all other stuff people wanted him to get for them. That's why he put up with all the other crap. When Hernando showed up, cold, broke and hungry, Julio let him sleep on his sofa, share his dope and talk till dawn about the old times when they were kids in the slums of Mexico City. Three days into Hernando's stay Julio said they were short handed at CRIMPERS and would he like a job?

"I don't have a license," said Hernando. In America, he knows, you gotta have a license for everything.

"They don't care," said Julio.

Hernando wanted to know why.

Julio shrugged. "Sometimes it happens. People go on vacation. Other people get sick, so then they don't care. They just need a pair of hands to help out, you know? To wash the hair and keep the place clean. When the people come back from wherever they were, maybe they don't need you no more."

Hernando said it sounded fine to him.

"Tips are good," said Julio.

Hernando was broke. He said that would be fine too.

Three weeks in at CRIPMERS and Hernando had a belly full mostly because of Mr. Warren, a faggoty old princess who was on his case the minute he got there. Mr. Warren ran the floor and told everyone what to do. First he came on to Hernando. Then he wanted a blow job in return for some nice treatment. "It could be nice for you or hard, please pardon the pun," he told Hernando in that sing-song voice of his.

Hernando chose the hard not understanding what a pun was and not wanting to give Mr. Warren a blow job. So now the guy was on his case all of the time. Driving him crazy. Snapping his fingers. Always with the loud voice. Hands flapping around like he's in a minstrel show. Calling him

Pedro. Pushing him. Taunting him. And now Hernando's had enough. This hairdressing shit left a lot to be desired. Things aren't bad enough with Mr. Warren, he's not getting laid, the tips are bad and this bowing and scraping thing is driving him crazy. He's off, man, far and away.

Mr. Warren had a thing for eye drops. He had allergies or something like that and as a going away present Hernando spiked them with poison. The same poison that killed Jerry Lewis. His going away present to cousin Julio was to steal everything not nailed down in that apartment of his. This is the same cousin Julio Hernando heard talking to Mr. Warren over some lines in the basement the other day.

"I want him out of my house," said Julio to Mr. Warren between loud snorts. "He smokes all my weed, smells up my bathroom and he's got that look on his face that says pretty soon he wants to be my partner."

Oh yes. Hernando heard all of this and a lot more. He's not stupid and understands just enough English to know when he's getting fucked up the ass. He ran into Julio as he was leaving the apartment, bag in hand.

"Where you goin man?" asked Julio.

"Some place far away amigo," said Hernando and kept on going. In his bag were his few clothes, a gun he found in Julio's room, all the man's weed, some pills, five grams of coke, $5,000 in cash and some jewelry. He took the train to Chicago and on the first night there blew most of the money, the gun and the jewelry in a poker game in a late night bar on the South Side. He rolled a drunk for some walking cash and got on a bus to Seattle, but he only found that out later. When he stepped off he'd been traveling for three days sprawled on the back seat of the half empty bus in a glorious haze. Popping pills. Smoking dope in the bathroom with his head hanging out the window, thinking about Mr. Warren. They called him "Mister Warren" as a mark of respect for CRIMPERS most senior hairdresser. CRIMPERS most senior blind hairdresser now, thought Hernando, and stifled a giggle.

It was damp and cold in Seattle, the suicide capital of America. Hernando could see why that was so. The drizzle was already beginning to depress him and he only just got off the bus. He couldn't imagine living here. He'd sell a little dope and maybe some pills and move on to some place warmer. He had no idea how he got to Seattle. He was so stoned when he bought the ticket he could have ended up anyplace, but this is where he was and he intended to make the best of it. He hailed a cab and told the driver to take him to where the action was. "I'm new in town, man and I wanna have a good time."

The cabbie, Roleigh Singh, thought Hernando was an asshole. He took him the long way around to the main drag and deposited him in front of the Whiskey A- Go-Go, a club he had a business arrangement with. $50 for every customer he brought to their door. There's a tenderloin in every city where the bright lights are and the hookers and the people who want to buy stuff they can't get in Wal-Mart. And the folks that want to sell it to them. It's a DMZ where everyone comes together and feels safe. Buyers and sellers. Every town has one.

Hernando paid the cabbie and got out, but he didn't go into the club. "Fuck that, man," he told the crestfallen Mr. Singh and headed down the road where guys were standing in doorways. Black guys, white guys and a smattering of Asians all whispering to him as he went by, "Sens. Sens. Whatchoo want man? Sens."

He hurried past them till he saw what he was looking for. South Americans. A few at first, on the border so to speak, but soon there were lots of them and now they called from the doorways, "Mira mira. You wan some weed, man?"

One of them, Little Patty he's called, came up to him and looked him up and down. "Wha you want, man?" he asked.

Hernando said he needed some money.

"What for?" the man wanted to know.

"Food. Expenses. Things like that."

"What have you got to sell?" asked the man.

"A little weed. Some pills."

"What do you want for these things?"

"I think $500 is fair," said Hernando.

"Show me," said Little Patty.

They walked to a doorway. Hernando looked around to make sure no one was watching, then reached into his duffel bag and came up with the package he'd put together for this very purpose. It's how it's done. How he'd done it all the way across America. Ripping stuff off from someone and selling it to somebody else. You can get rid of anything if you can find the right guy to do business with. Hernando felt Little Patty was such a man.

Little Patty was impressed. The weed smelled good and the pills were in big demand. He said for Hernando to keep walking. That someone would contact him along the way. Then he went back to his doorway, took out his cell, punched out a number and made his report.

Little Patty's the local shop steward. The floor manager. The guy that makes sure things go right in the territory. He kept the peace and made sure no freelancer came around to fuck things up. A freelancer could destroy agreements that have lasted for years without even realizing it. Then war could break out and everybody loses.

"He's pedaling pills and weed," he said into the phone. "Wants $500. Had it all ready for me. My guess is he's got more. Says he's moving on after this score. Letting me know he's not looking to set up shop."

"You believe him?" said the voice on the other end.

"Nahh," said Little Patty.

"You know what to do," said the voice and clicked off.

They dumped Hernando's body in the cool Pacific. They weighed it down with rocks, but after an unanticipated storm it broke free from its moorings and washed up on a remote beach farther down the coastline. Stuck to the sole of his left foot was the green card he'd paid so much money for when he started this journey. It's how the police were able to identify him.

Chapter 46

After they left Julio Perez and the Williamsburg station house, Morgan put Jimmy on the subway for Grand Central and they parted company, each making the phone signal and telling the other he'll keep him up to date. Then Jimmy found himself squashed like a cigarette butt against a humanity he'd lost touch with a long time ago.

The trip home was, like the kids say, a trip. In the middle of rush hour no less. Rush hours more like it. It makes him realize how much of a country boy he's become The subway station is filled to capacity, the platform is mobbed and the train is packed like they're giving away hundred dollar bills. He's thankful it's not the summer, with all the human smells that turn revolting in the heat. He remembers when he used to do it all the time. It didn't seem to bother him then, but it sure would now. After snaking up crowded stairs and through long winding tunnels, he gets to a Grand Central Station jammed full of people crashing and bashing and hurling themselves at one another. He's one of the first to get on the next train to Columbia and gets himself a window seat. He begins to relax the minute the train leaves the station. Trundling along with that calming clackety-clack. Like a metronome. Steady and monotonous. Hypnotic too, judging by the people nodding off all around him.

The ride up the Hudson is a picture show of beauty and peaceful relief. He catches a spectacular sunset and watches in awe as the shimmering orb disappears a little at a time behind the Palisades as if in slow motion. And when it's gone, the sky is fiery red, as if the horizon's ablaze. But it doesn't last for long as the twilight quickly takes over and by the time he gets to his stop, it's almost dark. Mary's waiting for him there.

A little while later they're at the diner, sitting in their regular corner booth by the window. After they've ordered food, fried chicken and mashed potatoes for Mary, meat loaf and extra gravy for him, Jimmy tells her about his lunch.

"We've got to eat in the City more often," he declares like it's a new rule for the relationship along with, "no more moving in talk," and "staying off the wine." Then he describes what he had and how it tasted in such detail that he sounds to Mary like someone who's never seen food before. They're catching up on their days, the two of them. Mary spent hers on the phone with her lawyer drawing up the papers for her investment in Josephine's Scarsdale salon.

"What are they calling it?" asks Jimmy.

Mary doesn't know.

"Do we still have to pay for haircuts now you're an owner?"

"Investor," says Mary. "I'm an investor. They own it. Her and Mitchiko."

"What's that got to do with paying for haircuts?"

Mary shakes her head and fakes a sob. "Sorry, Jimmy," she says and dabs a nonexistent tear from the corner of her eye, "I can't help you on this one."

He tells her about the Collis file that's missing from Jason's house. "I had to check the patrol schedule to make sure so no one would see me there, can you imagine? This afternoon they put me back on the case and I can do what I like again." He tells her what Jason said was in the file.

When he's finished she says, "'And Jason thinks that's why Collis might have it in for him?"

"Jason's lawyer is checking out Collis's career record, but Jason definitely thinks it's Collis who took the file."

"Why?"

"He says Collis is the only one who has any interest in it."

"How would Collis know where it is?"

"If he's been harassing Jason all these years he probably knows where everything in that house is."

"What do you think?" she asks him.

"Lots of people have marched through there in the past couple of weeks. Any one of them could've taken that file."

She agrees with him. "So what's the plan Sam?"

"A friend of mine's going to dust Jason's house for me. Then I've got to get a set of Collis's prints. He's not in any of the data bases."

"How will you do it?" She's looking at him with those goo goo eyes now. Like he's ten feet tall and able to leap tall buildings in a single bound. It gives him a little flutter in the pit of his stomach. "I'll show Collis pictures of suspects on something I've been working on. We should be able to get a set off of them."

This is what she likes most. The telling of it. The going over it. The hashing it out. She knows how to do it now. At the beginning she'd be too eager. Wanting to show she was listening, or into it, or something. Anyhow, she'd jump in too soon and ask a question at the wrong time and break the rhythm of the thing. Then he'd lose his way. And then he'd get mad. Because she'd spoiled it for him. And ruined the telling of it. That's when they first started going out. Now she's learned to keep her mouth shut, at least till he's finished.

They work on their food a while, then Mary tells him how cute Lucy looked in her Brownie outfit. That's where Lucy is now. At the Brownies. Mary's got to pick her up in an hour.

Jimmy says he's sorry he missed it. "You took pictures?"

She looks at him like he's crazy. "Of course I took pictures."

Of course she took pictures. Only he wouldn't take pictures because he doesn't have a camera. Another thing for him to learn in this increasingly digital world. He's still trying to get used to his computer.

"Mitchiko was a big help to the NYPD," he tells her. "Morgan was able to get to this guy Julio Perez because of her. Julio works at CRIMPERS. He's an assistant there. Apparently he gets everyone their drugs. And guess who Julio gets his coke from?" He pauses a beat. "Marc Hilliard."

"Sandra Ellison's boyfriend?"

"The plot thickens, eh Watson?"

He tells her about Morgan wanting him in on Julio's interview.

"How come?" she says. "It's not your case."

"He says I got the ball rolling on this one. If I hadn't turned him on to Mitchiko he might never have gotten this far. They've also got a flu epidemic down there. Everyone's out sick including Morgan's partner. Morgan told his skipper I'm working the case from the Westchester end so he let us partner up." He tells her how Morgan let him do the good cop thing and how he got Julio to tell them his cousin Hernando sold the poison to Jerry Lewis. And that Jerry Lewis got the poison for William who wanted it to kill his partner."

"Jeez," she says. "What a rough bunch. So what's with the poison in Lewis's safe being water?"

"You got me," says Jimmy. "I can't figure it out. Neither can Morgan."

There's more munching and chewing, then Mary says, "Quite the trip down memory lane for you today, Sherlock."

He shakes his head like he still can't believe it. "It was like being in a time warp. Everything was just like it used to be. The food. The subway. The precinct houses were really weird, especially the one in Brooklyn. I used to be in and out of that place all the time and you know what? Not one thing's changed. And working with a partner again, that was fun. And breaking out the old soft shoe shuffle which, it turns out, is no different from the new soft shoe shuffle except they wear different clothes these days."

"Where's Hernando?"

"Skipped town. Julio blames him for everything that's happened."

"Everything?"

"They found traces of coke, weed and the poison that killed Lewis in the locker they share at CRIMPERS, and the same traces in their apartment. Julio says it all belongs to Hernando."

"You believe him?"

"Not a word."

She smiles.

The waitress drops the check on the table and keeps walking.

"So what happened?"

"Morgan had to release him."

"Why?"

"Because nothing Morgan had would stand up in court."

She pokes at her potatoes.

"I have to go at Ted Butler again tomorrow," he tells her and fills her in on that story including the part where Smith and Monahan told him it's their collar no matter what happens.

"What did you say?'"

"Nothing. What do I care? Being back on the case is the more important thing. Now I can work on this Jason stuff without sneaking around. I never told them about Collis or that I'm close to finding the gun owner."

"Why?"

"Lets see if the pieces fit first."

She leans back and gives him a proud smile. "That's why they pay you the big bucks."

He puffs out his chest and flexes his muscles like Popeye, then he pays the check and they leave. After a quick kiss in the parking lot he tells her he'll call her later and heads for home.

Wednesday

Chapter 47

The ride to see Harvey Collis the next morning is a nice one. It's all back roads and country byways with undulating countryside and no traffic, just the way Jimmy likes it. The music for today's excursion features "Walk on the Wild Side" by Jimmy Smith. The opening track drives Jimmy crazy with that big band sound banging away and Smith's fabulous solo on the Wurlitzer or whatever it is he plays. Jimmy turns it up loud for the crescendo and when it hits he has tears in his eyes and chills down his spine.

It's that sort of morning. A clear blue sky. Bright sunshine. Perfect music. No more pressure about moving in with Mary. And to top it off something new to see in nature. This morning's treat is an old gnarly oak tree with long sweeping branches and a bunch of wild turkeys milling about underneath it. A huge tom, his head tucked into his feathers, is sound asleep on a low branch directly above them. The girls are waiting for him to wake up. They peck at the ground and cluck and groogle at him like they're talking about the weather or their favorite movie stars, whiling away the time till the tom gets up and decides what he wants to do.

Hillsdale Middle School is one of those sixties educational facilities that all seem to look alike. It's a two story cinderblock structure with arms and legs that stick out at odd angles all gussied up with green paint so it doesn't look so bleak for the tender young minds that crawl all over it. Jimmy parks in one of the visitor's slots and makes his way to Collis's office. He stands there now, at the door of Collis's basement cubicle, unannounced and uninvited. This time with a manila envelope in his hand and a pleasant smile on his face. The envelope contains the photos he wants Collis to touch.

"Whaddya want?" says a scowling Harvey Collis. He's sitting at his desk working his way through a stack of papers. The desk is covered with brochures, manuals, papers on spikes, old newspapers and assorted rubbish. He's not pleased to see Jimmy on this horrible morning. The toilets are backed up, the boiler's on the fritz and the principal's office has a leak in the ceiling that needs to be fixed before it rains. Now here's this cop nosing around again. Is it possible things can get any worse?

"Sorry to bother you, old chum," says Jimmy. He's pleased to see Collis flinch from the familiarity. "Old chum." He hasn't used the term in years. He got it off an English detective show and used it all the time back in Brooklyn when he wanted to annoy someone. He'd even affect an English accent. That would really piss them off. But not this time. No accent for Mr. Collis today. Only "old chum," to annoy him just a little because the man's so rude. Then he tells him about the investigation he's running at the Columbia High School. The pilfering that's getting out of hand and how it's turning out to be a county problem, so many districts are having the same trouble. "We've got a task force working the case, I'm part of it," says Jimmy explaining his presence.

Collis's demeanor changes. The scowl disappears replaced by something not quite so mean. He puts down the invoices and pays more attention.

"Have you seen any of these guys hanging around the school?" Jimmy asks him. He slides out the photos from the manila envelope and hands them to him. Five 8 x 10 glossies. All clean and shiny. Untouched by human hand except on the corners.

Collis grabs them and looks them over. He has huge hands and sausage-like fingers with hair on the backs of them and dirt under the nails. There are five mug shots. Two are real suspects, three Jimmy threw in for good measure. Collis keeps shuffling through them sometimes frowning, sometimes staring at just one. This goes on for a while till he finally settles on one in particular. "This one," he says and holds the print up to the light and squints at it. "I've seen this one around here a lot. I thought he was a student."

"At the middle school? He's a bit big, isn't he?

"We have some high school classes here because of the overcrowding. He looks like a senior to me. I've definitely seen him on the campus. He carries a very big back pack and wears a Red Sox hat. You don't see a lot of those around here." Collis shuffles through the pictures some more, then shakes his head. "That's the only one I recognize." He hands Jimmy back the prints.

Jimmy says, "When was the last time you saw him?"

"Last week, I'd say."

"Anything missing?"

"Apart from the usual?"

"What's that mean?"

Collis smiles for the first time. It's not much of a thing really, more of a crease in his face. "Lost book bags. The occasional watch." The crease gets a little wider. "There's been a run on fancy sneakers, but that's been going on for a while."

"Doesn't sound like what we're looking for," says Jimmy. "What's the deal with the sneakers?"

"Poor kids ripping off the rich ones. Some kids have everything, some have nothing. You know how it is."

Jimmy said he did. "But nothing major?"

"Not that I know of," says Collis. "What does he take?"

"Computers. Electrical stuff. He starts small. Watches the reaction. Does it again, a little bigger. Then the third time, when he's got the lay of the land and feels confident, he backs up a truck and takes everything he can get his hands on."

Collis suddenly gets worked up. "Not on my watch," he says vehemently and runs a hand over his shaved head. "He won't be doing that on my watch, I can assure you of that."

Jimmy believes him and makes a note of the quick wind up.

"Can I have copies of that photo to show the guys?" asks Collis.

Jimmy says he'll get him some.

"We'll keep an eye out for him. I'll speak to the principal and let the teachers know. If he shows up again, I'll give you a call."

Jimmy's got to smile at that. Here he's come on one thing and scores on another. Sometimes it works out that way. He's thinking he should buy himself a lottery ticket. Things come in threes or so he's heard. The turkey spotting was one. Collis picking the kid out is two. A winning lottery ticket would round the day out nicely. "Thanks, but don't call me," he says to Collis. "It's not my patch. I'm just doing the leg work for the task force. I'll call the locals and tell them what's going on. Someone will get back to you on this and they'll tell you what they want you to do, but believe me Mr. Collis this is huge what you've done here. Absolutely huge. This ID could bust things wide open for us." He sticks out his paw and shakes Collis's hand vigorously. "You've been a big help Mr. Collis, and I can't thank you enough." He says it with great enthusiasm and means every word of it.

There's a smattering of small talk after that, but Jimmy can see Collis's head is already down and back to his invoices. He says goodbye to Collis's bald spot, then he's off to his car and heading back to Columbia.

Chapter 48

Ellis Jones is sitting at his desk in the county crime lab in White Plains playing a video game on his computer. It's been a slow day crime-wise. He's got nothing else to do. He's a duster. A fingerprint man. Part of a four person crime scene crew ready to go at a moment's notice only there are no crime scenes to investigate. The county has three crews. One's already at a crime scene, the other two are sitting around waiting for something to happen. It's been this way for a couple of weeks now. One team's out and the rest sit around doing nothing. Everyone's caught up with their paper work, and dotted the I's, and crossed the T's and taken care of stuff they thought they'd never get to. So when he gets Jimmy's call, Ellis thinks it's some sort of miracle. A perfectly timed rescue from death by boredom you only see happen in the movies. After the obligatory chit chat Jimmy calls in his favor. "You know what this is for, don't you?" he asks.

"Bailing out my son?"

Jimmy caught Ellis's son buying weed by the library not long ago and after a phone call to Ellis, forgot about the incident for a favor to be named later. "This one's for Jason Friendly," Jimmy explains. He hopes Ellis will consider it a favor to Jason so he'll still have his favor in the bank.

Ellis says he knows all about Jason's troubles. "I really like that guy. We've worked on a couple of things together and he's always done right by me. Even on the stand he's polite and respectful. I don't think Jason could kill a fly let alone a human being, he doesn't have it in him. You want my opinion I think he's getting a bum rap for this so whatever I can do to help out, count me in."

Jimmy explains the situation with Collis and how he's got a set of his prints.

"On the photos?"

"Clear as a bell," says Jimmy. He tells Ellis about the intruder he disturbed at Jason's house. "We only got one room then. I need the whole house done, including the basement and the bedside table in the bedroom where the file was supposed to be."

"I can do that."

"Now?"

"Why not," says Ellis. "We're the last crew up this week and things are as slow as molasses."

"You're in?"

"I'm in."

Jimmy gives him the address and directions. "I'll see you there in half an hour."

"No problemo," says Ellis and hangs up the phone. He tells his boss he's taking a couple of personal hours, unless there's anything he wants him to do. The boss says he can't think of a thing, so Ellis turns off his computer, saves the game he's been playing for later and makes his way over to Jason's house. Jimmy's already there. Key in one hand, envelope with the photos in the other. Jimmy gives Ellis the envelope and lets him in the house. Then he puts the key back under the stone and heads back to the office. But not before Ellis tells him he'll probably have something for him by tomorrow afternoon.

Chapter 49

Jimmy rounds up Eddie and tells him they're going to take another run at Ted Butler for Smith and Monahan. He explains how they want him to check out this drug business. "Then the boys will come in like the cavalry and collect the collar."

"Nothing for us," says Eddie.

"Not even an honorable mention."

Eddie grunts and mutters something unintelligible. He tells Jimmy he's waiting for the pictures of Collis and Butler from the DMV. They're telling him first thing tomorrow morning now.

Jimmy makes the call to Butler and tells him there are a couple of details they need to clear up. A little while later they're back in his basement office lowering themselves into those comfy chairs again.

Butler's behind his desk.

"Mr. Butler," says Jimmy, all smiles and friendliness, "we want to see if we can help you find a way out of this trouble you're in."

"What trouble?" asks Butler. A sheen of sweat appears on his forehead.

"I've got a witness who says you've been distributing cocaine at the Rolling Hills Country Club."

"What a lot of nonsense," is all Butler can come up with. He looks uncomfortable. His beady little eyes flit from Jimmy to Eddie and back again.

"Do you know what distributing means, Mr. Butler?"

Butler doesn't answer.

"Dealing, Mr. Butler. Dealing, that's what it means. In this state, what with the Rockefeller laws still on the books and all, this is the end of your life as you know it, sir. The rest of it is going to be spent behind bars."

Butler looks very unhappy. "I don't see how any of this is helping me," he says miserably.

"You help me and then maybe I can help you." Jimmy looks over at Eddie. "Right Eddie? Isn't that how it works?"

Eddie nods. He loves this stuff. It's better than TV.

"How can I help you?" asks Butler.

"You can tell me things."

"Like what?"

Jimmy thinks for a second and decides to take a leaf from Smith and Monahan's routine. That old fashioned, sledgehammer approach of theirs just for the sake of it. To give it a try. To rattle Butler's tree before the surprise wears off and see what falls out. "Why'd you kill Sandra Ellison?" he barks loudly which makes Butler flinch.

"What are you talking about 'kill Sandra Ellison;'" moans Butler who looks like he's just been zapped with a taser.

"Shot her. You shot her didn't you? That's what we think, right Eddie?" Jimmy looks at Eddie for confirmation.

Eddie nods again. Sagely this time and with much more feeling. He rarely speaks in these situations. It's why he likes them so much. There's nothing to do but watch.

"I never killed anyone," says Butler. "You're crazy."

"Maybe you were pissed off at Jason because he gave you a hard time at the Club that time, so you tried to wing him when he was out on his run. A payback situation, something like that, but the shot went wild. You didn't mean to kill anyone. It's accidental homicide. Certainly not murder."

Butler looks like he's having a nightmare.

"What do you say Mr. Butler? Accidental homicide. How does that sound to you? A good lawyer can have you out in no time."

Butler suddenly calms down. Some sort of Zen thing they think when they're going over it again in the car on the way home. First he closes his eyes, then he takes a couple of deep breaths, then he opens his eyes again and someone else shows up. "You're making this all up," he says almost laughing. "You're out of your jurisdiction and you've got nothing on me. Now please get out of my house."

Lesser men might have left, but not Jimmy and Eddie. They sit in those comfy chairs holding their ground staring at the new Ted Butler like he's a boardwalk oddity. Jimmy shifts tack and takes a softer tone. Less belligerent. More accommodating. Discarding the Monahan-Smith routine since nothing seems to be falling out of Butler's tree.

"What about the coke?" he asks.

"Coke?" says Butler, like he doesn't know what Jimmy's talking about.

"Cocaine. Did you pass it to her?"

"Who?"

"Sandra Ellison."

Butler doesn't answer.

"We've got Marc Hilliard, you know that don't you? He's locked up in the City. That's how we got to you. He gave you up. That's why we're here. Hilliard told us he was your supplier. That you had quite the operation going on here. Is that right what he says, Mr. Butler? Have you got quite the operation going on here?" Jimmy waits for Butler to say something. Anything. But Butler maintains his silence. He's been around the block a few times has our Ted and he knows when it comes to the cops the less you say to them the better. Every word you utter can and usually will come back to bite you in the ass.

"Hilliard ratted you out," says Jimmy. "He's who told us about your action at the club and the favor you did for him, giving coke to Sandra Ellison. The same Sandra Ellison who got killed last week. The same Sandra Ellison you said you didn't know. And the same Sandra Ellison we think you killed."

Butler blinks.

"Jason saw you, right? That night at the club. He thought you were trying to hold her hand. He didn't know about the coke. Then what happened?"

Butler stiffens. No Zen this time, just meanness." I don't have to say anything and I don't have to answer any of your questions. I've asked you once already, please get out of my house."

"This is what *we* think happened," says Jimmy, ignoring him and plowing on. "Jason got mad when he saw you touch her. He never saw the coke, he thought you were coming on to her." Jimmy makes a face like the very thought of it is disgusting. "It was all very embarrassing for you, so you left the club in a hurry, we're told, and you haven't been back since."

"Two people canceled policies because of that night," Butler grumbles.

"And?" says Jimmy.

"And what? They held Jason back and I got the hell out of there. What? You think I was going to hang around for another ass whooping. You see the shape I'm in? No sir. Not me. That guy could've beaten the living daylights out of me if he wanted to."

"So you're holding a grudge?"

"Against Jason?"

Jimmy nods.

"I don't like the guy, if that's what you mean."

"C'mon, Mr. Butler. It's more than that."

"Maybe it is, but what's that got to do with anything?"

"You wouldn't be sorry if they gave him the needle."

Butler hesitates. "I wouldn't say that."

"Or put him away for life. That would be okay, right Mr. Butler? Putting him away for life?"

"Better than killing him, sure."

"So you set him up, isn't that what happened? To get back at him for the lost two accounts and all that embarrassment at the club. Those boys at Rolling Hills don't like scenes very much, do they Ted."

"Set him up?" says Butler. Standing up. Face reddening. "What the hell does that mean? Set him up."

"Left things around so we'd think he killed Sandra Ellison. Making a frame so he gets the blame. Listen to me," he says to Eddie. "I sound like Johnny Cochran."

Eddie smiles. He's never seen Jimmy do humor before.

Butler takes a couple of gulps of air and draws himself up to his full height behind his desk. He reminds them of a cornered mouse on its hind legs. Clawing at the air. Flailing to ward off its adversaries. "You've got no proof of any of this crap," he says angrily. "If you did you'd be reading me my rights by now, so I'm asking you nicely one more time. Get out of my house."

When he sees they're not moving he picks up the phone and hits a button. "I'm calling my lawyer. You're trespassing on my property. You're out of your jurisdiction. Anything you want to say to me from here on goes through him." He starts speaking to whoever's on the other end.

When he's finished Jimmy is undeterred. "Tell us about Sandra Ellison while we're waiting for them to show up. Who was that, by the way?"

"My lawyer."

"Is he coming?"

"He's on his way."

"How long till he gets here?"

Butler looks at his watch. "Half an hour, maybe."

"Good. I'm gonna call my guys now and see how they want to play it. Then you can tell me some things about Sandra while we're waiting for everyone to show up." He punches Smith's number on his cell phone and when Smith picks up, tells him what's going on.

"You sure he's lawyering up?" asks Smith.

"We're waiting for the guy to show as we speak," says Jimmy.

Smith says, "Hold the fort a while longer. We're getting a search warrant and pulling a team together. Figure us for 45 minutes," and hangs up.

Jimmy looks at Butler. "We got a while till anybody gets here. Tell me some stuff about Sandra I don't already know."

"Why should I do that?"

"It might help you later on."

"With what?"

"Whatever my guys are gonna get on you."

"How's that?"

"They're coming in with a search warrant. Who knows what they're gonna find."

Butler squirms uncomfortably. "My lawyer told me not to say another word to you. I've probably said too much already."

"If you did, I never heard it. What do you say Eddie? Did you hear anything we can use on him?"

Eddie shakes his head.

Butler picks at a nail. "What do want to know?"

"Was that the only time you met Sandra Ellison? That night at Rolling Hills?"

"You think this is going to help me?"

"It can't hurt."

Butler thinks about it, then he says, "I saw her before."

"Where?"

"At Marc Hilliard's place."

"The three of you?"

"There was another guy there too."

"What was his name?"

"Julio."

"The kid from CRIMPERS?"

"That's the one," says Butler.

"Three guys and one girl. What did you do?"

Butler shakes his head. "You can just imagine."

Jimmy got the picture. "So you liked her?"

"Not really."

"Why's that?"

"She asked too many questions. And it's not just me saying that."

"Who else?"

"Julio. He said the same thing."

"You did this all the time with these guys?"

"Just the once. I don't know what else went on when I wasn't around."

Jimmy says, "What else didn't you like about her?"

"The sex meant nothing. You could see it was some fantasy thing where she was really getting off on it. But she had her eyes on a bigger prize."

"What was that?"

"She wanted a piece of the business."

"Hilliard's business?"

Butler nods. "We told Marc, me and Julio, but he wouldn't listen to us. He said she was good entertainment and he knew what he was doing. We kept telling him a word from her can put you out of business."

"What about your business?"

Ever the cautious one Butler says, "Who said I had a business?"

"Or Julio's business?"

"I don't know anything about Julio's business. But I didn't kill her, detective. You have to know that. I did not kill that woman."

"I know you didn't, Mr. Butler," says Jimmy like a priest offering absolution. "I know you didn't."

But that was before he heard from Ellis Jones and his fingerprint report

Chapter 50

That night Mary and Jimmy retired to their separate corners. Lucy's in a school play tomorrow so they all decided on early nights to be fresh for the big day. Jimmy picks up some Boston Chicken and gobbles it down as soon as he gets in. Felix hovers in the background sniffing the air and purring like a freight train waiting for his turn. Then Jason's lawyer calls to tell Jimmy he found out why Harvey Collis left Harrison and Kegly. "I told you I had a friend there," the lawyer brags in that rat-a-tat style of his like this puts him ahead in the, "friends helping Jason" competition.

"The letter to the Friendlys was his downfall. It showed an incredible lack of judgment on his part. The Friendlys' lawyer faxed it to Harrison Kegly and the next day the partners hauled Collis's ass over the coals. Then they fired him. They still talk about it there, says my friend. They use it as an example of what not to do if you want to have a successful career in law."

"You can see why the guy might hold a grudge," says Jimmy. "And then?"

"No one knows. He wasn't very popular and everyone was pleased to see him go. No one kept tabs on him after he left."

"I'm not surprised," says Jimmy, then he tells him about getting Collis's prints and how he's had Jason's house dusted. "A favor from a friend," says Jimmy, evening up the score in the "friends helping Jason" competition.

The lawyer says he'll see if he can find out what happened after Collis left Harrison Kegly. "I've got an investigator I like to use. I'll have him make some calls." The lawyer yawns. "We better come up with something soon, time's getting short."

Like Jimmy needs reminding. He tells the lawyer he'll be in late tomorrow, says good night and breaks the connection. After that he clears away his mess and leaves the dishes to soak. He brews some tea and pads over to the couch. Stretches out and makes room for Felix who jumps up and snuggles himself in. Then he turns on the TV for the 10 o'clock news and promptly falls asleep.

Thursday

Chapter 51

Lucy's dressed all in pink for the school play. Pink tutu. Pink leotard. Pink wings. Mary stayed up all night sewing. Pink dancing shoes with pink laces. Pink ribbon in her blonde hair. Even a pink wand. She's a pink fairy in case you hadn't figured it out. There's a lot going on right now and Jimmy should really be at the office pushing things through. Instead he's driving to Lucy's school with Mary sitting next to him and Lucy in the back trying not to mess up her tutu. He's as excited as a three year old and hopes Lucy remembers her lines this time and doesn't throw up which is what she did last year. She was a bumble bee then with just one line. When it was time for her to say it she threw up all over her bumble bee outfit, the kid standing next to her dressed as a toad, and the girl standing in front of her wearing a sunflower costume. It brought the house down. You couldn't help laughing, especially if it wasn't your kid getting thrown-up on. Jimmy and Mary managed to keep straight faces and rushed Lucy off the stage. No one says a word in the car today. No one has to. Each one knows what the other's thinking. But Lucy's more self-assured this time and a year older. Pushing eight now. With many more lines and a truckload of confidence. Still no one speaks, not wanting to jinx her and she not wanting to jinx herself.

The play, or ballet or whatever you want to call it, goes well. Lucy delivers her lines with gusto and panache. The frog she touches with her pink fairy wand is turned into a prince to the accompaniment of oohs and aahs from an audience of parents, family and friends. Jimmy's filled with a parental pride he never knew existed and gets all teary-eyed when the kids come out and get a standing ovation.

When he gets back to the station house he bumps into Eddie outside. Eddie's in a froth. "Where've you been?" he wants to know. "I've been calling you all morning."

Jimmy explains about the school play.

"Don't you check your messages?"

Jimmy's still aglow from the good time he just had. How well Lucy did and the big round of applause she got when she took her bow. He'd turned the phone off, but he doesn't tell Eddie that. Instead he tells him he's been having trouble with the thing and he's sorry.

Eddie lets it go. He's got good news and he doesn't want to spoil it. He tells Jimmy that he got Butler's fingerprints. "He was in the army, not for long though. There's some mystery there." Eddie doesn't elaborate, but moves on to his next bit of news. "The DMV sent me Collis and Butler's pictures first thing this morning. I've been showing them around ever since. No one's seen Butler, but the liquor store owner says he remembers Collis parking at the end of the lot then disappearing on the night of the murder. He was the first stop I made. That's how long I've been trying to get hold of you."

"How come the liquor store owner didn't say this before?" says Jimmy. "We canvassed that whole area. Why didn't he say something then?"

"He never gave it a thought till I showed up with the pictures. He says people park there all the time. Joggers. Walkers. Then he reminded me that all we showed him that time was Jason's picture. We never said we might be looking for someone else and he never made the connection."

"When did he see Collis?"

"About fifteen minutes before Jason heard the shot."

"And Collis's car?"

"A beat up old Chevy Malibu. Brown with lots of dents is what the liquor guy says. DMV has a brown Malibu registered in Collis's name."

"What does Butler drive?"

"A Mercedes."

"He must be doing well."

"Not necessarily. It's a lease. Probably a write off. These days you can't tell who's rich any more by the car they drive."

"Anyone see it?"

"No."

Jimmy says, "Did the liquor store guy see Collis carrying anything?" Eddie shakes his head.

"Did he see him come back to the car?"

Eddie shakes his head again and looks at his watch. "The late guy at the deli comes on soon. I'm going over there to talk to him."

"This is very good stuff Eddie."

Eddies preens.

There are voice mail messages for Jimmy when he gets back to his desk. The ones from Jason's lawyer are the best. Each one is more frantic than the last. They run from polite, to angry, to just plain nasty. Jimmy's got to smile at that. He's the only friend Jason's got and here's this lawyer giving him a hard time. The phone rings as he's listening to the rest of the messages. It's the Westchester County Records Department. It's taken them this long to get back to him. They're calling to tell him that Mickey Swan died nine months ago. The records state that his last job was at the Hillside Middle School where he was employed as an assistant janitor. Hillside Middle School is where Harvey Collis works.

Then Jason's lawyer calls. He's all ready to give Jimmy a mouthful, but before he can get going Jimmy interrupts him. "That last message of yours was a bit harsh don't you think, counselor?"

It stops the lawyer in his tracks.

Jimmy repeats the question and adds, "People say things like that when they're never going to speak to the other person again. Now here you are calling me up, wanting me to help you some more after you've used language like that on me. What were you thinking when you said those things?"

The lawyer mumbles an apology and says how hard it's been to get in touch with him.

"Apologies accepted," says Jimmy magnanimously still feeling toasty from Lucy's performance, Eddie's report and the news he just got about the gun. "I told you last night I was coming in late."

The lawyer mumbles something unintelligible and babbles on obsequiously till Jimmy cuts him off. "So what's on your mind?" he asks him.

The lawyer says his private detective got him some information on Harvey Collis. "There's not a lot, but it's very suspicious." Suddenly the lawyer's back on track. Strong and commanding with a just a hint of pomposity.

"They threw Collis out of Harrison Kegly for writing that letter to the Friendlys. After that he must have had a hard time getting work. The only employment we could find was with a temp agency in New York. Then nothing until nine years ago when he was hired as a janitor at Hillside Middle School. Obviously something went very wrong for him."

Then Jimmy fills the lawyer in on what he's found out: the positive ID on Collis that Eddie got at the liquor store and the gun owner Mickey Swan being dead and having worked at the same school as Collis.

"That's fantastic," says the lawyer. "I can't wait to tell Jason."

Ellis Jones calls a little while later. Jimmy gets no attitude from this guy. No, "Where the hell have you been?" or worse, which is what everyone's been saying to him each time he picks up the phone. That warm and toasty feeling is long gone now, lost in a barrage of attitude and pique from a multitude of callers pissed off because they couldn't reach him.

Ellis talks like a long distance runner in the middle of a marathon. "Collis's prints are all over the house," he says breathlessly. "Doors. Windows. Basement. His prints match a bunch I found in Jason's bedroom, especially on that bedside table you wanted me to look at." He pauses for breath then hurtles on, spewing out information like he's being chased. "He's has been in every drawer and closet in that room. Even under the bed. I found a thumb print on the main frame. Creepy when you think about it, someone going through your things like that. Some prints are quite old. He's been in this room a lot over a long period of time. There are partials in the basement and in the bathroom down the hall from Jason's bedroom. Must've needed to take a piss I suppose. His prints also match prints they got from the back room." He pauses as if he's going to end the conversation, then he throws in the kicker. "There are also some other prints in the upstairs bathroom on the medicine cabinet. I ran them through the system. They belong to someone called Ted Butler. Ring any bells?"

Jimmy's surprised and fills him in on Butler's story. It never occurred to him that Butler might actually be involved in this. Now, with his prints showing up at Jason's house, he's wondering if Butler and Collis are in it together.

"Nowhere else?" Jimmy asks

"Nowhere else."

"Just the one set?"

"Just the one set," says Ellis.

"Mmmmm," says Jimmy.

Chapter 52

Jimmy gets a call from the chief to come and see him right away. It's more of a summons, really. A brief bark down the phone that goes something like, "Get in here now." The chief is following up on what's going on with Ted Butler, making sure Smith and Monahan's account is being serviced correctly. The chief hopes Jimmy has stopped persisting with this "Free Jason" nonsense. The chief's head is starting to hurt. He puts two fingers to his temple to try and locate the source of the pain and pops a couple of aspirin in an attempt to head it off at the pass.

Jimmy knocks on the door and enters.

The chief doesn't look up, neither does he offer Jimmy a seat. Such is the barometer of the Skipper's affections. If you were In you'd get a chair and a smile. Maybe even a cup of coffee. But if you're Out you get this sort of treatment. "What happened with Butler?" he snaps.

"The boys have him," says Jimmy with a grimace. "They showed up at his house with a search warrant and a bunch of troopers. They made a whole big whoopdy doo for the press they brought with them and told us in so many words to fuck off."

The chief asks, "Who's us?"

"Me and Eddie."

That gets a groan.

Jimmy pays it no mind. He stands close to the edge of the desk marveling at the way the chief looks at the end of the day. Crisp and clean and all spit and polish. He even looks freshly shaved. Jimmy on the other hand has the beginnings of a five o'clock shadow, his white shirt is rumpled and his dark blue suit that looked okay when he put it on this morning now looks like it needs pressing. It's a contrast in styles and personality. Freud would have a field day with it.

Unfazed by their differences Jimmy's confident and sure of himself. He doesn't care if the chief's pissed off at him. He thinks he's got this thing figured out and he's sure the chief will be on board once he's finished his presentation.

"So we're done with this now, right?" says the chief forcefully. His blue eyes bore into Jimmy. "Jason killed Sandra Ellison, Butler's a drug dealer and has nothing to do with Sandra's death or us, Smith and Monahan can go back to wherever the hell they came from, and we can all go home and give ourselves pats on the back for a job well done." His expression is hopeful. Like Jimmy's really going to see it this way. He's searching his temple. Gently probing. Cautiously applying pressure to different parts of his head. The aspirin not yet kicked in.

Jimmy doesn't see it that way. He doesn't gloat and he's not looking for revenge, though he thinks Smith and Monahan could have been more gracious with the Butler bust. "But," as he tells the chief looking him squarely in the eye, "what I'm about to tell you is going to cause those boys a great deal of embarrassment."

Without waiting for the chief to react he walks him through the case he's got on Collis. The prints all over Jason's house. Mickey Swan and the gun. The liquor store owner who saw Collis that night at the place where the shooter stood. And the missing file on the history between the two families. He's making his report detective to boss. Following procedure. Something they've done a great many times over the years. The Chief slips into form too and assumes his usual position when listening to a presentation. Leaning back in his chair. Arms folded across his chest. One leg crossed over the other. His eyes half closed in a posture of deep concentration. It's so hammy Jimmy wants to smack him one. Stifling the temptation he finishes his story by telling him, "We also found Butler's prints in Jason's bathroom."

"Who found them?" asks the chief.

Jimmy tells him how Ellis Jones dusted the place for him.

The chief wants to know what Ellis was doing in Jason's house.

"He owed me a favor," says Jimmy and leaves it at that. "Butler denies having anything to do with Sandra Ellison's death. Up till now I believed him. This print thing is bothersome. It makes no sense. I can't see him being involved with Collis, but you never know."

The chief sits up straight. He looks like a lion getting that first whiff of something good to eat. Sniffing the air. Nostrils aquiver. He's coming around. His features are softening. The more opportunities he sees for himself, the more he begins to relax. That's when he stops massaging his temple and gets down to business. "Tell me more about the rifle," he says.

"Mickey Swan, the original owner, died nine months ago. His last place of employment was the Hillside Middle School as a janitor on Collis's crew."

The chief nods approvingly. "How come Smith and Monahan didn't come up with this stuff?"

"You got me," says Jimmy, "but my guess is after a couple of runs at it they gave up. It took me a lot of digging and calling in some favors, and with all of that I only got the word an hour ago. Those boys like to move fast and get on to the next thing. They're also very lazy."

"They are that," says the chief.

"But there's still this fly in the ointment," says Jimmy.

The chief's head gives a twitch. His fingers go back to his temple.

"Butler's prints in Jason's upstairs bathroom. He was definitely in that house."

The chief rearranges the stuff on his desk. It's a nervous thing he uses to buy time when he hasn't finished working things through. When he's finished his housekeeping, he looks up at Jimmy with a broad smile. "Well," he says with a chuckle, "you've certainly gone and done it this time. Those boys are gonna be pissed to beat the band when they get a hold of this. This is the second time you've shown them up on a murder case and they sure as hell aren't going to forget it. On the other hand," this time he gives Jimmy a friendly wink, "who gives a shit. It sounds to me like you've got Collis cold. How are you going to play it?"

Jimmy says he wants to go for a confession.

The chief raises an eyebrow. Confessions are hard to pull off. "What about Butler?"

"Let me go at Collis first," says Jimmy. "If they're in it together, it's sure to come out."

The chief agrees. "I'll call the DA," he says, "and tell her what's going on." His headache has miraculously lifted. He's suddenly clear of eye. Firmly in charge. The Skipper. "I want to get Jason out of jail just as quickly as you do," he pronounces. Suddenly brimming with confidence and self -importance. Like this whole thing was his idea from the start.

Jimmy smiles. He's got to, the whole thing's so ridiculous, but who cares. The chief's on board isn't he, and talking like he's never been anywhere else.

"How will you go about it?" asks the Skipper, poking about his desk looking for the DA's number. He's in a hurry now, anxious to get his friend Jason out of jail before anyone else comes up with the idea.

"I'm going to need one of your, 'Thanks From the Community,' letters to make it work. A big fat juicy one praising Collis for identifying the suspect we had our eye on in the school rip off case."

The chief looks puzzled.

Jimmy explains. "The photos I showed Collis to get his prints. That's when he picked out the kid who's been ripping off the schools."

"Who's 'we'?" the Skipper wants to know.

Jimmy doesn't understand.

"You said, 'We had our eye on him.' I wondered who the 'we' is."

"The task force. Westchester detectives. County cops. Troopers." Jimmy gives him a squinty look. "Don't you remember any of his, Skip? There were memos up the kazoo about it. I even sent you one myself."

The chief has no idea what Jimmy's talking about. Such is his grasp on events that don't impact him directly. He mumbles something incomprehensible and quickly changes the subject.

Jimmy lets it go and files it away for Eddie who loves stupid Skipper stories. "Make the letter an over the top one," he says, sitting down now and not waiting to be asked. "Me and Eddie will deliver it tomorrow and put on a show for the guy. Then we'll see where we're at."

The chief raises an eyebrow but he doesn't say anything. He figures now's not the time to quantify his objections to Eddie being involved. Instead he calls for his secretary and dictates a letter to Harvey Collis so filled with treacle that Jimmy hopes they haven't gone overboard.

Chapter 53

Mary threw a school play cast party. It began at three and is still going strong as Jimmy drives up to the house. What seems like hundreds of kids, though there are really only twenty, are running around the house like wild animals. Some of them still have their costumes on. Others are in regular clothes. Lucy's swatting everyone that comes near her with what's left of her pink wand. Twenty kids bring twenty parents who look on in bewilderment as the noise and running around appears to be reaching a crescendo. Jimmy catches Mary's eye. She shrugs. "What can you do?" is what she's saying. She's surrounded by young mothers who daintily sip at their glasses of wine and look forlornly at the carnage taking place around them.

Jimmy's arrival signals the beginning of the end to the festivities. One by one a mother corrals a child and tears ensue. The kids are hopping and jumping about like they've got St. Vitus Dance. Through it all Lucy's still the ringmaster. Yelling and screaming at the top of her voice, only to be drowned out by answering shouts from the remaining crowd. Jimmy's just about to take a hand in calming things down when his cell phone goes off. He takes the call, but there's so much noise he can't make out who it is. By the time he breaks free of the racket and makes it outside the connection's broken. He hits the redial button and Morgan Flynn picks up.

"I was about to call the riot squad. What's going on there?"

Jimmy explains.

"You all right?"

Jimmy assures him everything's okay.

"Got a few updates for you."

Jimmy's all ears.

"Smith and Monahan scooped up Butler."

"I know," says Jimmy. "I was in on it. They threw me and Eddie out so they could get themselves all the publicity, not to mention the collar."

"Not even a share?"

"They told me up front the collar was theirs. That's how they keep their numbers up."

Morgan lets go with a string of profanities.

Jimmy tells him about Butler's prints in Jason's house.

"That's something you weren't counting on. What do you think about that?"

"It's just the one set. The other guy's prints are all over the place. It makes no sense." Then Jimmy fills him in on Harvey Collis and how he's going to go at him tomorrow. "If they're in it together, it'll come out."

"Sounds like you've got Collis cold. The boys aren't gonna like that?"

"That's what makes it so much fun."

Morgan tells him about Marc Hilliard and how they flipped him and got him to wear a wire. "It's either that or going up the river and becoming someone's boy toy for the rest of his life. Not much of a choice unless you like that sort of thing. Then, I suppose, it's like going to paradise. One of the first things we picked up on Hilliard's wire is a conversation between Hilliard and Julio Perez who, it turns out, is not the innocent party he'd have us believe."

"We never thought he was."

"Julio's not in such good shape. They fired him from CRIMPERS. We couldn't charge him with anything, but we made sure they knew what he was doing there. So they threw him out. According to the wire he's got no product to sell because Cousin Hernando stole it all from him. Plus his cash. And some jewelry. He wants Hilliard to front him some coke so he can make a living."

"How sad," says Jimmy.

"And there's a lot of talk between Julio and Hilliard about Butler," says Morgan. "He's not as small time as you think he is. I've got to speak to Smith and Monahan about that. Also there's a lot of chatter from Julio about how glad he is that Sandra Ellison's dead. How dangerous she was to them, Butler included. Hilliard's arranged a meet with Julio tomorrow to give him some coke. We'll grab Julio after that. Between possession and what we have on the wire, we should be able to put him away for quite a while. Lastly, we took William from CRIMPERS in for poisoning Jerry Lewis. That was on Julio's say so, remember? He told us cousin Hernando sold the poison to Jerry who gave it to William, so he could poison his partner. You with me with on this?"

Jimmy says he is.

"William confessed to the Lewis poisoning. It was an accident. He meant to poison his partner, but poisoned Lewis by mistake. He broke down and told us everything, so we charged him and locked him up. Case closed."

"Quite the day," says Jimmy.

"And you're closing your case tomorrow."

"Looks that way."

"Ain't we good," says Morgan.

"Yes we are," says Jimmy. "Yes we are," and that ended their conversation.

Back inside the house, order begins to prevail. Most of the kids and their moms have departed leaving just a few exhausted children who are now glued to the television watching a program about dungeons and dragons. These are the kids who are sleeping over tonight. Five of them including Lucy. Mary looks like she's ready for the funny farm.

"Drink, dear?" says Jimmy sounding like an upper class twit.

"I thought you'd never ask," she says doing her version of the same thing.

He pours her a glass of wine and she downs a big gulp. Then he tells her about his day.

"When are you going at Collis tomorrow?" she asks.

"First thing."

"What do you think?"

"I think I've got him. I just spoke to Morgan. They arrested your partner's ex-boss today."

"William?"

"That's the man."

She takes another slug of wine. "So that's why Mitchiko quit. She called me this morning to tell me she's moving up the opening date."

"Did you ask if we get free haircuts?"

"No I didn't ask if we get free haircuts."

But then one kid's pulling another kid's hair out, so that's the end of their conversation. Jimmy gets a snack from the refrigerator, watches as Mary separates the battlers, then blows her a kiss and leaves.

Friday

Chapter 54

When Jimmy drives up to the station Eddie's waiting for him on the steps. He's wearing a brand new, spotless uniform and fending off hoots of derision and catcalls from his fellow officers who are used to seeing him looking a lot messier. He gets in the car and gives Jimmy a nod. There's no talking on the way. Eddie knows better than to start an inane conversation before a show. Instead he contents himself with looking out the window. There was a shower earlier and the emerald green landscape sparkles and shimmers in the bright morning sunlight.

Jimmy's in lockdown mode. Quiet and pensive. He's always this way before a performance. He's going through his lines. Working it through. Planning for every contingency. Making sure he knows what he wants to do and how he's going to get there. Mary picked up his cleaning so he's able to sport his favorite suit, a double breasted grey pinstripe that makes him look thinner. Couple that with a white button down shirt and a solid dark grey tie and he looks and feels like a million dollars. A little while later they're standing in the doorway of Collis's dimly lit office in the basement of the Hillside Middle School. It's cold down there and damp. They wonder why anyone would put up with such working conditions. Jimmy introduces Eddie to Collis as his associate.

Collis is not happy to see them. He scowls menacingly and starts to say, "What the…" when Jimmy cuts him off with unaccustomed gusto and a flashy smile. Words of praise and appreciation cascade from his mouth in an avalanche of approbation. Syrupy plaudits of flattery and supplication bombard Collis's ears. And there's Collis. This six foot four gorilla in denim overalls and work boots. Sitting at his battered metal desk, his reddening face a mask of anger and displeasure. On the verge of hurling abuse at Jimmy and his associate. Stopped in his tracks. Not believing what he's hearing, he's so damaged and unaccustomed to praise. Listening intently as a symphony of compliments tumble from Jimmy's mouth. Collis's hand reaches up and grasps Jimmy's paw and shakes it with undisguised enthusiasm. Then he does the same thing with Eddie, all the time listening in amazement as Jimmy generously ladles out the soup.

"We'd never have arrested that kid without your contribution," says Jimmy and means every word of it. It's why he sounds so sincere, even to Eddie's finely tuned ear. It's Collis's ID that was the nail in the coffin in the case. The last detail the various departments needed to round out their investigation. Because of Collis, the Croton Police Department felt confident enough to run a sting that caught the kid red handed. No sir, credit where credit's due. And it's the task force, he tells Collis now, that's designated Jimmy to come here today and offer their sincere thanks and congratulations for the information he provided. Without Collis's ID, Jimmy gushes, they would not have been able to move forward on this one.

Jimmy hands Collis the letter. The one the chief dictated, so full off butter and cream. On official stationary with it's flag and eagle crest. Watching with fascination as Collis begins to preen, and puff out his chest, and raise his chin proudly as each word of dripping praise sinks into his unsuspecting brain. They watch with surprise as years of pain peel away from his face and for a moment they can see what he used to look like before all the troubles came upon him. When he was young and carefree and on his way up. For Harvey Collis is a happy man today. Happier than he's been in a very long time.

Then Jimmy says matter of factly, "That boy we caught, the one you ID'd. He was a real piece of work, you know?"

Collis is all smiles and friendliness and full of good fellowship. "How so?" he asks, looking at his new friends with all the warmth he can muster. He's not used to feeling so good and wants to share it with them.

"It took a while for him to see how we could help him," says Jimmy, turning all serious now.

Collis is perusing his letter again. He's even more pleased on the second read of this unexpected recognition, realizing that suddenly he's become a pillar of the community instead of a basement rat in overalls with dirt under his finger nails.

They stare at him, Jimmy and Eddie, from near the doorway. Not moving. Still as statues.

Waiting for him to ask them something. Waiting for him to show some interest in the direction Jimmy's taking them.

Collis is preoccupied with his letter. He's still reading it. Still smiling. Lost in a fantasy of public acclaim and redemption.

No one speaks.

Collis looks up and sees they're waiting for him to say something. "How could you help him?" he asks. Miles away. Not really concentrating on what Jimmy's saying. Imagining everyone's reaction when they hear of this. How they'll pat him on the back and heap more praise on him. The faculty, the principal. All of them that look at him like he's some kind of circus freak.

"We told him about the system," says Jimmy in a voice that makes him sound like an undertaker. "About the way it works. People don't understand much about it, so it's our job to explain it to them. Generally, if we do our jobs right, it saves everyone a lot of trouble."

Jimmy and Eddie are straight faced and solemn now.

Collis doesn't seem to notice the change in them. "How so?" he asks absentmindedly. Grinning. Grinning. He's still so happy as he fingers his letter, this masterpiece of praise, like it's some sort of holy grail. The ticket to a different way of life. He's thinking that he should put it up on the notice board so everyone can see it. Then everyone will know what a good guy he is.

"Their lawyers say they can get them off," says Jimmy. "That's what happens in these kinds of things. They say we've got a weak case and they can beat it. But if the guy's guilty, somewhere down the line the lawyer throws in the towel. He'll say he can't do any more in light of the strength of our argument. By that time you've run out of money. The lawyer recommends a plea which you've got to take, but it's too late. The deal you were offered at the beginning isn't there any more. You've got to take what's on the table and usually it's not enough."

Collis begins to look interested. He's still fingering his letter and beaming. Still flushed with this unexpected victory, but they've gotten his attention now, these two new buddies of his. "So what did you tell the kid?" he asks, looking from one to the other. Wondering when they're going to get back to telling him how wonderful he is.

"That if you cooperate," says Jimmy making eye contact with him now, staring hard at him, personalizing the dialogue and bringing down the boom. "That if you come clean now, not later but now, at the start of the process, and if you show remorse, explain that circumstances conspired to make you act the way you did, the sentencing process can often be more lenient. Not always, but most of the time. Especially if the details are ironed out beforehand."

There's a long pause then Collis clears his throat and asks, "What'd the kid do?"

They can sense the change in him. A smile is fixed to his face but it looks to Jimmy and Eddie like one of the frozen kind. Jimmy presses the bet.

"We had him cold is the thing." He's still using the undertakers voice. "Prints. Witnesses. Folks like you saw him all over the place. Plus there's a hidden camera that caught him in the act. There's no way he's getting out of this and he knew it. And it's not like he didn't do it, right? It's a slam dunk so far as we're concerned, but he's just a kid you know?" He looks at Collis who's listening intently now. "None of us wanted him to go away forever, and they wanted to try him as an adult. It didn't seem right him being a kid and all, so we got the DA to talk to his lawyer who told the kid what she wanted. How a plea would save him years in the slammer. It took a while, but finally he saw the light. He'll do a couple of years in juvie, two years probation and if he keeps his nose clean the record will be expunged. If he fought it out in court as an adult and lost, he'd have gone away for ten years maybe more, and be spending his time with the big boys. You can just imagine what would happen to him then." He looks to Eddie for confirmation.

Eddie nods sagely.

"See what I'm saying here?" says Jimmy. "It's a budgetary thing. They don't have the resources. The way things are today anything that saves money is good. That's why the DA's always ready to make a deal. Now in *your* case," Collis's head snaps up like someone hit him with a cattle prod, "the same thing is true. You and this kid have a lot in common. If you fight this thing with what we've got on you, you'll be going away for a very long time. I know what you're thinking," Jimmy puts his hands up in surrender. "You think if you get yourself a smart lawyer you'll beat it. You were an attorney yourself once, so it's natural you'd be thinking that way. Get yourself a dream team, something like that. But it's not their ass that's on the line here, so they can afford to be optimistic. It costs a lot of money to hire such optimism. I'm sure you know that already, given your background. You don't look like you've got those kinds of resources, Mr. Collis. They'll take every penny you've got and when there's nothing left they'll throw you to the wolves."

Collis hasn't moved.

Neither has Eddie.

Jimmy's voice turns soft and friendly. "I'm sure you didn't mean to kill that girl." Bringing him in close. Two friends scheming their way out of a difficult problem. "And I can't imagine you were trying to kill Jason. Am I right there, Mr. Collis?"

Collis's looks smaller than when they came in. Like he shrunk somehow.

"No one's going to believe you no matter what you say," says Jimmy. "By the time the press have finished with you, you won't be able to find a juror who hasn't already made up their mind about the case. Your face will be on every TV show and splashed across the front pages of every newspaper for weeks on end. Everyone will know how you persecuted Jason. How you went to his house and messed with his stuff. How you threatened his life and sent him those terrible letters. Jeez Harvey, do you have any idea how this is gonna sound to a jury?"

Collis is shell-shocked.

Jimmy keeps pounding away, breaking out a routine he hasn't used in a very long time. Not since Brooklyn when he did this sort of thing all the time.

"But I believe you, Harvey, I really do," he says kindly. "Much like that kid I was telling you about. As bad as things are, I'd still hate to see you go away for the rest of your life and at your age that's probably what it would be. You just wanted to shake him up a little, am I right? Get him back for all that pain he caused you. Isn't that right Mr. Collis? Isn't that how it happened?"

Collis nods his head imperceptivity. His eyes aren't focusing and he's turned a pasty shade of white.

"You come clean now," Jimmy purrs. "Put it all down on paper. A statement telling your side of things. What happened, why it happened. Showing how sorry you are. Remorse is a very important ingredient in these things. You do that Mr. Collis and I'm telling you sir, just like I told that kid I was telling you about, it's a whole different ball game."

Eddie brought along a legal pad for this very purpose. It's part of the drill. He's kept it out of sight up till now so as not to distract Collis. Now he hands it to him along with a pen.

Collis hasn't moved. His smile has been replaced by a look of terror.

Jimmy nods encouragement. "Go on, Harvey. Take your time. Write it down for us."

Collis looks up at Eddie pleadingly. Like somehow Eddie can get him out of this.

Eddie shakes his head and shrugs his shoulders.

Collis looks back at Jimmy.

Jimmy shakes his head too and gestures to the pad. "Write down what happened, Harvey. You'll feel better when you've got it out."

"That you didn't mean to kill anyone," says Eddie, speaking for the first time.

"That it was an accident," says Jimmy.

"You only meant to wing him," says Eddie.

"To shake him up a little," says Jimmy.

"It's your last chance to help yourself," says Eddie

"After that the system takes over," says Jimmy. "Then there's nothing we can do for you. Nothing anyone can do."

Collis looks back at Eddie, but Eddie's run out of things to say. He gives Collis an encouraging smile. It's the best he can do.

The lights dim for a second as the boiler kicks in. Collis looks from one of his new friends to the other, wondering how they got from a festival of praise to killing that girl so quickly.

Jimmy keeps working on him using that soft tone of his. A long monologue of gentle reasoning, then the hard facts to seal the deal.

"Look it," he says sternly and counts it out on his fingers. "We've got your prints all over Jason's house. We've got witnesses that place you where the shooter stood at the time of the shooting. The rifle belonged to Mickey Swan your co-worker. Your DNA is on the rifle and the ammunition." This is a stretch, but he's sure it's true. "And we've got a motive." He shakes his head sympathetically. "We've got you cold my friend, don't you see that?"

"You lose this in court," says Eddie sensing they're getting close, "and you'll die in prison. You come clean now and you'll save yourself a whole lot of time on the back end. I know it's hard to see it clearly when you're on the outside and free, especially if you've never been in prison before, but put yourself in a cell. Eight by ten. With two other guys and no window. No day or night, only a blaring light you have no control over, and an hour a day of fresh air *forever*. Think about it, Mr. Collis. Not another moment to yourself. Shitting in front of them and they in front of you and everything that goes with it. Now think of a chance to save yourself years of that because what's sure is you're definitely going to jail for this. It's just a question of how long."

Eddie stops to let his message sink in then he starts up again. A little slower this time. Making every word count. "Time stands still in a place like that, Mr. Collis. Every minute is an hour, every hour is a day. That's how slow it goes in that hell hole they're gonna put you in. With your cell mates. And their smells. And their habits. That is, of course, if they don't kill you first. And now, right now, there's a way to get years of your life back for yourself. Just the one chance. Because if you don't take advantage now, it's gone forever. We're offering you some of your life back here. Years you don't have to waste in that terrible place. Think about it that way for a while, then maybe you'll see what we're talking about here."

They watch Collis working it through. From the doorway. Where they've been standing all along. To give him space. To see it right. Jimmy looking like a million dollars. Eddie holding up his end nicely. Watching Collis as he runs through the permutations. Processing them. Weighing them. Testing them for their truth. For this is not a stupid man here. A lawyer no less, or was at one time. A Yale man. So he knows, though it's been a while, that what they're telling him is the truth.

And they, watching so patiently from their vantage point. From the moment of his euphoria. Till now. This moment. The moment Collis stops all his figuring and comes to a conclusion.

"Get me the DA," he says to Jimmy without looking up.

Chapter 55

Jason Friendly's mother won't look at me. She's seething. I can see it. I've aroused something deep inside her she never knew existed. Some maternal instinct so powerful she can't help herself. It's manifested itself before my eyes as she reads the letter, my letter, about her precious son. Her claws are extended. Her hackles have risen and she explodes in a frenzy of anger. Raving like a mad woman. Eyes twice their normal size. Screaming obscenities at me. Words you can't imagine from such a small woman. "Storm trooper?" she shrieks. "Is that what you called him? A twelve year old boy. A storm trooper?" Then there's another barrage of cursing. Like a fish wife. Like someone who works from the back of a barrow.

I head for the door as Mr. Friendly and the detestable Jason come down the stairs. Mr. Friendly looks horrified. He thought he'd put this thing to bed. So did I. But she's too far gone, this wife of his. You can see it in her eyes. She's out of control, this thing no more than five feet tall. Arms flailing. Pushing and slapping at me with my letter. My own letter. And that's when it hits me. When I realize she still has it. The letter. The one we wrote on headed notepaper. The letter we designed so carefully to cow them into submission.

The next day at the office I'm summoned to a meeting with the senior partners. A secretary fetches me to the conference room. The partners sit unsmiling around the large oak table. They all wear similar outfits. Dark suits, white shirts and conservative ties. They are all roughly the same age, white haired, wrinkled and mean. They are hard men with not a soft feeling among them. They're grim faced and unhappy as I walk into the room. Then I see the reason for their demeanor. My letter. The one we wrote on Harrison Kegly stationary. Each of them has a copy in front of him. They look like choirboys studying their song sheets. Then looking up at me. Then back down again. A constant bobbing of heads like some strange puppet show. The most senior partner calls the meeting to order.

A secretary is there to take notes. She sits to one side, not at the big table. I stand at the end of the table, opposite the senior partner who wants to know what the meaning is of such a letter? That someone in their employ could do such a thing? To involve the firm in such matters. To put the company at risk. To jeopardize the firm's stellar reputation in such a trivial matter. Who did I think I was? What was I thinking? When he's finished his soliloquy, each partner takes a turn throwing his own particular dart at me. For past transgressions. And present misdeeds. For tardiness. For appearance. For anything that comes to mind. It's open season on me and the partners enjoy my crucifixion. It's what they do so well, these men, and they warm to their task as they go around the table for another turn. This time asking questions about the Friendlys and what they did to deserve such a letter. No one cares for my excuses. That I never intended to send it. That it was just a threat. A bluff. Never supposed to see the light of day.

I'm punctured by their barbs, so carefully aimed and expertly placed, till finally the senior partner brings matters to a head and gives an assessment of the proceedings so far. A synopsis of my failings. A tally of the partners' disappointments. A summing up of my total incompetence. And then, delivered in a voice only Solomon could top, comes his irrevocable conclusion. That I'm no good to them any more, he says in mournful tones, me being so damaged and totally judgment-impaired. So, after weighing all the facts and, considering I'm still an associate and should've made partner years ago, his qualms about me have turned out to be justified. He looks around the room pugnaciously. To let them know this triumph of perception is the reason he's the senior partner. The boss. The one with the sharpest hatchet. And under these circumstances he says, his rumbling baritone rising to a crescendo of trembling righteousness, he no longer sees a future for me at Harrison Kegly. He thinks I should move on. Quickly. Post haste. This very hour. Keys are demanded of me for the men's room, my office, my desk and my filing cabinets. I'm given thirty minutes under the eyes of a security guard to clear out my things and vacate the premises. Boxes are provided. Boxes they have on hand for this very purpose. Then with my arms full of cartons, I'm out on the street. Shocked and bewildered. Without a job and no future. One minute I'm working on a brief, the next I'm pounding the pavement. All I can think of is how much I'd like to burn down the Friendly house.

I thought it would be easy to find work, but there's a recession on and a bear market. Everyone's cutting back. Whenever I get a nibble they call Harrison Kegly and that's the end of that. I'm on unemployment, but it's running out. I'm drinking more these days. Much more. You don't go down the tubes overnight you know. The wife is less understanding. We're getting to the end of our money and her job doesn't bring in enough to support us. I like the booze. It keeps me numb. Her black looks don't spoil it for me any more. What else is there to do? Even part time jobs are hard to come by. I did some work for an accountant, but he smelled liquor on me and threw me out. That was a bad day at home. She even heaved something at me. A first in a downward progression of aggressive behavior. The more she glares at me, the more I drink. Then one day, home from another fruitless search for work, they're gone. Mother and son. She'd cleaned out their things. And the checking account. And packed their bags and left without even a goodbye note.

They're taking my house. The one I worked so hard for. I got a foreclosure notice. I can stay on till the procedure works through the system, but after that? After that I'll be on the street, then what? I'm drinking more these days, much more than I used to. To tell you the truth it's all I like to do.

After they took the house, I ended up in New York. I got a few menial jobs at first. Then less. Till eventually I was on the street. The booze is what killed me. She knew it would. My wife. That's why she kept me off it. She'd seen me like that just once and it wasn't very pretty. Not that I didn't want to be sober back then, when all was nice and going right. My dad was a boozer. They found him in the gutter a long time ago. By the time they got him to the hospital he was dead. The thing of it is drinking's what I like to do most of all. Staying numb and number still. It's not so hard to pull off, you know. You stick your hand out and people give you money. Not all of them, but enough to get some wine or cheap whisky and catch yourself a buzz.

But it's getting cold now and winter's coming on. They sweep you off the streets in the cold weather. It's for your own good, they say, and put you in shelters. Armory auditoriums. Wall to wall cots. I don't care for them. There's always something going on there. A hierarchy, a pecking order, and they steal from you. Awake or asleep, eventually you lose it all. I'm sick now. I've got a hacking cough and open sores on my body. Someone took my boots last night and left me a worn-out pair of sneakers. It's harder to stay numb these days no matter how hard I try. It's the cold that seems to fight it off.

They found me in the gutter like my old man only it wasn't from the cold. I got hit by a car as I staggered off the sidewalk. The driver didn't know what he'd done and drove off. It's my own fault. I was drunk and crashed into the car as it went by. It spun me around and I fell and smashed my head on the curb. I broke my nose, three ribs, an arm and a leg. I was filthy from head to toe. There was blood all over my face and clothes. I'd shit my pants, thrown up all over myself and passed out. I got lucky though. I was scooped up by a Salvation Army truck that took me to the hospital and after they patched me up, got me to a group specializing in people like me. They took me in, fed and clothed me and got me into rehab. I got counseling, therapy and a whole lot of religion. Six months later they got me a job at the Hillside Middle School as a janitor. I've stayed clean ever since.

I was a regular success story until I heard that Jason was back. It didn't bother me at first. I'd been at Hillside five years or so when I heard about it. I'd kept my nose clean till then and stayed off the sauce. There was a story about him in the paper, that's how I found out he was back. I hadn't thought about him in years. Then, just like that, he was back in my life. Not long after that there's another blurb about what a great guy he was. A few weeks later he's in the paper again, a bigger article this time, with a picture. Just to piss me off. For a while it seemed like he was everywhere I looked. All I wanted to do was to wipe that smug grin off his face, so I sent him the furniture, then some pizzas for the opening of his office. To annoy him. And roses. And a whole bunch of other stuff. And after that it was easy. I could never resist another poke at him, so I'd take his newspapers and have other things sent to the house. Or the office. Or call him at all hours of the day and night.

Then he won the marathon. You'd have thought the Martians landed after that. Every time I picked up the paper he was there with that cocky grin of his plastered all over his rotten face. That's when I started going to his house all the time. I liked moving the statue around, the one he got for winning the race, to different parts of the house. Then he decided to run for mayor. I guess that's what pushed me over the edge. I realized that all the things I'd done so far hadn't even made a dent on his psyche.

Now his picture's everywhere. Billboards. Garden lawns. He's driving me mad without even knowing it. There's me trying to drive him crazy when it's the other way round. All I can think of is the pain he's caused me, so I step up the action. What else could I do? I sent him letters like you see in the movies. White sheets of paper with cut up words threatening to do terrible things, but nothing seemed to have an effect. I thought if I took a shot at him and winged him it would make him realize I meant business. Then maybe he'd go away and be out of my face. That's all I wanted really, for him to be out of my face. I didn't want to see him or read about him any more.

The rifle belonged to Mickey Swan. He's an old geezer I worked with. Mickey liked to hunt. Fridays, in season, he'd pack up his car after work and head up north to kill something. He'd lock the rifle in his locker. It was against school rules, having firearms on school property, and I was the only one who knew he did it. I caught him jamming it in the locker one time, that's how I found out. Mickey figured it was better in his locker than leaving it in the car and maybe have a student rip it off. One Friday, in season, he dropped dead of a heart attack while he was cleaning out the girls' bathroom. Mickey was a loner. He had no friends or family. Time passed and no one came to empty out his locker, so I did. And kept the rifle. Once in a while I'd take it out for target practice. I'm not much of a shot.

The night I tried to shoot Jason I couldn't stop my hands from shaking. Every time I lined him up they started to tremble some more, but then he changed direction and began running towards me. It made for a bigger target. An easier shot. So I aimed for his thigh. I figured it would put an end to his running career and ruin his life like he ruined mine. I squeezed off a shot, but my hands still trembled. He didn't go down. The sound alerted him. He was looking around to see where the noise came from. That's when I got out of there.

Chapter 56

They read Harvey his rights and took him back to the station. Jimmy and Eddie had the usual fight. Cuffs or no cuffs. This time Jimmy wins. "What's the point?" he wants to know. "Things are bad enough for the guy. Why humiliate him in front of everyone he knows. The kids. The faculty. What's the point? They'll hear about it soon enough." Jimmy's not a fan of the perp walk or this particular regulation.

Eddie says the rules are the rules. This from someone who takes a delight in breaking every one of them. "But this is different," he says with some passion. The guy's guilty and he's got to pay for it. Now's as good a time to start.

They don't cuff Collis till he's in the car.

The DA and the chief meet the trio on the station house steps. The DA spirits Collis off to an interview room where she makes sure he's been apprised of his rights and introduces him to the public defender she's managed to get for him on a moment's notice. After that the haggling begins. And then, after that, on the advice of his new attorney, Collis makes a deal and gives them a statement.

The chief embraces Jimmy like a long lost brother. You'd have thought they'd been on the same page from the very beginning. A press conference has been called for 3 o'clock. Smith and Monahan say they can be there by 4:00 which is why the chief calls it for 3:00. Jason's lawyer has been contacted as has Jason. It's possible he'll be released within the hour. The chief wants to make sure he's there for that one. The photo ops alone are worth a fortune in public acclaim and future votes.

Sunday

Chapter 57

Jason Friendly threw himself a party. At the club of course, where else would he have it? Sunday 4pm. Come one, come all. When he was in prison he had nothing to do but think about things. Like who came to see him? No one. Who offered him help? No one. Who believed in him? No one except for Jimmy. So when he got out of prison he figured it's pay back time, hence the party. To celebrate his freedom. And announce he's back in the race for mayor. So they can't refuse him, the people at the club. Because now they need him. And like him again. And want to be his friend. Again. All of them. Including Richard Charkham, who never came to see him either and wants to be his campaign manager. Again. But who needs him now? Not Jason. The polls say he's a shoe-in. And he doesn't need anyone's help. Least of all Richard Charkham's.

He's rubbing their noses in it is the thing. The board. The committee. All of them who turned their backs on him and now that he's clean can't wait to shake his hand. He's packed the place with the people he knows they don't like. The police chief and his wife. The fire chief and his missus. Jimmy and Mary. And Josephine. And Mitchiko. The cops. And firemen. And all the volunteers. The list is endless. He calls it an Open House of Celebration and the members have to bite their tongues and look the other way. They thought the party was just for them. Surprise. And who is this new Jason, they ask themselves. Certainly not that amenable young man they knew before the trouble began. This is a less obsequious Jason. A more aggressive Jason. A Jason more inclined to stand with the ordinary folk. At the club. Our club. And the police chief. And the fire chief. Strutting around like they own the place. Like they're members for God's sake. And these other people. Who are they? My neighbors you say. I don't think so. Though in truth I wouldn't know who my neighbors were if I ran over them in the street.

Jimmy's the man of the hour. Jason sees to that. From the little stage. Where he makes an eloquent speech about how he wants to be their mayor and why it's only possible because of Jimmy Dugan. He holds up the front page of the local paper. The headline reads, "The Shoe-in's a Shoe-in Again," and underneath is a picture of Jason with his arm around Jimmy's shoulder. The *New York Post* picked it up, he tells them. And so has the *Daily News*. The crowd claps delightedly. Then he asks them all to raise their glasses and join him in a toast to Jimmy Dugan. For services rendered. A job well done. For recognition of a performance above and beyond the call of duty. And they do. All of them. Town people and club members alike. All of them together. Standing up for Jimmy. And applauding him. With whistles and cheers and shouts of bravo. It's a magical moment and he wishes it would go on forever.

After the speech there's food and drink and dancing to a band whose main claim to fame is that they opened for Bob Dylan when whoever was supposed to couldn't. The club's picking up the tab. A board decision. There's too much at stake here and they don't want to piss Jason off. They all have lucrative contracts with the town and they'd really like to hang on to the business.

They've given Jason the ballroom for his party. The board. The members. It's an elegant room. More like a night club really, with wood paneling, and soft recessed lighting and a small stage with a dance floor in front of it. Then there are the tables. Lots of them. White-clothed and set with gleaming cutlery and sparkling glasses for water and wine. In the back of the room is a huge bar with a picture window that looks out onto nothing but distant forests and tree covered hills. The food is set up buffet style next to it. Everyone heads there now.

Jimmy finds himself at the back of the crowd standing next to the ME. He of the prissy manner and out of date clothing. Even now he looks almost Chaplinesque in a white stiff collared shirt, a black bow-tie and a black suit so tight it makes his rear end stick out. All that's missing is the hat, cane and mustache.

"They're picking up Sandra Ellison's body tomorrow," he says as if nothing special's going on here today.

"I didn't know we still had it," says Jimmy.

"Well we do. As soon as it's gone I'll send you the paperwork, the final report and the transfer papers."

Jimmy gives him a cheeky grin and moves off to greet Mary who's just then emerging from the ladies room. They run a gauntlet of smiles and handshakes and general good wishes, almost tripping over Josephine who looks great in her high heels, tight jeans and blazer. She's trailing the chief, she says breathlessly. To check out the wife. A short pudgy woman in her late fifties with tousled gray hair and a face that's ruddy and makeup free. "A dog," says Josephine with undisguised glee. Then she tells them how strange it is to see them together, the chief and his wife, she knowing all these things about them. When they ask her what those things are she won't tell them. Jimmy likes her for that. She may be promiscuous, but she's still got her standards. Their eyes met just once, Josephine tells them dramatically, hers and the chief's, but only for a second. Then she scurries off after them again. Suddenly lost in the crowd.

Mitchiko's at the party too. She's brought the entire staff from the new salon with her. They're a trendy looking bunch who fit into Rolling Hills like Hassids at a church social. They're undaunted, this energized little group, and mingle and talk, wearing giant 'Friendly for Mayor' buttons on their chests and big smiles on their faces. They're chatting people up like door to door salesmen selling religious conversion. Handing out cards for the new salon that say MJ AND FRIENDS, and the hairdresser's name in a solid print on extra thick stock.

Jimmy and Mitchiko meet up at the bar. Jimmy's getting white wine for Mary and a coke for himself. Mitchiko's moving into a vodka tonic. Bunches of people stop to shake his hand and say nice things.

"Morgan Flynn's very pleased with you," he says when there's a lull. "He wouldn't have gotten to Julio Perez or been able to charge William for Jerry Lewis's murder if it wasn't for you. Everything you told me turned out to be true." He smiles ruefully. "Maybe you should get into my line of work."

"Yeah. Right," she says.

"What was it like at CRIMPERS when they arrested William?"

Her face screws up in disgust. "They schlepped him out of the place in handcuffs, Morgan and some other dude. Boy those guys dress slick. I didn't much care for it. It was degrading. I suppose that's what it's meant to be, but there was something terribly sad about it. The way William looked at us when they carted him off. Like there was nothing left of him. All that strutting around and throwing himself about and he ended up with nothing but handcuffs and shame. Someone must have tipped off the press. They were all over the place. It was like a lunatic asylum there. Cops. Lights. Cameras. Just like a movie set only the real thing."

Jimmy says he saw it on TV.

"You've got to be some shmuck to put the poison in the wrong cup," she says harshly. "How hard is that to do, I'm asking you?"

He forgot what a tough cookie she was.

"It's not like they didn't always drink the same thing. Coffee with milk for Mr. Lewis. Coffee black for William. Chamomile tea for Daniel. Never different for as long as I've known them. So I'm asking you, how hard is it to put the stuff in the right cup?"

"How'd you know about the drinks?"

"It's been like that for years. We've all had to take it to them at one time or another and it's always been the same."

"I hear you quit. How come?"

"For the P.R."

They're walking back to Mary who's standing alone on the terrace leaning on the wall looking at the view. When they're together Jimmy says still he doesn't get it.

"Get what?" Mary wants to know.

"Why you left CRIMPERS," says Jimmy. "The new place won't be open for a couple of weeks."

"We hired a public relations person," says Mitchiko. Touching everyone's glass with her own in a silent toast. "A hot shot client of mine's in PR and lives in Scarsdale. We haven't exactly hired her. She said she'll see if she can get us some publicity in return for free services. When this thing with William broke she began to drool. She says she can get a lot of mileage out of it since I used to work there. We've already done a couple of interviews. She says there's more to come. We're not open yet and people are already calling for appointments."

Mary beams. It's what every backer longs to hear.

The chief comes over dragging his wife behind him. It's like he doesn't want to be seen with her is the way it looks.

Jimmy makes the introductions.

The chief asks Jimmy if he's got a minute.

They leave the ladies chatting and go to another part of the terrace where the chief asks him, "Did you ever find out why Ted Butler's prints were in Jason's house?"

Jimmy says he never got the chance.

"Well you will now. Morgan Flynn called me. The wire they've got on Marc Hilliard picked up something between Hilliard and Julio Perez he wants to talk to Butler about. Smith and Monahan have him in the county lock-up. They're too busy to do it is what they told me. They've designated you, since you've touched Butler before, to baby sit Morgan on this one for them."

"Sure. When?"

"Tomorrow," says the chief. "Morgan's gonna call you." He takes a slug of his drink, puts the glass down on the terrace wall and marches off to retrieve his wife and drag her someplace else.

Monday

Chapter 58

Jimmy gets his call from Morgan in the morning and arranges to meet him at the county lock-up after lunch. Morgan explains why he wants to talk to Butler. "We picked up Julio Perez telling Marc Hilliard *he* poisoned Jerry Lewis. I need to run it by Butler and get his take on it."

"Julio poisoned Jerry Lewis?"

"That's what he said he did."

"Why?"

"Julio won't tell us. That's what I want to talk to Butler about. "

"So you're letting William go?"

"We've got him on attempted murder now," says Morgan. "We've still got his confession saying how he thought he was killing his partner."

Jimmy spends the rest of the morning clearing his desk and assembling the paperwork for the Sandra Ellis file. At the end of a case there's a lot to put together. Interviews. Forensic reports. And endless notes. True to his word the ME sent over his records. Jimmy flips through them to make sure it's all there and finds the autopsy file is missing any details. No test results, no toxicology report. Not that it makes any difference since it was clear Sandra was shot to death. He can't be sure if the ME's yanking his chain or it's a genuine mistake. He picks up the phone to find out.

"I can't find the autopsy test results for Sandra Ellison," he says when the ME picks up.

"There aren't any," says the M.E.

"I thought it was standard procedure."

"Never mind standard procedure," snaps the ME. "She was shot in the chest wasn't she? That's what killed her, any fool can see that. What's the point in wasting valuable time and money on useless tests."

"You told me she did cocaine. How did you know that?"

"It was in her bag. I saw it so I just assumed."

Jimmy says, "You better hope there's no lawsuit."

"Why should there be a lawsuit," says the ME indignantly. "The family's only too pleased I didn't leave their precious daughter with a Frankenstein scar down her middle. That's all they wanted to know about when I spoke to them. Did I cut her up?"

"I'm just saying," says Jimmy. "You better hope."

Chapter 59

Jimmy and Morgan sit across from Ted Butler in an interview room in the bowels of the Westchester County Lock-up in White Plains. Ted, who's been in a cell for a couple of days now, looks haggard and old. He was unshaven when they brought him in. Now he's got a scraggly looking salt and pepper beard and puffy bags hang beneath his bloodshot eyes. His sallow face is grim and tense. Morgan's seen better days too. The bug sweeping his precinct house has finally settled on him. His nose is running and his normally perfectly groomed hair is tousled all over his head. His eyes are rheumy and his complexion is blotchy. His suit, though obviously expensive, hangs on him like it's a size too big, and his shirt has an uncharacteristic coffee stain down the front of it.

"Bad day," Morgan says catching Jimmy staring at it. He takes out a tape recorder and places it on the table and turns it on.

"What's he doing here?" says Butler looking at Jimmy.

"What's it to you?" snaps Morgan.

Jimmy gets up and leans against the wall and says nothing. It's Morgan's show, let Morgan handle it.

"So," Morgan says to Butler. "Here's the deal. Julio Perez has confessed to poisoning Jerry Lewis."

"I thought you had William for that," says Butler.

"Mmmm." Says Morgan. "So did we.

"So why did Julio step up for it?"

"He didn't. We've got a recording of him telling someone he poisoned Jerry and got William to take the fall for it. Julio's under arrest, but he won't tell us why he did it. What do you think Mr. Butler, why do you think Julio would poison Jerry Lewis?"

"How should I know?" says Butler, looking disinterested.

"I thought you said you were going to help us with this."

Butler sighs.

"Why do you think he did it?"

"Look," says Butler. "Julio had it in for Jerry big time. The guy was asking him to do impossible things and threatened to expose him all the time. He was blackmailing him for coke and pussy and all sorts of other things and treating him like a pimp. Always ragging on him around people and making him feel stupid and small."

"Did you know Julio was going to do it?"

"Oh right. Like I'm gonna say yes here and get myself into more trouble."

"You think Julio's capable of doing it?"

"You just told me you've got it on tape. What more do you want?"

"But why?" says Morgan. "That's what I don't get."

"Something bad happened. About a month ago. "

"Like what?"

"A foursome," says Butler. "That's what this is all about. It was an ambush for Julio. He wasn't expecting it. Wasn't prepared. I heard it from both sides. Marc told me what a mess it turned out to be. He said they were having themselves a party, Marc and Jerry and Sandra Ellison. I told you, she likes to party. Then Julio shows up and they invite him to join them. After a while Jerry and Sandra turn on Julio and things get out of hand. It turns out Julio's got an unusually small dick. When you've been doing blow all night and you're hopped out of your mind, it can get pretty hairy when things go bad. Julio pulled a knife on them and all sorts of weird shit went down. Marc had to cool the thing out and look like Mr. Straight, while all the time he was getting off on the whole deal. That's what he likes, Marc. A good show. Julio told me he was blindsided that night. He thought he was picking up some coke. He didn't know she and Lewis were going to be there."

"So why'd he stay."

Butler sighs. "Pussy's pussy, man. You know what I mean? After a couple of lines and she's flashing her snatch at him, what's a fella to do?"

"What did you think of her?" asks Morgan.

"I already told this guy." Butler looks at Jimmy.

"So tell me," says Morgan."

Butler sighs again. It's a pattern. He sighs every time he says something he doesn't want to. "That.bitch could've rolled us all up."

"Why's that?" asks Morgan.

"Why'd you think?"

"I'm asking you," says Morgan. "Seems to me you all got rolled up anyway."

"That's true," Butler says philosophically. "The hazards of the trade, you know? The risk you take. One guy rolls over, then another. Now I'm rolling over on someone else. That's the way it goes. But that bitch was a wild card. You didn't know which way she was going with things."

"What things?" says Jimmy. Speaking for the first time.

Butler says, "She was definitely angling for a piece of the business."

"How would you know?" says Jimmy.

"It was obvious. Me and Julio warned Marc about it. I told you this already."

"Did she get it?" says Jimmy.

"Not exactly. Marc said it hadn't gotten that far yet, but she was asking too many questions. Things she shouldn't be asking. It scarred the shit out of Julio."

"Why's that?" says Jimmy.

"Why d'you think?"

"What is this, twenty questions?" says Morgan. "Tell the man what he wants to know."

Another sigh from Butler. Then, "The kid was making a fortune out of CRIMPERS. He's already got trouble with Jerry Lewis. He was always afraid of what Lewis had on him. Another partner would do him in altogether."

"You're saying," says Morgan. "Julio killed Jerry Lewis because he was driving him crazy and blackmailing him."

"Yes. And it all came to a head that night when they all started ragging on him about the size of his dick. It was like that put him over the top."

Morgan thinks about it for a second or two and says, "Makes sense. What do you think Jimmy?"

Jimmy said it sounds right to him too. "On another subject, How come your prints were in Jason's house?"

Butler grins at him. "What is it? You think I'm working with Collis? Isn't that the name of the guy that killed Sandra Ellison, right? Harvey Collis."

Jimmy nods. "I can't figure out why your prints are in that house."

"I'm on a club committee," says Butler. "We had a meeting at Jason's house a couple of weeks ago. I went to the bathroom upstairs. Is that where you found them?"

"Inside the medicine cabinet," says Jimmy. "You must be one of those nosey people who are always checking things out."

Butler makes a deprecating shrug.

Outside Jimmy says, "Don't you think it's odd how everything seems to revolve around Julio Perez? Where is he by the way?

Morgan stiffens. "Why do you want to know?"

"I'd like to talk to him."

"He's got nothing to do with you."

"I know that."

"So?"

"I got a feeling."

"What kind of feeling?"

"You gonna let me see him or not?"

"We got him all wrapped up and ready to go," says Morgan."

"What's that mean?"

"He's going to Riker's at the end of the day."

"But you've still got him now?"

"We do."

"So let me have a minute with him."

"Why?"

"As a favor."

"Why?"

"For old times sake."

"What old times? We only just met."

"I knew your dad."

"Oh that old times."

Jimmy grins.

They agree to hook up later at Morgan's precinct house where Julio Hernandez is being held.

Chapter 60

Jimmy's on his way to the City to get his minute with Julio Perez. Every light's green on the Saw Mill River Parkway. Even the tough ones at Pleasantville and Hawthorne. Green and green again. And the music. "Old 55" by Tom Waites. Playing over and over at full blast. Tom's gravely voice hitting those rough notes like sandpaper on Jimmy's soul. And the hawks. So many of them today. Perched on the lampposts along the Parkway like a somber honor guard to salute Jimmy as he passes them by. He gets to New York in record time. Morgan's waiting for him outside as he slides into a rock star parking spot just vacated in front of the police station.

Now they're downstairs in the bowels of the building, in the interview room. Waiting for Julio, who's finally brought into them by a burly officer. Julio looks small in his orange jumpsuit with PRISONER printed in black letters across the back. His rat like features look pinched and drawn. The officer fastens Julio's cuffs to a chain attached to the ring in the center of the table and sits Julio down. Then he goes and stands by the door. Morgan leans against the wall sniffling and snarfling and trying to control a persistent cough. Jimmy sits opposite Julio. Julio stares at Jimmy with undisguised hostility.

"What are you mad at me for?" says Jimmy. "I'm the good cop, remember?"

Julio shifts in his chair but doesn't say anything, he just glares at Jimmy.

"I hear you've got a very small dick," says Jimmy, getting the show on the road.

Julio glares at him.

"I mean really small." He turns to Morgan. "Isn't that what we heard, Morgan?"

Morgan grins. He's got no idea where Jimmy's going with this. Jimmy wouldn't tell him what he had in mind. Just that he wanted a minute with Julio. And a minute, he argued, couldn't make much difference to anyone. To which Morgan could do nothing but agree. Now he's glad he did. This is the best fun he's had all day. He holds up a finger and thumb an inch apart.

"With a dick like that," says Jimmy, "you'll be catching the whole time you're in jail. That pretty little mouth of yours will be doing all the heavy lifting."

The guard snickers. Julio steams.

"A small dick keeps the ladies wanting. I hear the girls you tried to screw had a hard time keeping a straight face."

"I don't have to listen to this shit." Julio turns to the guard. "Get me outta here."

The guard gives him the dead stare.

"We heard Jerry Lewis thought your dick was the funniest thing he ever saw," says Jimmy.

"Yeah?" says Julio. "So look what happened to him."

"That's why you poisoned him?"

"Fuck you," yells Julio.

The guard steps forward and places a hand on Julius shoulder. Julio relaxes a little.

"Is that why you poisoned him? Because he thought your dick was so funny?"

"Read my statement."

"Sandra Ellison thought your dick was smallest thing she'd ever seen, that's what Ted Butler told us. Isn't that right, Morgan? A Guiness Book of Records sort of small."

Morgan says it was, grinning some more.

"What did she say to you?" says Jimmy.

No answer.

"C'mon Julio, she must have said something really bad to piss you off so much."

Nothing.

"What did she say?"

"Leave me alone, man. You got no right to do this to me. Get me my lawyer."

"What did she call you?" Jimmy's stifling a laugh.

"Fuck you man."

"Whaddya think it could be Morgan?"

Morgan's smiling broadly now. Joining in. He holds up his finger and thumb again an inch apart and says, "Maybe she just did this."

"That would piss me off too," says Jimmy. All sympathy now. "Is that what she did to you, Julio?"

Julio is steaming.

"C'mon man," says Jimmy. "Tell us what she said. We're not gonna let you go till you do."

"Yeah, tell us," say Morgan.

Julio's fidgets in his chair. He's angry and pulls at his chains.

"C'mon tell us," says Morgan. Both of them laughing at him now.

"It had to be a good one to get him to pull that knife on them," says Jimmy.

"Maybe it was the other guy said something," says Morgan. "Jerry Lewis. Maybe he came up with it."

"Was it Lewis?" says Jimmy. "What did he say, Julio? "

Julio glares at them both. Furious.

"I think it was her," says Jimmy. "She must have said it for sure."

"Why do you say that?" says Morgan.

"Because this girl liked to screw. With a dick like Julio's, he's no good to her. That's when she said it to you, am I right Julio? Right then. When you were all hot and bothered. She took one look at that thing of yours and said it right to your face. Right Julio? That's when you went for the knife. When you couldn't take it any more. She really got you going didn't she, kid? She wanted a piece of your business, but nothing to do with your piece." He bursts out laughing at his punch line. Morgan too. Both of them laughing at Julio. The guard joining in now. Everyone laughing. Except for Julio. Who sits there scowling at them. Angry. Rattling his chains at them. Saying "Fuck you man," over and over.

Jimmy throws him a couple more one liners to keep the thing going then he slips it in gently. While it looks like Julio's looking the other way. "And that's why you poisoned her isn't it, kid?" he says softly.

Freeze frame. Another freeze frame. A moment where time stands still and no one moves. For a single beat. Then Julio takes a conspicuous swallow and says, "I never killed no woman."

"Not directly."

No one's laughing now. There's absolute silence.

"You got nothing on me," says Julio.

"I know you had Sandra Ellison poisoned," says Jimmy.

"How'd I manage to do that when all the time I was working at CRIMPERS."

"You paid someone to do it for you."

"Like who?"

"Some illegal up in Albany," says Jimmy. "A dishwasher. It's easy if you know how. A phone call. A couple of hundred bucks. Easy."

"Why would I want to do something like that?"

"She wanted a piece of the action."

"What action?"

"Your action. Butler told us."

"How would he know?"

"Hilliard told him."

"Told him what?"

"She was angling for a piece."

"Of what?"

"Everything," says Jimmy. "Yours, Hilliard's and Butler's."

"So how come Marc didn't off her? Why me? How come you don't think he did her?"

"Because he's got a bigger dick than yours," says Jimmy and starts to laugh again. They all do.

Then Jimmy says, still laughing, "C'mon man, no one likes to be laughed at. "

"You can't prove nothing," spits Julio.

"Except for the size of your dick," says Jimmy and there's more laughter from everyone. Raucous laughter. The three of them. Morgan, Jimmy and the guard. Gasping for breath they're laughing so hard.

"You got nothing on me," says Julio. Looking from one to the other then back at Jimmy. Glaring at him. Challenging him.

Then Jimmy stops laughing. "Probably so," he says, "but I'd still like to know why."

Everyone gets silent again, Julio too, as he and Jimmy pull back to assess their positions.

Then Jimmy says, "Look, whoever you paid to do it is long gone now. Whatever you paid him must have seemed like a fortune. Or was it a her? Someone who thinks your dick isn't as small as everyone else does."

There's more snickering from the gallery

Julio glowers.

"How did you get the poison up there?"

Nothing.

"How did you know where Sandra was going to have lunch?"

Silence.

"How did you know she was in Albany that day?"

"Lotta questions, man," says Julio. He's finally got his rat-like features under control and now he manages a small smirk. "Sounds to me like you're fishing."

"Hilliard told you, right?"

Nothing.

"How'd you get it up there?"

For the first time there's a twinkle in Julio's eye. "You tell me," he says. "You're the detective."

Jimmy puffs out his cheeks and shakes his head. "You got me, kid. You're the genius."

"You can't prove nothing."

"Agreed," says Jimmy.

"So what's all this about?"

"I just want to know."

"Oh, you just want to know do you."

Jimmy nods.

"But you can't prove nothing."

"I know that."

"I'm in the clear on this one."

"You are."

"'Cos you can't prove nothin."

Jimmy says, "Not a single thing."

And it's true. He can't prove a single thing. He's already had the restaurant checked out. A dishwasher left a couple of days ago. An illegal. No one knows where he came from or where he's gone. Even if Julio tells him the absolute truth he wouldn't be able to prove it in a court of law. But this he does knows for sure, everyone likes praise. A little credit where credit's due. Some recognition for a job well done and a pat on the back, and Julio here, now that they've established that nothing will rub off on him, can't wait to tell him how he did it. Jimmy looks at Morgan. "A free ride on this one buddy, whaddya say?"

Morgan's looking at Jimmy with a new found respect. Not that he thought Jimmy was a rube or anything like that, but the City's the City and a City cop's the best there is. This is a great move he's watching Jimmy pull off here. He nods at Jimmy now. Agreeing that no matter what, they'll never be able to prove what he tells them. So what the hell, he wants to hear the story too.

Julio cracks his knuckles and sits up a little straighter. "Tell you what," he says conspiratorially. "Let's use Hernando's name on this. That way there'll be no blow back. It's not like I don't trust you guys, but we're living in the real world here."

Jimmy shrugs.

Morgan too.

"She was up in Albany the whole week," says Julio.

Jimmy says, "Sandra Ellison?"

"Who the fuck do you think I mean."

The guard steps forward.

Jimmy shakes his head. "S'alright buddy. Julio's getting his five minutes of fame here. We'll let it slide for the time being."

The guard steps back.

"Sandra told Marc where she liked to eat," says Julio. "This place off the Albany mall. Hernando took a ride up there. Cased the joint. Found himself an illegal. Told him what he wanted. When he wanted it done. And how to do it. He gave him a grand to do it and another grand to get lost when the job was done. End of story."

"Why?"

"Why what?"

"Why'd you do it?"

"Hernando, you mean?"

"Okay," says Jimmy. "Why did Hernando have her poisoned?"

Julio stares at him.

Jimmy asks him again, "Why?"

Julio lets out a stream of air then looks Jimmy in the eye and says, "Like you say, man. No one likes to be laughed at."

Epilogue

Morgan and Jimmy are standing on the street outside the precinct. Jimmy's about to get into his car.

"How did you know?" says Morgan.

"I didn't."

"But you went straight at him."

"It was just a hunch."

"Some hunch."

Jimmy grins.

"What twigged it?"

Jimmy shrugs

"What made you think it?"

"Julio had a temper. He pulled a knife on them when they were all laughing at him. I got to thinking, if he could kill Jerry Lewis for driving him crazy and putting pressure on him, why not Sandra too? Especially because, as it turned out, she was angling for a piece of his business."

"But you had your guy. Collis, right?"

Jimmy nods.

"And the autopsy results."

"That's another thing. The ME didn't do any tests."

"What are you talking about?"

"We got a budget problem up there. It was obvious she was shot, so the ME figured he'd save some money."

"You've got to be kidding me."

"I wish I was."

Morgan says, "So was she shot or poisoned?"

"Both, I suppose.

"What killed her?"

"Someone else is gonna have to figure that one out."

"How come it took the poison so long to kick in?"

"I'm guessing the coke screwed the timing up. I've read somewhere that can happen."

"You know this for sure?"

"It was just a hunch, I told you."

"Some hunch," says Morgan.